PITY PRESENT

WHITNEY DINEEN

Made in the United States. October 2024

Print ISBN: 979-8-9912328-4-5
E-book ASIN: B0D3VLQRT4

https://whitneydineen.com/newsletter/

33 Partners Publishing

ALSO BY WHITNEY DINEEN

It's My Party

You're So Vain

Head Over Feet

Queen of Hearts

At Last

She Sins at Midnight

Going Up?

Love for Sale

The Accidentally in Love Series (with Melanie Summers)

Text Me on Tuesday

The Text God

Text Wars

Text in Show

Mistle Text

Text and Confused

A Gamble on Love Mom-Com Series (with Melanie Summers)

No Ordinary Hate

A Hate Like This

Hate, Rinse, Repeat

Visionary Fiction

The Celestial Contract

Conspiracy Thriller

See No More

Non-Fiction Humor

Motherhood, Martyrdom & Costco Runs

Middle Reader

Children's Books

CHAPTER ONE

MOLLY

If I had a dollar for every time my sister Ellen interfered in my life, I'd have enough money to buy everyone in Chicago their own pizza, and I'm talking the deep-dish delicious kind, like Pizzeria Uno. Well, maybe only a slice and not the whole pie—we're not gluttons here—but that's still a lot of meddling.

Ellen has been invested in every aspect of my existence since the day I was born—which is when she decided I would become her lifelong pet project. I'm pretty sure that makes me the oldest living pet in history, if you don't include parrots or those giant tortoises that live two-hundred-plus years.

As I ram another sweater into my suitcase, my sister lies on my bed and jabbers on about her favorite topic du jour. "Heath and Trina's lodge is amazing! You're going to love it there." Ellen's the one who told them that I'm the best gift shop designer in the tri-state area.

"It certainly looks nice from the article you wrote about it," I tell her. *Gorgeous lodge set in the middle of Elk Lake, Wisconsin— what's not to love?* "I can't help but wonder why they didn't have their gift shop organized before opening." I mean, who goes public without being ready to charge eight dollars for a tooth-brush to all the poor suckers who come unprepared?

Ellen shrugs her shoulders in response before saying, "I wish I was going with you."

I don't really want her to come, but she *is* responsible for my getting this job, so I feel obliged to say, "You're welcome to join me. We can share a room."

She exhales loudly. "I'll be with Henry visiting his parents in St. Louis." Ellen and her boyfriend have been an item for nearly two years.

"Do you think he's going to propose?" I ask with cautious optimism. If Ellen gets married again, surely she'll be too busy with her own life to dissect every aspect of mine. That's my pie-in-the-sky dream, anyway.

"Maybe." She sounds neither expectant nor particularly excited. Her tone is more reminiscent of how she might respond if you asked her if she'd rather eat turnips or radishes. She hates them both.

"But you love him …" I prompt.

"I do."

"And you'd like to get married again."

"I guess." Ellen and her husband, Don, divorced on their first wedding anniversary. As most of their union was fraught with turmoil, my sister never really got a chance to enjoy wedded bliss. She has since likened the institution to starring in a season of *Squid Game*—never knowing where the next attack was coming from. I suppose it's lucky that Don didn't hurt my sister physically, but the emotional abuse left one heck of a mark.

"If you got married, you'd still have time to have your own family." *Please procreate, Ellen, so you can have a new creature to smother with your devotion.*

"Henry's kids are enough," she says matter-of-factly before adding, "I'm not sure I want to take the risks associated with late-in-life pregnancy."

"You're only thirty-eight," I tell her. Which is ten years older than me, which is probably why my sister behaves more like my mother than my sibling.

"Mom had *you* at thirty-eight," she reminds me like my existence is the sole reason our mother acts like a crazy person most of the time. After I was born, she suffered from postpartum anxiety —an affliction that never fully went away. *Talk about helicopter parenting.*

I finish tucking rolled-up pairs of underwear into their packing cube before carefully placing the pale pink square next to the sock cube. "Just because Mom had hormonal problems doesn't mean you will, too. Every pregnancy is different."

"Maybe. But having the hormones of a sixteen-year-old one day and then returning to middle-aged hot flashes the next is not my idea of a good time."

"Thirty-eight is not middle aged."

"It is if you die at seventy-six." Ellen glares at me pointedly. Strangely, that's the age both of our grandmothers passed.

I'm not ready to give up hope of my sister finding a new hobby, so I tell her, "Cameron Diaz had her kids at forty-seven and fifty-one." I don't mention that both pregnancies were with a surrogate or the fact that the movie star most assuredly has a staff of helpers to aid her in the travails of later-in-life motherhood.

My sister rolls her eyes before pushing herself toward the side of the bed. After throwing her legs over the edge, she stands up. "Yeah, me and Cameron could be twins." Running her hands along the sides of her curvy body, she shimmies. "Except she's seven inches taller than I am and probably seven sizes smaller."

"And more than seven years older than you when she became a mom." I *really* don't want to let this go.

Ellen adjusts the waistband on her three-pleat wool pants that are almost identical to the kind our mother used to wear. She claims with the extra room from the gathered fabric, she can fit into a size smaller than normal. "Call me as soon as you check in. In fact, call me as soon as you pull into the parking lot."

I fold my suitcase over on itself before zipping it closed. Setting it on its wheels, I respond, "I'll do my best."

Ellen suddenly turns toward me and throws her arms around my neck. "I love you to the moon, Molly Boo! Have a great time!"

"I'm sure I will," I tell her, somewhat confused by her enthusiasm. "It's just another business trip, you know."

Tipping her head to the side until her left ear is nearly touching her shoulder, she says, "Exciting things happen in December."

"There's Christmas and New Year's Eve," I tell her. "And I'll be back home for both."

Ellen ignores me. "This could be like your very own Hallmark movie. Stylish young city gal flees her urban home for a quaint inn and falls in love with the surly lumberjack who lives next door."

"Except I'm going to Wisconsin and all those Hallmark movies take place in Vermont." Pulling my suitcase out of my bedroom, I add, "And I'm not looking for a lumberjack to share my life with. I'm perfectly happy the way things are."

"Liar," Ellen hisses.

"I'm not lying. I love my life in Chicago. I have a great job, and a nice apartment. I have friends. I'm perfectly content."

"You're still pining after Kyle, aren't you?"

"Kyle and I broke up over two years ago," I remind her. "I'm not pining, nor have I ever pined. I was sad, then I got over it."

She cocks her left eyebrow like she's inspecting an invasion of tiny laugh lines around her eyes. "Which is why you never date. Because you're over it?"

"I don't date because I'm not interested in dating right now," I tell her. "I'm building my career. I'm taking care of myself. You of all people should understand the importance of that." Ellen is always talking about how women should put themselves first. Case in point, she called Henry on his last birthday and told him she couldn't go to the party celebrating his big 4-0 because she'd booked herself a spa weekend. And while I admire her love of self, she can take it too far.

My sister finally concedes. "If you say so. Just keep an open mind."

"I'll be gone for two weeks, Ellen. No one falls in love in two weeks."

She slides into her parka and zips it. "Christmas is a time for miracles."

"Yes, it is," I agree. "Maybe our Christmas miracle will be you getting engaged so you can make me an aunt."

Instead of playing along, Ellen picks up her purse and blows me a kiss. "Call me as soon as you get there. Love you, Boo!"

I wait until she's gone before opening my refrigerator and chucking out the things that will go bad before I get home. Being that I travel a lot for work, my fridge is usually bare bones. As such, the only items I toss are a pint of milk for my coffee, a wedge of brie that's been in there for months, and a bag of lettuce that's past rusty and has started to resemble a thick soup.

Once I dump the garbage bag down the chute, I go back into my apartment to retrieve my suitcase. Looking around, I decide that my bachelorette pad looks sad. I decorated it when I was in the height of my beige phase, so pops of color are few and far between. I wonder if that's how people see me. Boring, beige Molly with no boyfriend and no life outside of work.

The fact that I haven't put up any Christmas decorations yet adds to the feeling of sterility. I have to force myself out of my current contemplation before I fall into a real existential crisis. No good can come from this kind of navel gazing. *I'm fine*, I tell myself. My life is good. I'm perfectly content.

That's my story, anyway, and I'm sticking to it.

CHAPTER TWO

BLAKE

"I moved to Chicago to cover sports," I remind my boss with a death glare. "You know, the Bulls, the Bears, the Cubs?" *The Black-hawks, the Sox, the Windy City Thunderbolts ...* If a ball or puck is involved, I'm all over it.

"That was the plan," Gillian says, still typing away on her computer like my presence is of no consequence whatsoever. When I first interviewed for this job, I thought Gillian was a total bombshell—all sleek and sophisticated without a single hair out of place. While not my normal type, she made such an impression I considered venturing beyond the LA standard of bleach blonde, fake tan, and often more than one surgically altered feature. It wasn't until I saw a wedding picture on my new boss's desk that I realized she wasn't looking.

Widening my stance like a boxer squaring off with his opponent, I respond, "That was not the *plan*, Gillian. That was the *job* I was offered."

She continues to click on the keyboard for several moments before deigning to look up. "I agree that was the job you thought you got, but what can I say? Things change."

I'm so boiling mad right now I feel like I'm standing on the Vegas Strip at high noon in the middle of an August scorcher. I inhale slowly, and on the exhale tell her, "I left LA to cover Chicago sports. I'm a sportswriter. It's what I do and why you hired me."

She finally lifts her fingers from the keyboard before pushing her chair back from the desk. With one well-manicured hand, she gestures for me to sit down. "Blake," she sounds like she's talking to a preschooler, which I find highly condescending, "we had a little bit of a snafu when Charlie decided he didn't want to retire until basketball season was over."

Not only is Charlie Clark a legend in sports journalism, he's also a hometown hero. He played for the NBA for a record twenty years before retiring. Yet, as much as I respect the guy, I can't help but say, "I don't see how that's my problem."

"I understand your confusion." *I'm sorry you wet your pants, and I'll call your mommy to pick you up if you need me to.*

"My contract states quite clearly what my job title is," I remind her.

"And that's the job you're going to have when Charlie retires."

"In April ..."

She shrugs her slim shoulders while simultaneously executing a disdainful eye roll. *How did I ever find this woman attractive?* "Which is four months away. Being that you're already on the payroll, I've decided to give you other assignments until you step into Charlie's shoes."

Dropping into the chair across from her, I run my hands through my hair like I'm endeavoring to rip it out. "By sending me to some lodge in Wisconsin to interview the Midwestern Matchmaker?"

"Partially," she says cryptically.

Trina Rockwell used to star on a show called *Midwestern Matchmaker* before it got cancelled. Then she and her fiancé, Heath Fox, opened a lodge in the town where they fell in love. Now she's apparently hosting dating encounters to match singles en masse.

"Gillian, I don't cover crap like dating getaways for the hopelessly lonely and unattached. I'm not a romance writer."

She raises one arched eyebrow so high it nearly hits her hairline. "The thing you need to ask yourself, Blake, is how you want to start out this job. Do you want to be thought of as a team player or do you want to set yourself apart as a troublemaker?"

"I'm not the troublemaker, Gillian. I'm just the guy who wants to do the work he's been hired to do."

Her expression relaxes to the point where she almost looks pleasant. I'm not buying it. "I'm a newspaper editor who needs her staff to be willing to step outside the box if that's what the paper requires."

"You think *Chicago Wind* needs an exposé on a dating getaway in Wisconsin?" I try my darndest to make sure my tone conveys every ounce of contempt I'm feeling.

"Yes, Blake. This kind of thing is why we created the Windy Season circular. Chicagoans want to know the dish on all thing social. And being that you're our shiny recruit from the West Coast, you're the guy for the job."

I can't seem to stop myself from asking, "Because I have a tan? You don't have very high standards, do you?"

"You're the man for the job because you're currently the only single person without a permanent assignment." Smack. Down.

While I could go on pleading my case for the next hour (day … month …) I know it won't do any good. I can either walk away from my dream of writing about the sports teams I grew up with, or I can do this favor in hopes of garnering the best possible work environment. "What does the assignment entail?" I sound as though I'm accepting a death sentence.

"Two weeks in Elk Lake, Wisconsin. You'll be back by Christmas Eve."

"You just want me to interview people about their experience? Ask them what they think of the event and all?"

She shakes her blonde hair from side-to side, making it look like a silk curtain swaying in the breeze. "No one can know you're a reporter."

"Excuse me?" *Wait a minute, she just said I was the only single person on staff without a permanent assignment. She can't mean ...* "You can't possibly want me to pretend I'm one of the singles being set up?" *Please don't mean that.*

The slow smile that crosses Gillian's mouth makes my blood run cold. "I'm not interested in dating right now. I've only just come out of a serious relationship." I don't mention that relationship ended three years ago.

"You don't have to marry anyone."

"I don't have to date anyone, either. I'm not a piece of meat for you to pimp out for the entertainment of your readership."

"That's unnecessarily harsh, Blake. All you have to do is be social. Act like you're interested, then write about your experience and let other singles know whether you think this getaway is a worthwhile endeavor."

I feel like I did that time my parents told us we were going to Disneyland, and we wound up at some county fair in Kentucky. It wasn't their fault our alternator broke, and they couldn't get a new one for three days, but I still felt duped. Taking one last stab at freedom, I ask, "How in the world am I supposed to go to a bunch of singles' events without people knowing who I am? They'll suspect I'm writing about them."

Gillian looks confused. "Why? Who *are* you?"

Is she purposely being obtuse? "I'm a well-known sportswriter from Los Angeles."

She snorts disdainfully. "Nobody in Chicago cares about LA. In fact, I think it's safe to say that nobody in Chicago even knows who you are."

Ouch. "I did grow up here," I remind her.

She smirks before scooting her chair back under her desk. "If you see your parents or childhood friends up in Elk Lake, tell them to pretend they don't know you. But don't you dare tell anyone else who you are or why you're there or you may not have the job you came here for." She starts typing again like she didn't just threaten my livelihood.

I don't move for what feels like an hour, although I'm sure it's only a couple of minutes. I just sit there staring at my boss like she's a newly discovered life form from another planet. It isn't until she picks up her phone and makes a call that I realize she's done talking to me.

Standing up slowly, I force my unhinged jaw to close. Meanwhile, Gillian spins her chair around and starts to talk to the person she just called. What just happened here? Have I really just been sent to Elk Lake, Wisconsin, for a dating getaway?

As I walk out of the office, I fantasize about moving back to LA. The only reason I left was to fulfill a childhood dream of reporting on my hometown teams. But what if Charlie decides to hang on for another year, or ten? God knows what hellacious crap I might have to put up with then.

Once I'm out on the street, I hail a passing taxi and take it back to my apartment in Wrigleyville—a neighborhood so named for its proximity to Wrigley Field. Talk about serendipity. I knew the minute I found it that my move home was meant to be. Now I'm not so sure.

By the time the cab turns onto West Addison Street, I've reluctantly accepted my fate. And while I'm about to spend two weeks in snowy Wisconsin, that doesn't mean I have to like it. It also doesn't mean I'm going to write the kind of articles Gillian expects me to.

I'm not overly hopeful a miracle will occur that will help make this trip bearable, but I'm not opposed to a little divine intervention. If such a thing exists.

CHAPTER THREE

MOLLY

A train full of commuters can be overstimulating, as is currently the case. The woman across the aisle is filing her fingernails so aggressively, it sounds like nails on a chalkboard, not to mention the acrylic dust filling the air—gack. The guy next to me is so disheveled, he looks like he's recovering from a days-long bender. He's hogging our shared arm rest, and is slumping in my direction, so that his head is nearly on my shoulder. If that's not bad enough, he reeks of garlic and regret. The topper is the little kid in front of me who is standing on his seat trying to burp the alphabet as loudly as humanly possible. It's times like this I wish I owned a car.

I have another hour before I reach my destination, so I pop in my earbuds, close my eyes, and try to escape my current reality by listening to a crime podcast. There's nothing like murder and mayhem to settle the nerves.

When the train pulls into the Elk Lake stop, I jump to my feet and practically run for the exit. Unfortunately, I don't see the foot blocking the aisle. As such, I wind up making a spectacular display as I trip up the aisle for several yards. My performance is akin to a vaudevillian physical comedy routine. Luckily, a hand reaches out to steady me before I hit the ground. "Whoa there. I've got you."

I take a moment to catch my breath before turning to thank my rescuer. One look at his hazelly green eyes and chiseled jaw renders me nearly speechless. *Is that a tan?* I finally manage to say, "Thump queue."

The Adonis stands up and reaches toward his overnight bag. "Excuse me?"

"Thump queue," I repeat before forcing my mouth to form proper words. "I mean, thank you."

His lips curve ever so slightly before he responds with a wink. "You're welcome."

I know I just told my sister I wasn't interested in dating and that she was crazy to suggest I might be about to embark upon my very own cheesy movie experience, but for a split second, a wave of possibility washes over me. Before I can stop myself, I ask, "You aren't a lumberjack by any chance, are you?"

His eyes widen. "No."

Feeling foolish, I try to think of something to say that will make me seem less weird. I decide to go with, "Me neither."

He cocks an eyebrow. "Good to know. I hear it's hard work."

I'm going to be single forever. While I claim to be fine with that outcome, I secretly want to find the man of my dreams, get married, have two point five children, and then adopt a Bernese Mountain puppy or three. The house in the suburbs and white picket fence are a given.

Turning around, I continue to make my way off the train while chastising myself for being such an idiot. I step down to the ground before lugging my suitcase to my side. The gorgeous stranger is behind me, but he doesn't stick around to continue our inane small talk. Instead, he veers to the right and exits the platform.

I don't move as quickly. I simply look around at my charming surroundings. There's nothing like a small-town train station decorated for the holidays. The depot windows are strung with colored lights. The old-fashioned streetlamps lining the walkway are festooned with flocked wreaths, and Christmas carols are booming from the speakers against the side of the building.

Laughingly, I tell myself, "You're not in Kansas anymore, Dorothy." Not that Chicago is at all comparable to Kansas, but a certain *Wizard of Oz* magic seems to have overtaken me.

I appreciate my surroundings for long enough that by the time I turn around, I'm the only person left on the platform. The text I received from the Elk Lake Lodge said they would send a driver to pick me up. As such, I make my way through the depot to the other side of the building.

The sidewalk is covered in fresh snow, so I'm careful to step into the footprints left by others. I look around for a van with the hotel's name on it, but the only vehicle at the curb is a dark blue Suburban. Before I can approach it, a gaunt middle-aged man wearing a gray parka steps out. "Molly Anders?"

I throw a hand up in the air and reply, "That's me!"

He walks over and takes possession of my suitcase before putting it in the back hatch. Then he opens the door for me. "Name's Paul. You're my last pickup which is good because we're expecting more snow." I'm glad I decided to come tonight and not wait until morning.

Getting into the back of the truck, I'm greeted by a familiar face. "Hey, there." It's the hottie from the train.

"Hey, hi. Fancy meeting you here."

The driver gets in and asks, "You two know each other?"

Before I can answer, my seat mate explains, "We met on the train. Neither of us are lumberjacks." *Kill me now.*

"I'm Molly," I tell him hoping he'll forget that whole lumberjack fiasco.

"Blake," he says.

"You're staying at the lodge, too?" He nods his head, so I needlessly tell him, "So am I." *Duh, Molly. Obviously, you're both staying at the lodge, or you wouldn't be in this car.*

Blake remains quiet which is my cue to ramble on like a lunatic. "Do you live in Chicago?" But before he can answer, I decide, "You must. I mean, why else would you have been on the same train as me?"

"I might have come in from the suburbs to catch a train that goes to Elk Lake," he suggests.

I hadn't thought of that. "Did you?"

Another pained smile. "No. I live in Chicago. I just moved there."

"Really? Where are you from?"

"I'm *from* Chicago, but I've spent the last ten years in Los Angeles," he says.

"Winter is a crazy time of year to come home."

As Paul pulls out onto the road, Blake explains, "I got sick of all the beautiful days in LA. I missed real weather."

Neither one of us says anything else as we turn onto a road that leads through the woods. I don't mind snow so long as it doesn't stick around for months on end—which it tends to do. Yet, the current scenery replaces my disdain for an endless winter. The vision of huge evergreen branches laden with its white bounty is better than any of those calendars nature photographers shoot. I feel like we're driving into Narnia or something.

By the time Paul turns onto the road in front of the lodge, I'm lock, stock, and barrel in love with Elk Lake.

Paul pulls around the circular drive leading to the giant log-style building. When he gets out, cold air that makes me shiver fills the cab. Blake and I take this as our signal to exit our warm confines and retrieve our luggage.

We both thank Paul for the ride before wheeling our possessions through the expansive double doors leading inside. The interior of the lobby is a warm honey oak from floor to ceiling. Roaring flames leap in a giant fireplace and the overhead chandeliers are fashioned from elk horns. My eye is drawn to what must be a twenty-foot-tall Christmas tree in the great room beyond the lobby. The whole scene is stunning.

Blake doesn't appear to be quite as impressed as I am, but he still says, "Nice."

I walk toward the front desk and am greeted by an affable-looking older man. "Welcome to the Elk Lake Lodge," he says.

"Thank you. My name is Molly Anders."

He clicks away on his computer. "I have a suite that just opened up if you and your friend would care for more space."

I turn around and lock eyes with Blake which causes my heart rate to pick up speed like I just ran a 10K in under thirty minutes. I know my face turns bright red because I can feel the heat. The reasonable side of my brain says, *Turn around, Molly, and tell the man you're here alone.*

The devilish side has other ideas. *Think of the fun you could have with this smoke show. Go, girl, take the suite!*

As I juggle the possibilities of staying in the same room with a total stranger, Blake announces, "We're not together. I have my own room."

The clerk nods his graying head. "Very good, sir."

I belatedly spin around and confirm Blake's statement. "Yes. Right. No, I'm alone. All alone. Not here with anyone. Just me." I briefly wonder if I always sound like such an idiot when talking to members of the opposite sex. I'm not flirty by nature, but my visceral reaction to Blake has rendered me positively stupid.

The clerk reaches into the drawer in front of him and takes out a plastic card. He runs it through what looks like a credit card machine before handing it to me. "We have you in room 214," he tells me. "Would you like someone to bring your bag up for you?"

While I love the perks of staying in five-star accommodations, I only brought one suitcase with me. "No, thanks, I've got it." But instead of moving along, I just stand there blocking the path.

Blake looks over my head and tells the clerk, "Name's Blake Walsh."

I tell myself to leave but I don't listen. Instead, I take two baby steps to the side and lean against the counter. Then I scan my phone with the same intensity the president might while reading a message from the Pentagon.

Yet, my messages aren't quite so impressive. There are two and —surprise, surprise—they're both from Ellen.

> BS
>
> It's your big sis! How is it? Are you there?

And ...

> BS:
>
> Where are you? Call me!

I type a quick response letting her know I've arrived and promise more details once I get settled. Glancing at Blake, I watch as he takes his keycard. I'd better get moving so he doesn't think that I've been waiting for him—which obviously, I have been. I stop short when the clerk announces, "The first singles' event takes place tomorrow night at five, Mr. Walsh. Make sure you're in the great room on time. Miss Rockwell has a lot of fun activities planned."

Singles' event? He's here for a singles' event? Not only does he not look like the type who needs help dating, but I didn't sense any "bachelor on the prowl" vibes from him. And believe me, I would have noticed.

"Thank you." Blake sounds like he couldn't care less. Then he maneuvers around me and walks toward the elevator.

My feet finally start to move until I'm nearly sprinting after him. I follow him into the elevator and watch as he pushes the button for the second floor. I want to ask about the singles' event, but I don't want to come across as nosy. Also, what would I say? *I'm single, too!* I'm sure that wouldn't come as a shock.

I nearly giggle out loud as another possible comment comes to mind, but there's no way I'm going to say it out loud. At least that's what I tell myself. So, imagine my surprise when I declare,

"Look at us, two single, non-lumberjacks, staying at the same hotel."

Blake turns his head slowly until he's looking down at me. With what appears to be bionic effort, he forces a smile, but the overall impression is not one of joviality. It's more of a constipated grin. "Yes," he says. "Look at us."

CHAPTER FOUR

BLAKE

Getting off the elevator, I scan the wall for an arrow pointing in the direction of my room. I turn right as soon as I spot it. The odd woman from the train is still behind me when I stop at room 215. That's when I discover she's staying right next door to me. It's not that I don't find her attractive, because I do, but I'm here on a loathsome assignment which has completely soured my mood. I'm here to write about pathetic singles and not act like one of them by trying to pick up the first person I meet.

I tap my keycard against the lock mechanism, and as soon as the light turns green, I open the door and walk inside. The room isn't huge, but it's big enough to hold a large, four-poster bed and the standard hotel room furnishings of a chest of drawers, a TV stand, nightstands, and a small round table by the window.

The dark browns of the furniture are complimented by the wide-ribbed, dark green, corduroy bedspread. The curtains match the duvet and look as soft as newborn sheep. The whole set up makes me feel like the lord of the manor and I'm not complaining. My current mode of home decorating—just the basics—not only lacks finesse but lends the impression that I'm still in college.

I leave my suitcase in the small hallway next to the bathroom before checking to see what the bathing situation is. I'm a shower guy, but one look at the deep copper bathtub, and I'm seriously considering changing my ways. This whole lodge seems to be the perfect backdrop for romance.

After taking off my coat and hanging it up, I open the desk drawer and find the room service menu. There's no sense going down to the gallows a night before I have to. Scanning the offerings, I decide to get a cheeseburger and fries, but before I can place my order, I hear a knocking sound. *Who in the world could that be?*

Opening the door, I discover Molly standing there holding a basket full of pears, wine, and what appears to be truffles— although from where I'm standing, they look more like poop emojis. If I didn't know better, I'd think she was trying to seduce me. "Hello?"

"Hi," she says which signals a bloom of color to stain her cheeks. Holding out the basket, she offers, "I think this is yours."

"You've brought me a food basket?"

"Yes. No. It was in my room."

I turn around and scan my surroundings. "Maybe I got one, too."

"I don't think it's from the hotel," she says.

I face her again before taking the proffered basket. Sure enough, there's an envelope with my name typed on the front. I turn around and put the container on the console table before pulling out the note.

Blake,

You're a real champ for doing this. Now go have some fun. Who knows, you might get lucky and come back to Chicago a nice guy.

Gillian

Wow, a thoughtful gesture and rude comment all wrapped up into one. Putting the note down, I open the clear plastic box holding the chocolates. Then I pop one into my mouth. They're chocolate-covered cherries, but not the sickly-sweet kind they used to sell in those pharmacy chains when I was a kid. These are brandied cherries covered in a high-quality dark chocolate. They're sensational.

"Oh, dear," my neighbor gasps, as I release a groan of pleasure. Molly looks like she's about to faint.

I quickly retrace my steps until I'm once again standing in front of her. "Thanks for bringing the basket over."

"You're welcome. I hope you enjoy it." She doesn't make a move to leave so we wind up standing there in the doorway, awkwardly staring at each other for a few beats. It's about as comfortable as being at a high school dance with a girl your cousin set you up with. *Ask me how I know how much fun that is.*

"I'm just going to go … Thanks again." I begin to shut the door, but my neighbor suddenly pushes against it to keep it open.

"WouldYouLikeToGrabABiteToEatWithMeDownstairs?" Her words are as rapid as machine gun fire and it takes a minute for my brain to realize that she's asking me to eat with her.

"I was about to call room service." I don't want to offend her, even though the look on her face suggests I just did. Molly is average height, but she carries herself regally, so she seems taller. Her dark hair is so shiny and thick, I kind of want to run my fingers through it to see if it's as soft as it looks. Her eyes are a piercing blue … *Where am I going with this?*

"They close at eight. The dining room is open until nine."

"Oh." So much for my cheeseburger. "Well, then, I guess I'll just eat my way through my gift basket." Her expression drops as though she's suddenly become an old hound dog. Hoping to mitigate any offense, I hurry to add, "I have a work call in a few minutes."

She inhales deeply before releasing her breath in a staccato fashion. "Fine. Have a good night." Then she turns and proceeds down the hall like a soldier under attack. In other words, she nearly sprints.

Part of me wants to call her back and tell her that I'll eat with her, but I'm not here to enhance my own social life.

Closing the door, I pick up the basket and carry it to the bed. Using the included corkscrew, I open the bottle of cabernet before pouring myself a coffee cup full. Then I eat a bag of cashews and some truffle crackers before finishing off the chocolates. Too bad the pears aren't quite ripe, or I'd have one of those, as well. While not exactly the supper of the gods, it's not half bad.

After refilling my wine, I open my laptop and read through the notes for my assignment. Essentially, Gillian wants to run an article a week in the Sunday magazine insert for the first three weeks of the New Year. She doesn't care how they're structured; she just wants compelling stories about what the Elk Lake Lodge dating events are like.

Rubbing my hands together like some old penny opera villain, I start to type.

Some of you know Trina Rockwell from her hit series *Midwestern Matchmaker*. Even though her show has been cancelled, Trina has not given up on her dream of matching Midwestern singles. Quite the opposite, in fact. She's partnered with her fiancé to run singles' events at their newly-opened lodge in Elk Lake, Wisconsin. I'm the lucky guy who's been enlisted to find out if she's as good at her job as her press would have us believe.

I don't have anything against people being set up by friends or office mates, but I don't have the same kind of faith in matchmakers. How can a person you've never met know enough about you to help you find your soulmate? Why would you ever trust them to do so? And more importantly, what kind of person takes money to bring people together?

I'm here for two weeks for Trina's first non-televised date-a-palooza. While on the frontlines, I won't rest until I give you the full story behind her quest. But if I were you, I wouldn't hold my breath that I'm going to become a convert to this kind of thing.

It's my humble opinion that love does not stem from a business transaction.

CHAPTER FIVE

MOLLY

What possessed me to invite Blake to have supper with me? I try to convince myself it's because I thought we'd formed a connection on the train/car ride/walk up to our rooms, but that's not the real reason. The truth is, my hormones have a mind of their own and they've developed an interest in Mr. Tall, Dark, and Hunky.

I stomp my way to the elevator like I'm trying to kill an army of cockroaches under my feet. I don't believe for one minute that Blake is expecting a business call at 8:30 on a Friday night. He just didn't want to eat with me. I suppose that's understandable, given my somewhat bizarre behavior, but it still smarts.

Exiting the elevator, I follow the signs to the restaurant. When I reach my destination, the hostess smiles at me and asks, "How many in your party?"

"Just me," I tell her. As a rule, I don't mind eating by myself. I actually do it a lot, but there's something about staying at a gorgeously romantic lodge during the holidays that makes me sad about my current state of aloneness.

The hostess picks up a menu and leads the way to a four-top

in front of the vaulted wall of windows. "I know the table's a bit big," she says, "but you have a great view of the outside here."

"Thank you," I tell her before sitting down on a chair facing the aforementioned vista. There are dozens of large pine trees covered in colored lights. Nestled among them are several clusters of decorative deer standing around adorned in twinkling lights. It's pure magic.

After opening the menu, I quickly choose my meal. As I'll most likely eat my body weight in my mom's gingerbread cookies when I go home for Christmas, I conclude a salad is my best bet. When the waiter comes to take my order, I add a salmon filet to it, to jazz it up.

While I wait for my meal, I take out my phone and text Ellen back.

ME:

> I'm here and all checked in. You're right, this place is outstanding.

BS

> Send pics! I want to see how they've decorated for the holidays.

When the waiter drops off my diet soda, I tell him, "I'm just going to get up and take a few pictures."

"You'll want to get one of the singing chipmunks in the great room. Just touch the paw of the big one and they'll perform for you."

"Thanks for the tip," I tell him as I stand. "I'll make that my first stop."

I'm not sure singing chipmunks are my idea of classy Christmas decor, but I know my dad would love it. He's forever sending me videos from social media of people who have made it look like their dogs are singing rock music. If the chipmunks are any good, I'll have to pass along a clip.

Entering the great room feels like I'm walking into another era —a time before everyone was distracted by their electronic devices. Families are sitting at tables playing board games, and more people are nestled in overstuffed chairs conversing in front of the fire. There's another group standing near a grand piano. No one is currently playing, but I'm guessing it's only a matter of time, given the audience that's begun to assemble.

I spot the chipmunks in the far corner and make my way toward them. These aren't your ordinary rodents. They stand about four feet tall and they're wearing red scarves and Santa Claus hats. I gingerly reach out and touch the largest one's paw and the trio immediately starts singing "Rockin' Around the Christmas Tree." It's so surprising that a loud giggle erupts out of me as they wiggle their hips back and forth.

Several people join me to watch the stuffed animal serenade, and when the first song is over, someone else touches the big chipmunk. This time they sing "Jingle Bells" while I take a video and send it to both my dad and Ellen. My sister texts back immediately.

BS

That is the funniest thing I've ever seen!

ME

This place is cool, El. Thanks for making the connection.

BS

Have you met with Trina yet?

ME

We have an appointment in the morning. I'm heading back to the dining room to eat.

BS

Send more pics on your way.

I snap photos of the Christmas tree and the fireplace with

stockings hanging from the hearth. Then I take a couple shots of the outdoor light display and fire them off to Ellen.

When I return to my table, the waiter is standing there holding my salad. "Great timing," he says before putting the plate down on the table. "Can I get you anything else?"

On a whim, I decide, "Hot chocolate with whipped cream if you have it."

As I sit down and dig into my meal, I'm not surprised that it's delicious. Everything at this lodge seems to be the epitome of perfection. Once again, I feel sad that I'm alone. This is the kind of place you want to share with someone special.

Unbidden, Blake pops into my mind, and my previous annoyance returns. I know we're strangers and he doesn't owe me anything, but the guy *is* here for a singles' event. Doesn't that suggest he's looking for female companionship? And here I am— a female. You can see how I might take offense.

A tall, dark-haired woman walks toward me carrying a mug with a mountain of whipped cream on top. Stopping in front of me, she says, "I think this is yours." Then she sets it down on the table in front of me.

I hurry to swallow the bite of salmon I just took. "Thank you."

"Are you by chance here for the singles' event?" she asks. That's when I recognize her. She's Trina Rockwell from *Midwestern Matchmaker*.

"I'm not," I tell her. "I'm Molly Anders. I'm here to help you with your gift shop."

"Molly!" she says enthusiastically. "I'm Trina. Do you mind if I join you?"

"Not at all." I gesture to the assortment of empty chairs. "My sister Ellen told me what a beautiful place you have, but she didn't do it justice."

Trina sits across from me. She looks so sophisticated and put together, I take a minute to be grateful she's not single anymore. No one needs competition like this. "We really loved meeting Ellen when she came up to do a story on our opening," Trina says.

"She enjoyed meeting you too," I tell her. "I understand you have a singles' event going on."

"We do! It starts tomorrow night." With an expression of pure glee, she adds, "I guess I couldn't give up my love for matchmaking."

"I'm sure it will be very successful," I tell her.

"I hope so. It's a jungle out there in the dating world."

The reality of her words settles like a weight on my chest. "That's the truth."

Sounding surprised, she asks, "*You* aren't still single, are you?"

I take a moment and enjoy the fact that I don't present myself as the hopeless singleton I am before confessing, "I work a lot, so it's hard to meet people."

She signals a passing waiter and asks for a glass of wine. Turning her attention back to me, she commiserates, "I barely dated at all before Heath and I got together."

"How did you meet?" I quickly follow that up with, "If you don't mind me asking."

Trina puts her elbows on the table and teepees her fingertips in front of her. "I don't mind at all. We went on one date for charity a couple of years ago, but Heath told me he didn't want to get serious with anyone. Then we both spent the summer here. We were neighbors and, well, the rest is history."

"It sounds like the two of you were meant to be."

With a large smile on her face, she says, "We're getting married in June."

"Congratulations!"

"It's amazing how your life can change when you least expect it," she says.

I nod my head slowly. "My life has been pretty much the same for the last few years. I'm not sure I have any surprises coming my way."

"You know what?" Trina leans toward me like she's about to share government secrets. But instead of telling me that aliens are real and they're walking among us, she says, "I just had a last-minute female cancellation. You should join our event."

My nervous system responds in overdrive and beads of sweat pop up on my forehead. Suddenly, I'm burning hot and freezing cold at the same time. I wonder if I'm getting sick. "I couldn't," I tell her. Stammering along, I add, "I … I … I'm here to work."

She waves an elegant hand in front of her which gives me a chance to check out the giant rock on her left-hand ring finger. I knew Heath Fox was loaded, but he must also own a diamond mine to find a doorknob like that. "There will be plenty of time for you to work *and* enjoy the activities I've lined up."

My mind spins with possibility. What are the chances Trina would have a cancellation the same time I'm here, the same time Blake is here? "Can I think about it?" I ask.

"Of course you can. And there won't be any charge. I couldn't fill the spot with such short notice anyway, so think of it as my gift to you."

"That's very nice, thank you." If I decide to do this, I can never tell my sister. At least not until after the fact. She'd make me crazy asking questions and giving me advice.

Trina and I chat for a few more minutes before she stands up. "I'll see you in the gift shop tomorrow morning at ten."

"I'm looking forward to checking out what you've done so far."

"It's not your standard store." Trina says this like she's warning me not to expect too much.

"Don't worry. We'll have you up and competing with the Ritz in no time," I tell her.

"I hope not," she says cryptically. Waving her fingers, she adds, "See you in the morning, Molly. We're very happy to have you here."

I can't help but feel glad to be here. I love my job and while I usually enjoy my stays at the beautiful hotels I work at, there's something about the Elk Lake Lodge that feels very different from any place I've been before.

CHAPTER SIX

BLAKE

The quiet of rural Wisconsin is rather unsettling. I've become so used to hearing police sirens and traffic noise outside my window that I barely slept a wink last night. After getting out of bed, I make a beeline to the coffee pot and start it up. While the promise of caffeine drips down, I walk across the room and open the draperies.

Holy heck! There must be a foot of fresh snow out there. The tree branches are so heavy with it that they're bowing under the weight. The smaller trees are unrecognizable and look more like oddly shaped snowmen.

I take a moment to enjoy the scenery and let the pristine whiteness settle any lingering annoyance I have about being here. I remind myself that this is the kind of thing I've been missing living in LA. The first few years I was there were great, but after that, I started to long for a real winter. By the looks of it, Elk Lake takes the season very seriously.

Once the coffee is done, I pour myself a cup and crawl back into bed. Then I grab my laptop from the nightstand and open a new doc to make a list of questions I want to find the answers to.

- Why have a two-week dating getaway instead of simple weekends? *I'm guessing it's so they can charge more money.*
- How many singles are participating? Probably a hundred. *There seems to be no end to how many suckers are out there willing to spend a fortune to find love.*
- Is it an even number of men and women? *My money's on more women because they have that whole biological clock thing going on.*
- How did everyone find out about the event?
- Where do the participating singles live?

While I want all the questions answered, I find the last one most compelling. I mean, if people are coming from all over, how are they expected to make enough of a connection to keep dating after they leave? The answer to that might be why the event lasts two weeks. The extended time could be enough for real feelings to develop, although I doubt it. I mean, who signs up for a relationship after such a short time?

My last girlfriend and I had been together a full year before she got a great job offer in San Francisco. That felt like long enough that we might actually make a go of it. The problem was that I worked a lot of weekends, and she didn't want to be the one always commuting. So, what I thought was a relationship on track for the long haul turned out to be the beginning of the end.

By the time we'd missed three consecutive weekends, she declared she needed more. I agreed long-distance wasn't working like we thought it would and accepted that we should move on. In retrospect, I wonder if we should have fought for each other. It seems the older you get, the harder it is to find someone you're innately compatible with. Which is apparently why people are willing to spend a fortune on the pipe dream of a matchmaker.

Before closing my laptop, I pop onto the internet and do a quick search on Lana. It's probably been two years since I've done that, and I'm curious to know how she's doing. Being that she's a well-known interior designer, Google spits out several pages of matches for her name.

Clicking on her Instagram page, I discover that my ex is not only happily married, but she's also a new mother of twins. A wave of sadness hits me like a semi running into a brick wall. I'm not sure why this affects me so much; it's not like I'm still in love with her. After some reflection, I realize it's probably because she has the life I thought I'd have by now. I'd like to be a husband and a father. And now that I'm past thirty, I guess my own biological clock has started to make noise. How depressing.

Once I close the computer, I get out of bed and take a hot shower. While the rain pulse beats down on my head, it hits me that I *am* at a singles' event. If I want to find someone to date, this could be the perfect place to do so. Then I remind myself I don't believe in this kind of thing and the feeling of possibility passes.

Every relationship I've been in has started organically. None of them included paying an overpriced pimp to help me secure romance. I briefly consider the fact that none of my past girl-friends are still around, but at least our relationships weren't the byproduct of some busybody who thought she knew what was best for me. I've got my mom for that, should I ever need it.

After getting out of the shower, I put on a pair of jeans and a flannel shirt before venturing out of my room. I'd like to get a lay of the land downstairs before I'm thrown to the wolves, or they're thrown at me. Whichever the case, there's a definite wild animal metaphor playing in my brain.

Walking out into the hallway, I almost expect to see Molly there, but she's not. I briefly glance at her closed door before turning in the other direction and heading to the elevator. Inside, there's a woman standing with a small child leaning next to her. He's very slender and has a pale pallor. He doesn't look well.

"I'm sorry," she says. "I'm waiting for my husband." She moves to push her child out of the way so I can go down.

"I can wait for a minute or two," I tell her. I smile at her son and a wave of compassion comes over me. My brother had a severe case of cerebral palsy when he was born. His death when he was only three left a hole in our family that we never fully recovered from. Tommy was five years younger than me and seven years younger than my sister, Melissa. It's hard to remember what our lives were like before him.

"What's your name?" I ask the boy.

"Ben," he tells me proudly, showing off a crooked smile.

"This is a pretty cool place, isn't it?" I ask him.

With his swim cap sitting sideways on his head, he declares, "I'm going to the swimming pool!"

I smile while telling him, "I hope you have a great time."

A minute or two pass when I see the woman's husband hurry down the hall. He's carrying a plastic inner tube and what appears to be blow-up fins. Getting into the elevator, he says, "Sorry it took me so long. I was looking for the beach ball but couldn't find it."

"Shoot, there was so much to get ready, I think I forgot to pack it."

He reaches out and takes his wife's hand before tenderly telling her, "You did a great job."

I suddenly feel like I'm witnessing a highly personal moment, so I stare at the lighted panel of buttons. I don't want them to feel like I'm intruding. When the doors open, I stand back and let the family exit. Instead of following the signs to the dining room, I walk into the lobby and stop at the coffee station. I pour myself a cup before taking it into the great room.

There are several families sitting around playing games, and that's when I realize there are more than a few children with obvious disabilities. I wonder if they're all part of the same group.

Sitting in front of the fire, I sip my coffee and watch the room with interest. So far, I'm the only person by myself, which I take to mean that most of the attendees for the singles' get-togethers are probably going to arrive today. Either that, or they've come to their senses and realized this is a waste of time.

Releasing a breath I hadn't realized I'd been holding, I pick up my phone and do a search on the lodge. I click on an article written by a reporter named Ellie Strand.

> Heath Fox is not only a major real estate developer, he's also a philanthropist with a heart of gold. Mr. Fox has reserved ten percent of the Elk Lake Lodge's occupancy for families with disabled children. These rooms are on a first-come first-serve basis, and they are free to the families who qualify to use them.
>
> Mr. Fox says, "It takes a lot of time and energy to raise a special needs child, and I feel strongly that our facilitating a getaway for them is the least we can do to be of service." Fox doesn't have children of his own, but his brother has a diabetic daughter. As such, he knows the kind of worry these families have and he wants to do his part to bring them some joy.

I'm impressed. Billionaires don't always strike me as the most community-minded people and their contributions often seem to have a self-serving purpose. From outward appearance, Heath Fox seems like he might be an exception to the rule.

Putting away my phone, I continue to crowd watch. That's when I notice a familiar face enter the gift shop across the hall.

CHAPTER SEVEN

MOLLY

I hurry into the gift shop feeling slightly disheveled. I slept so well last night that my normal six a.m. wake-up alarm came and went while I remained blissfully unaware. The only reason I got up when I did is because the sun was shining in my eyes. That's when I looked at the clock and saw it was already past nine.

Trina is standing behind the counter when I walk in. She finishes ringing up a guest's purchases before greeting me. "Hi, Molly, how did you sleep?"

"I overslept by three hours," I tell her.

"It's the sedatives we put into the water," she jokes. Then she says, "I sleep like a baby here, too."

"You're from Chicago originally, right?"

She nods her head. "Yeah, but I traveled a lot for work when I was hosting *Midwestern Matchmaker*. I love staying in one place now that the show is over."

"I can understand that," I tell her. "Traveling for work is a different kind of life."

I expect her to take this opportunity to pressure me about joining her dating event, but she doesn't. Which I appreciate because I haven't made up my mind whether I'm interested or not.

Looking around, I tell her, "You're better stocked than I thought you'd be. I was under the impression I'd basically be starting from scratch." My gaze stops on a shelf full of diapers and coloring books.

"We didn't want to open without having the basics."

"I'd say you've got that covered. I'm not sure why you even need me." Looking at a rack of keychains on the counter, I ask, "Why are you only charging three dollars for those? Most hotels price items like that around the ten-dollar mark."

"We're not looking to make money with the gift shop. We just want it to pay for itself."

"Why not be profitable, too?"

"Every t-shirt, keychain, and branded item we sell is good advertising for the lodge."

"Yes, but you could still make money on them," I tell her.

"We could, but we don't need to."

I think of all the high-end hotels I work for that make a ton in their gift shops and wonder why Trina and her fiancé aren't of the same mind. Picking up a toothbrush from the display, I tell her, "You could get eight or nine dollars for this." They have theirs priced at two.

"People already spend a lot to stay here; there's no reason to punish them for forgetting necessary items." Segueing off the topic of oral hygiene, she says, "We're interested in knowing what other kinds of things you think we should offer."

"I'd normally suggest an array of expensive luxury items. You know, perfumes, adding a jewelry case, silver flasks or things along those lines."

Trina nods her head thoughtfully. "I can see how those might be in demand in big cities or resorts, but I'm not sure they would be as marketable here in the middle of nowhere."

She's right and once again I wonder why I'm here instead of someone who specializes in more rustic locations. "I don't normally work for places like yours." I think, but don't add, *places that aren't looking to rip off their guests at every turn.*

Trina walks around to the front of the counter until she's standing next to me. "People are people. I figure you can get a feel for who our guests are and then advise us on what else you think we should carry."

"I can't imagine I'll need two weeks for that." Maybe two days …

"Then you'll have plenty of time to participate in the singles' event while you're here." If I were a conspiracy theorist, I might surmise my being here at the same time Trina was having her first matchmaking session was less of a coincidence and more of a planned happenstance. As in, maybe Ellen paid for me to be offered the spot and there really was no cancellation. But there's no way my sister would pay to have me participate without a guarantee that I'd do so. She's more careful with her money than that.

Also, why would Trina and Heath pay me to organize their gift shop if I were here for their singles' event?

"I'm still not sure I'm interested."

Trina looks nonplussed. "I thought you were intrigued by the idea last night." Waving her hand in the air, she decides, "But it's neither here nor there. Join us if you want, and if you don't, there are no hard feelings." Her attitude helps convince me this wasn't a set up.

"I guess I'll look around at the things you already stock. Then I'll put together some ideas of what more you could do."

"You don't have to stay in the shop," Trina says. "We want you to participate in all lodge activities and really get to know the ins and outs of the place so you can get a feel for what being a guest here entails. Just charge any expenses to your room and they'll be comped."

The Elk Lake Lodge is very different from my usual jobs. While I've worked at some of the most exclusive resorts in the world, I generally only get my room covered, along with a daily per diem for food.

"That's very nice of you, Trina. Thanks."

She smiles as she turns to leave. Before walking out the door, she spins around and adds, "If you change your mind about joining us for the singles' event, we'll be in the great room at five." Then she's gone.

I pull a notepad out of my purse as a youngish woman walks through the door. She's probably a few years younger than me. "You must be Molly! I'm Lorelai. I work here."

"In the gift shop?"

She nods her sandy brown head. "I live in Elk Lake. I was so excited when the lodge opened, I knew I wanted to be a part of it in some way."

Lorelai is the perfect person for me to talk to. "Is there anything your guests are looking for that you don't carry?"

She tilts her head as her face scrunches up in thought. "You know, I think we should carry more warms socks. You wouldn't believe how many people I hear complaining about cold, wet feet."

"Do they ask for socks?"

She shakes her head. "No, but they can see what we have and what we don't. The trick is listening to what they say to each other."

I'm suddenly convinced Trina and Heath just need to talk to their current employees. Regardless, I jot down warm socks on my pad before saying, "Thanks, Lorelai. Let me know if you can think of anything else."

Before starting my research, I exit the shop with the sole intention of finding a cup of coffee. I immediately forget my destination when Blake nearly runs me over.

"Molly, hi," he says.

I merely nod my head. I'm in no mood to embarrass myself with the inane drivel that constantly comes out of my mouth when Blake is around.

He looks over at Lorelai and asks, "You don't by any chance carry cinnamon gum, do you?" Glancing at me, he adds, "It's surprisingly hard to find."

"I'm sorry, we don't," Lorelai tells him. "I've got some Juicy Fruit if you want that."

Blakes eyebrows furrow as though he's having a hard time making the connection between cinnamon and artificially fruity flavors. "No, thanks." Then he looks at me and asks, "What are you up to today?"

Why is he suddenly being so friendly? Last night he treated me like I was a case of poison ivy looking for a hug. I remind myself to keep our interaction brief and words at a minimum. "Not much," I tell him. "Just working."

"What do you do?"

"I'm a gift shop consultant." Taking my notebook out, I write something down. "I've just made a note to order cinnamon gum."

The smile he gives me is enough to melt my butter. "Thank you."

Nodding my head again, I tell him, "Sure thing." Then I scurry around him. If I stick around, I'm sure to embarrass myself again.

Although, I *have* suddenly developed an interest in going to tonight's mixer. I don't know if I'll participate in the rest of the activities, but what can it hurt to see what kind of things Trina thinks will bring singles together?

Not only that, but it might also be interesting to find out what kind of woman Blake finds attractive. Especially as he's made it abundantly clear that *I'm* not his type.

CHAPTER EIGHT

BLAKE

I have no idea why I asked for cinnamon gum. Cinnamon rolls? Those are great. But chew straight cinnamon on purpose? It burns the taste buds right off my tongue. I guess I just wanted a chance to talk to Molly, and for some reason cinnamon gum popped into my mind.

I feel bad about the way we left things last night, but her behavior this morning made it perfectly clear she's no longer interested in talking to me. This isn't the first time I've sent a woman running in the opposite direction. I reference the time I told a waitress at The Ivy that I couldn't stay and have a drink with her because I was busy stalking Danny Green. She rolled her eyes and announced that her gaydar must be broken before walking away. Fine, she ran.

I didn't bother explaining that I was supposed to write an article about the Lakers star, and he wouldn't return my calls. I just beat it out of the restaurant in hot pursuit.

Walking out of the gift shop, I make my way to the front desk to see what kind of activities there are to pass the time. I find a stack of brochures of things to do in the area as well as a list of indoor and outdoor happenings that can be enjoyed right here at the lodge. Zip-lining looks like fun, but I worry that after last night's snowfall I might wind up wearing all the snow in the trees. Cross country skiing is an option, as is snowmobiling. I make a mental note to try both later in the week.

I finally decide to walk around the grounds before choosing an event. After tromping around the woods for a good half hour, I'm about to go back inside and warm up when I see a guy about my age sitting on a log. His head is resting in his hands. There's something about his posture that makes me think he might be in distress.

Walking up behind him, I ask, "Excuse me for interrupting, but are you okay?"

"No." He doesn't so much as look up.

"Can I help you into the lodge?" Call an ambulance, a priest …

He finally lifts his head and turns around. His eyes are so dark I have a strange sensation they lead to a black hole. "You wouldn't happen to be a therapist, would you?"

A burst of laughter shoots out of me before I can stop it. "Not even close," I tell him. "Did you and your wife have a fight?"

"No wife," he says before letting his shoulders sag. "No girlfriend. No one."

My head bobs up and down like a bobblehead on a speeding dashboard. "Same," I tell him before walking over to him. Gesturing toward his log, I ask, "Mind if I join you?"

"It's a public log."

Since I'm here to write an article about single people, I might as well talk to one. After brushing the snow off the spot next to him, I gingerly sit down. *Man, it's cold!* My butt immediately goes numb as it makes contact with the frigid wood. "What are you doing here at the lodge?"

A look of embarrassment crosses his face before he answers, "I'm here for a dating thing. Trina Rockwell from *Midwestern Matchmaker* is having her first big mixer tonight." He pauses for a beat before adding, "It's actually a two-week-long event."

Sticking my hand out, I introduce myself. "I'm Blake."

He mimics the gesture. "Kyle. Kyle Williams."

"So, Kyle. Are you fresh off a breakup or something?" I ask. I might as well get some information for my article. Who knows? Kyle might even be the perfect guy to follow so people know what a waste of time these things are.

"Not fresh off, no. My girlfriend, Amelia, broke up with me six months ago. She met someone else."

"Ouch." I don't ask any follow up questions and wait to see if Kyle divulges anything else on his own. He does.

"We were together for a year and a half when we went on vacation to the Bahamas. I brought along an engagement ring." Closing his eyes, he shakes his head and inhales deeply. On the exhale, he opens them. "I mean, is there anything more romantic than getting engaged on a tropical beach at sunset?"

"I can't think of anything," I tell him. Although halftime at a Bulls game on the Jumbotron pops into my brain.

"I thought we were forever, man. I really did."

"What happened with her and the other guy?" I realize this might be an intrusive question, but I'm curious.

"They got married last month. Which is the reason I booked myself on this excursion. I figure, I could either continue to sit around and feel sorry for myself or I could pick up the pieces of my shattered heart and start over."

If Kyle wrote his story on paper, he'd have a country western song. All he'd need to add is a broken-down pickup truck and a mutt with gout. "So, you thought a matchmaker was the way to go?"

He shrugs. "I've never tried it before and nothing else has worked, so I figured, why not?" Then he asks, "Are you on vacation with your family?"

"I'm actually here for the same singles' thing you are," I tell him, feeling like a world-class phony.

"Really?" He sounds so excited I can only surmise that misery really does love company. The only thing is, I'm not miserable.

"Yup," I tell him. "I just moved back to Chicago from LA and I figured this was the perfect way to get back into the Midwestern dating scene." More like the perfect way to keep my job so I can finally do what I moved to Chicago to do—write about sports.

"Is dating in Los Angeles a lot different than dating here?"

"LA is generally thought of as its own planet," I tell him truthfully. "There's no other place on earth where out of shape, fifty-year-old men think it's their due to date twenty-year-old swimsuit models."

Kyle's face contorts in disgust. "Do the women really go for guys like that?"

"If the men profess to be producers they do. LA is the land of bartering your body for career advancement."

"Dude, that's so gross," he says. Although part of him looks intrigued. "What's keeping everyone from pretending to be something they're not?"

"I guess some people have morals. Also, smart women will look up potential suitors on IMDB to confirm their identities. Although, drunk ones at random parties often find out the truth too late."

His expression is priceless: revolted, with a side of *I wonder if that would work for me?*

"Did you ever do that?" he wants to know.

"No way," I tell him. Then, for emphasis, I add, "Not only am I *not* a predator, but I want to date women who are interested in the real me." Which, of course, is another reason I can't pursue anything with Molly. She can't know who I am until this event is over.

His chin lifts in agreement. "I guess the teenager in me got a little excited at the prospect of being a hot ticket."

"Yeah, but that stuff doesn't last." Even though none of my relationships have gone the distance, I console myself that at least I've never been a sleaze bucket.

"How did you find out about this event?" he wants to know.

"I heard about it at work. I'm a barista." While that's not

currently true, I did work at a coffee chain for two years while I was getting my sports-writing career off the ground.

"You moved back to Chicago to make coffee?"

"I'm working on a novel," I tell him. "The coffee gig pays the bills."

"You can make enough as a barista to support yourself in Chicago?"

Letting the lies pile up, I tell him, "My folks have a small apartment in the city for when they come into town to shop or see a show." Now I'm making myself sound like I'm a Rockefeller or something.

"That's cool," he says. "I'm a lawyer."

"I guess you can afford a fancy place then."

"Yeah, but what fun is a great apartment when you're all alone?"

"Which is why you're here," I remind him. "Maybe in two weeks you'll have met a nice woman to date and you'll be well on your way to becoming a couple." More likely he'll have wasted a ton of money and still be miserable, but that's his problem.

"I had a really nice girlfriend before I met Amelia," Kyle says.

"What happened to her?"

He pinches the bridge of his nose like he's trying to stop a throbbing pain, before telling me, "I left her for Amelia."

"Oh man, that's rough."

"It's like karma is gunning for me. I knew enough not to fool around, but I did it anyway. Then I got the same that I gave. It's poetic justice, I guess."

"They do say that what goes around, comes around ..." I agree.

"I know I deserve to be in the boat I'm in," Kyle says. "But I justified my behavior because my girlfriend and I weren't engaged. Heck, we weren't even living together. I figured I was still single, so I was allowed to change my mind."

"Were you exclusive?" I ask.

"That's the fine line, isn't it?" He pauses before saying, "We were, but she traveled a lot, so it didn't always feel like it."

I think about Lana and realize that even if we'd tried harder, we weren't destined to be. You can't live long distance forever because inevitably one of you will start to feel you're not receiving enough attention, and that can easily develop into a wandering eye.

As I ponder what might have been, Kyle stands up. "It's been nice talking to you, Blake. I guess I'll see you tonight."

"You bet," I tell him. As I watch him walk away, I wonder at what age we start to realize there aren't an endless number of people we might wind up with. I'm not a fatalist, but I have been starting to wonder if we might not pick our mate before we arrive on Earth.

That thought leads me to consider that by a series of near misses I might have already lost my opportunity to meet my person. What if she got itchy and decided I wasn't getting to her fast enough? What if she settled for someone she knew wasn't right for her but didn't want to wait anymore?

I'm about to have a panic attack when I hear a voice inside my head ask, *What if she's still out there looking for you?*

CHAPTER NINE

MOLLY

I spend the morning nosing around the lodge, trying to put myself in the place of the average guest. The problem is, I can't quite pinpoint who that is. Not only are there a lot of families here, there's also a sizable singles' event about to take place. I open my notes app and write down mouthwash. That's something everyone can use.

Sitting in the great room, I noodle around on my phone to find out more information about Trina's new matchmaking endeavor. I discover there will be thirty women and thirty men. While that feels like a big number, it's probably better than too small of a group. How horrible would it be to get here and find out in the first two days that no one was right for you? Then you're stuck for days on end without any other options.

As I continue to read about the event, I learn that it's specifically for singles in or around the Chicago area. That's smart because if they were from farther away, it would make it difficult for couples to continue to see each other after the two weeks are up. It's hard enough to make a go of things when you're based in the same town.

I eat a late lunch in the dining room where I further observe the lodge guests. While the room is mostly full of families—strangely, a large number with disabled children—there are also a few singles which leads me to believe more people have started to arrive for the big event.

Taking a bite of my club sandwich, I once again consider whether I'll go tonight. Even though I occasionally watched *Midwestern Matchmaker*, I never considered auditioning for the show. In retrospect, I guess I was a bit judgy about the whole thing. It's one thing to be entertained by other people's struggles, but it's another to make yourself vulnerable and be the one everyone is watching. Having said that, this gathering won't be televised, so that alleviates some pressure.

After signing the check for my lunch, I go upstairs to look at my wardrobe to see if I brought any clothes that might be suitable for a mixer. I mostly have pants and sweaters, but only one dress. It's my emergency black dress that never leaves my suitcase. It's not the height of fashion. It's more of an all-purpose number that can be worn to a meeting, a funeral, or if I don't mind looking borderline Amish, a party.

Picking up the phone, I call the front desk. "Are there any shops in town that carry nice dresses?"

The woman on the end of the line answers, "There's Bride's Paradise."

I unsuccessfully try not to laugh. "I'm not looking for a wedding dress."

"They carry a lot of other dresses, too. You know, for going to weddings, proms, and such."

"Do you have a shuttle I can take into town?" I ask. I normally stay at the hotel I'm working for and don't visit the actual town it's in, but I don't want to go to a mixer in pants, and my emergency dress is not going to attract the kind of attention I *might* be looking for. I'm still not fully committed here.

"We have a shuttle that goes into Elk Lake every hour," she says. "They should be leaving from out front in five minutes."

I'm not sure I can get there that quickly but I'm going to try. After thanking the clerk, I hang up the phone before running out of my room and practically sprinting down the hallway toward the elevator. The doors miraculously open on my approach, which is why I don't slow down right away. As a result, I practically run over Blake.

"Hey." He grabs my arms to stop the momentum that might have otherwise thrown us both to the ground.

Disengaging myself from his grasp, I tell him, "No time. Gotta go." Then I hustle into the elevator and hit the button for the lobby.

"What's the emergen …" The doors shut right in his face, which I find particularly gratifying.

When they open again, I dash through the lobby and out the front door in time to see the same SUV I took from the train station pull away from the curb. Throwing my hand up in the air like I'm hailing a taxi in the middle of Times Square, I shout out, "STOP!"

The car turns toward the curb and stops. Opening the door, I discover Paul, the same driver I had last night. "Going into town?" he asks.

"I am," I tell him while getting inside. There's no one else here. "Why are you going alone?"

"I'm picking up some people who went earlier," he says with a smile. "Come on then."

Once I'm nestled inside the warmth, I tell him, "I'm going to a shop called Bride's Paradise."

Paul nods his head but doesn't offer any comment. As we drive through Elk Lake, I once again find myself totally enchanted. One thing this town has in common with all those Hallmark-style Vermont towns is the unparalleled charm. Elk Lake's downtown is decorated for Christmas like it's the North Pole. Almost every store has a Christmas tree in the window along with wrapped presents and other assorted festive decor. There are even a couple with blue and silver menorahs. I still find those festive, even though I'm not Jewish.

As Paul pulls off the road, he announces, "Will an hour be enough time for you?"

"It'll have to be," I tell him. "I need to be in the great room by five tonight."

With a twinkle in his eye, he says, "I expect you'll have a wonderful time."

"Maybe." Getting out of the car, I tell him, "Thanks for the ride, Paul."

From the outside, the store appears to be nothing more than a bridal shop. I would have never suspected they would carry other kinds of dresses. Walking in, I'm greeted by a beautiful woman with red hair and a noticeably pregnant stomach. "Hello, welcome to Bride's Paradise," she says. "I'm Melissa."

"I'm Molly," I tell her. I'm immediately put at ease by her welcoming demeanor. "I'm looking for a cocktail dress to wear tonight."

Melissa points toward the back of the store. "We keep those in the far corner. Are you going to a wedding?"

I decide to come clean. "I'm going to a mixer up at the Elk Lake Lodge."

She claps her hands enthusiastically. "Trina's big do?"

I nod my head but remain mute.

"Trina's a good friend of mine. She set up my best friend Paige with her husband, Tim."

"Really?" I suddenly feel less awkward about confessing to being part of a dating mixer.

"Paige and Tim were on the last season of *Midwestern Matchmaker*. They caused quite a stir."

"I must have missed that season," I tell her.

"Paige will be delighted to hear that," she laughs. "Trina really saved her bacon by making sure a particularly embarrassing scene didn't get aired."

"I could never go on a dating show," I tell her.

"I was going to go on with her," Melissa says. "But I met my husband right before we applied."

I point to her stomach. "It looks like things are going well."

"So well!" she exclaims proudly.

A girl who looks a lot like Melissa walks out of the back room. She must have overheard what we were talking about, because she says, "I'm going to be a big sister."

"You've got quite an age gap there, huh?"

Melissa answers, "This is Sammy. She's my husband's daughter from his first marriage."

Sammy adds, "But I consider Melissa as much of a mom as my birth mom." That's a sweet sentiment you wouldn't necessarily expect to hear from a teenager.

"You must be thrilled to have a sibling on the way."

"I can't wait!" Sammy says.

"I already know we couldn't do it without her," Melissa adds while giving her stepdaughter a loving smile. I'd never considered the idea of marrying a man who already had kids, but I have to say, these two make the possibility seem kind of appealing.

"Molly is going to Trina's mixer at the lodge tonight," Melissa tells Sammy.

"Oh, fun! What are you going to wear?"

"That's why I'm here. I'm in Elk Lake to consult with Trina on the gift shop at the lodge. I didn't even know there was a singles' event going on until I got here, which is why I'm not prepared."

Melissa and Sammy share a mysterious look before Melissa announces, "That sounds like a premise for a romcom movie."

"I want to hear all about your 'meet cute' when it happens," Sammy announces.

"I'm not sure real life is anything like the movies," I tell her. "At least that hasn't been my experience."

"It isn't, until it is," Melissa says before explaining, "My dating life had to be the most boring in history until I met Jamie. Then it was straight out of a Julia Roberts flick from the nineties!"

"I suppose I can dare to dream," I tell her. "But so far, if my social life were a movie, it would get record low scores on Rotten Tomatoes."

"Trina's going to change that," Sammy says. "And when she does, you have to get your wedding dress here."

"At cost!" Melissa adds excitedly. There's something about Melissa that makes it feel like we've been friends our whole lives.

"I promise that if I meet the guy I marry here in Elk Lake, I'll not only buy my wedding dress at Bride's Paradise, but I'll pay full price for it."

Melissa beams. "Not if, but when, and we'll discuss pricing later. For now, we need to make you feel like a million bucks."

I spend the next forty minutes trying on several dresses. Each one makes me feel more glamorous than the one before and I have a hard time deciding which to buy. As a Christmas gift to myself, I pick my favorite three. My reasoning is that if tonight goes well, I'll surely need other dresses over the course of the next two weeks.

As I'm checking out, Sammy calls out, "Paul is out front!"

Melissa hands a shopping bag over the counter. "Come back and tell us how it goes."

"Please!" Sammy adds enthusiastically.

I don't know why, but I agree. "I'll come back in a couple of days." Then I take my purchases outside and get into the SUV.

If I were prone to flights of fancy—which I'm not—I might confess to feeling optimistic, which I haven't felt in a very long time. If I let my imagination go, I might even confess to feeling like a heroine in her own romcom. One who's about to find everlasting love.

CHAPTER TEN

BLAKE

After talking to Kyle, I head upstairs to my room to write down some notes. Ever since getting this assignment, I've been curious about the kind of people who use matchmakers. If you believe what you see on television, it's easy to assume that every single person is attractive, successful in business, and the victim of bad luck in their previous dating experiences.

This afternoon I met another man who's going to take part in Trina Rockwell's new matchmaking adventure. He told me that in his relatively recent past, he left his girlfriend for another woman. Ironically, the other woman left him for another man.

Some might say he got what he deserved, but I'm guessing it's probably more complicated than that. Nothing in the dating world is as cut and dried as it seems on the surface. There are always mitigating circumstances and details that people on the outside looking in don't see.

While I'm here, I hope to be able to bring you a variety of

stories so that you can find something relatable. The truth is, I'm not sure we need matchmakers as much as we need to use our common sense. But I should know more after my first mixer, so stay tuned.

I fire off an email to Gillian to let her know I've accepted my fate. Even though I'd much rather be covering a basketball game, my curiosity has gotten the better of me, and I commit to do my typically stellar work on this assignment.

I'm not sure what the dress code is tonight, but I decide to put my best foot forward. By the time I'm ready to go downstairs, I'm wearing a slim cut pair of grey pants and a black button-down shirt with the sleeves rolled up. The black loafers say that I'm cool but don't take myself too seriously. My mom would say that I look dapper, and I wouldn't disagree.

Looking in the mirror I run a hand over my slight scruff and decide it makes me look like a tough guy. I think back to last night talking to Molly. I might not be lumberjack rugged, but I have an edge.

On my way downstairs, I pass the same family I saw earlier in the day. They're wearing snowsuits this time, full-on with matching Santa Claus hats. I smile as we pass in the hall. "Looks like you guys are having a full day."

Ben, whose smile is bigger than you'd think possible on such a little face, says, "We went snowmobiling! It was so cool!"

"Based on your glowing recommendation," I tell him, "I'll make sure to give it a try."

Getting into the elevator, I realize I'm kind of apprehensive— like a steer looking for a buyer at the county fair. It's one thing to go out for a night on the town where no one knows your status. It's quite another to go to a cocktail party where everyone is there hoping to find love. And even though that's not why I'm going, I still feel vulnerable.

I briefly glance at my watch and see that it's a few minutes after five. I didn't want to show up early and look too eager, and I certainly don't want to arrive so late that I draw everyone's attention as I walk into the room.

When I walk into the lobby, I see that it's been roped off and there's a sign declaring a private event is taking place. Thank goodness there's no banner announcing the kind of gathering. I walk through a break in the rope in time to hear Trina announce, "There are no rules this evening. This is a meet and greet with no expectations. Just do your best to talk to as many people as you can. We'll start more formal activities tomorrow night."

As I don't know anybody here, I look around the room for Kyle. I figure he'll be an interesting story for Chicagoans to follow. Making my way toward him, I discover that he looks like he just buried his dog. Sidling up next to him, I suggest, "You should smile. You know the old saying that you attract more flies with honey."

"Blake, right?" he asks.

"That's me. What do you say we walk around and introduce ourselves?"

"I don't know," he says nervously. "I'm not sure I'm ready for this."

"What's to be ready for?" I ask. "All we're doing is saying hi to people." I look around the room and discover everyone has put forth a real effort to look their best. "I bet they're as anxious as we are."

"Are you nervous?" he asks.

"I'm not exactly comfortable," I tell him truthfully.

Kyle slowly stands up straighter. With each inch he looks more in control. Once his shoulders are fully squared, he says, "Let's do this."

The first couple of women we walk up to look like models from a runway show. They're both remarkably tall and beautiful. If I were on my own, I might not have had the courage to approach them. Yet they're here at Trina's event, so they must be interested in meeting men.

"Hi there, I'm Blake," I introduce myself before pointing toward my partner in crime. "This is Kyle."

"Krista," the blonde says with a coy smile. Then she gestures toward the brunette next to her. "This is Marley."

"Cool name," Kyle says to Marley. He moves closer to her side and asks, "Can I get you a drink?"

As they walk away, I focus on Krista. "So, what do you do, Krista?"

Her previous confidence seems to waver as she answers, "I'm a kindergarten teacher."

"Lucky kids," I say more flirtatiously than I was planning. Then I tell her, "I'm writing a novel."

"Really?"

"It'll be my first so I'm not a big deal author yet." Even though I'm lying about why I'm here I don't want to come across as a jerk.

"I used to want to write romance novels." A faint pink blush overtakes her face.

"But not anymore?"

One slim shoulder lifts. "It's scary, you know? I mean, I don't want people to judge me based on what I write."

"Are you planning on writing smut?" I ask with a grin.

Her eyes pop open so wide she looks like a startled fish. "Not necessarily. I mean, maybe if the story called for …"

"You know what I think, Krista?" Her head moves from side to side, so I tell her, "I think you need to keep everyone out of your head while you're writing. You can't worry about the critics and the naysayers. You've gotta just let your story out the way it wants to come out."

"Is that what you do?" she asks.

I think about the hundreds of articles I've written and tell her, "Pretty much."

She smiles prettily. "Thanks, Blake. That's good advice."

Before we can continue what's turning out to be a very pleasant exchange, I see Molly walk into the room. She's wearing a sleeveless red cocktail dress that's both quite festive and very sexy. She also looks like she's about to cut and run.

"I hope we can chat later," I tell Krista before asking, "Will you excuse me? I just saw somebody I know."

Krista smiles nervously. "Sure, I'll see you in a while."

I turn toward Molly and notice that she's looking around the room awkwardly. Approaching her from the side where she doesn't see me coming, I say, "Hey."

She nearly jumps out of her skin. In fact, if this were a dark alley instead of a hotel great room, I'd half expect her to follow the action with a karate chop to my neck. As soon as she recognizes me, she says, "Oh, it's you." She does not sound thrilled.

"Yes, it is. Blake Walsh."

Her face remains un-emotive, so I add, "Single, non-lumber-jack, at your service."

Her icy blue eyes dart around the room like she'd rather be anywhere else than talking to me. "Have you met any nice women?" she finally asks.

"I met a kindergarten teacher who seemed pretty sweet."

Her eyes narrow as she asks, "What do you do for a living, Blake?"

I need to be consistent with my lies so that no one suspects why I'm really here, so I tell her the same thing I told Kyle. "I'm a barista."

She looks at me dubiously and her lip curls in what appears to be pure hatred. "You had an urgent call last night regarding making coffee?"

It takes me a beat to realize she's referring to the excuse I gave her for not having supper with her last night. "No," I say. "I'm also a struggling author and I had a meeting with my agent."

"On a Friday night?" Yeah, she's not buying it.

"I haven't sold anything yet so I'm not exactly his top priority. He fits me in wherever he can."

"What's your book about?"

Before I can stop myself, I tell her, "Alien robots taking over the Earth."

"Excuse me?"

I guess she was expecting something more normal. "It's a dystopian love story, really."

"An alien robot dystopian love story ... Don't give up your day job, Blake."

Even though I'm not really writing a novel, that kind of hurts. "Hey, the storyline worked in that movie *Rebel Earth*."

"You're stealing the plot from a movie?" I'm not sure how I ever thought Molly might be interested in me because she's currently being downright rude.

"I'm just taking inspiration from it," I tell her before commenting on her appearance at the mixer. "I thought you were staying at the lodge for work."

"I am." She sounds uncomfortable. "But Trina had a last-minute cancellation, so she asked me if I'd like to come tonight."

"So you're not here for the full two weeks?"

"I'm at the lodge for two weeks but I'm not sure I'll be joining in on all of the singles' events." Then she asks, "Why are you doing this?" She asks this in such a way as though she's enquiring why I'm attending the circus in my underwear.

My eyes briefly drop to my feet before returning to her gaze. "Because I'm single, I guess." *Liar*.

She crosses her arms in a defiant pose. "And you can't find anyone to date on your own?"

She might mean that as a compliment, like she thinks I'm so hot I shouldn't have any trouble finding dates, yet there's an underlying judgment that makes me wonder. "I could ask the same of you," I tell her.

"What's that supposed to mean?"

"It means you're a beautiful woman. One might suppose you have an easy time finding dates." Although, it might be her personality that's the problem.

"I'm not big into swiping my way to love," she says. "And that's kind of the culture we live in, especially in Chicago."

"I get that," I tell her. "It was actually worse in Los Angeles."

"I can't even imagine what that's like. I couldn't compete with a bunch of skinny starlets."

I smile at her appreciatively, thoroughly enjoying the sight of her soft curves. "I once heard someone say that nobody wants a bone but a dog."

The comment catches her by surprise, and she releases a short bark of laughter. "I like that. Do you mind if I borrow it?"

"Not at all," I tell her.

Just as I start to think we're getting along like a house on fire, she looks behind me and declares, "Oh, hell no. Not him."

I turn around and see that she's looking at Kyle. Then I notice Kyle's expression when he sees Molly. I'm about to ask Molly how she knows him, but my fear for her physical health takes precedence. Her skin turns so red I'm afraid she's about to spontaneously combust. I ask, "Are you okay?"

"I'm … well … no … not good."

"Can I get you some water or something?"

"I'm thinking more along the lines of a double gin with a tequila chaser." Before I can offer to retrieve that for her, she adds, "Maybe with a nice tranquilizer garnish …" I'm about to tell her I'd be happy to fetch that for her—sans the tranquilizer, because where in the world would I find that?—but before I can, she turns and practically runs out of the room.

CHAPTER ELEVEN

MOLLY

What in God's name is Kyle doing here? He can't have broken up with Amelia, too, can he? Thoughts spin through my head like a tornado tearing through a mobile home park. No freaking way is my ex at the same singles' event I am. What kind of heinous crime did I commit in a past life to warrant this kind of rotten luck?

Before I can continue my flight to safety, I hear Kyle call out, "Molly, is that you?"

While I want to run, I'm suddenly overcome with the desire to confront him. Whipping around, I force what feels like a maniacal smile onto my face. Through clenched teeth, like I've come down with a bout of lockjaw, I sneer, "Kyle. What are you doing here?"

He shoves his hands into his pockets, but he doesn't answer. In the silence, I stare at him long and hard and decide that he's as handsome as ever, but there's something else that wasn't there before. Is that humility? If so, it looks good on him.

He finally says, "I … um … Amelia and I broke up."

Excellent. "Really?"

"Yeah, um … well … the thing is, she married someone else."

"Oh." What else is there to say? *You certainly got what was coming to you, didn't you?* But I don't go there. He'd have to be an idiot not to have already worked that out for himself.

Before I can ask for further details, Blake walks up and joins us. "How do you two know each other?"

Kyle's face forms into a wince. "Molly is the girl I left for Amelia."

Before Blake can comment, I ask, "How do *you* know Kyle?"

"We met this afternoon," Kyle says. "We were both out walking."

"You told a complete stranger that you left me for another woman?" Well, this is embarrassing. It's also not something I would have ever thought Kyle would cop to. The man I knew wasn't particularly keen on taking responsibility for actions that made him look less than stellar. Case in point, he told all of our mutual friends that our breakup was a joint decision.

Addressing Blake, Kyle asks, "Would you mind giving us a minute?"

Apparently, Blake does mind because he stands riveted to his spot. I'm glad too, because I think I might enjoy having a witness while I rail against Kyle for wasting so much of my time. Having an audience will embarrass him more.

Barely controlling my anger, I announce, "I'm not sorry Amelia left you, Kyle. In fact, it's exactly what you deserve. And while I no longer fantasize about you getting run over by a semi-truck, I really don't think there's any point to you and me talking."

"You wanted to kill me?" He looks appropriately chagrined.

"Not personally," I tell him. "In my fantasies, I liked to be on the sidelines watching you meet your end." *Your grizzly, untimely, painful demise, you big turd.*

Kyle's complexion turns a dingy sort of grey. "Oh."

I continue, "I'm not sure how many of these mixers I'm going to attend, but I'd like to make it clear that you are to avoid me like I'm the bubonic plague and you're a midwife. Because that's how I see you."

"You see me as a midwife?" He sounds genuinely confused.

"No, you get to be the bubonic plague."

"I suppose it's too late to say I'm sorry then." If I didn't hate Kyle quite so much, I'd almost feel some compassion for him.

"Not at all," I answer. "In fact, I'd very much like to hear your apology." It won't do me any good now, but I find I'm quite enjoying my ex's discomfort.

Taking a deep breath, Kyle says, "I'm so sorry, Molly. From the bottom of my heart, you deserved better than what I did to you, and there's no excuse that would justify my past behavior."

Darn if he doesn't sound sincere. But I'm not about to let him off the hook. "Better late than never, I suppose," I tell him. Then for good measure, I add, "Now, stay away from me."

Kyle's gaze shifts from me to Blake and then back to me. "If that's what you want." I nod my head once, which is all the energy I deign to expend on his behalf. I can't believe I let Kyle scare me away from dating, and I'm really starting to resent him for that.

Kyle turns to walk away but Blake does not follow suit. Instead, he steps closer to me. "That was brutal," he finally says.

I take a giant step to the side to regain my personal space. "What was brutal?"

"Kyle and you. You know, the whole leaving you for another woman thing?"

In attempt to recoup my dignity, I tell him, "It's over and done. Kyle doesn't mean anything to me anymore."

"Yeah, but still. It must have been a shock at the time."

"A shock?" I ask before saying, "Yeah, it was a shock, but you know what they say, don't you?" He shakes his head, so I tell him, "All's fair in love and war."

"It sounds like you're defending the guy." Blake sounds surprised.

"No. I'm not defending him. But Kyle did teach me a valuable lesson."

"What's that?"

"He taught me trust is something that needs to be earned. I gave him my trust too easily, and I won't make that mistake again."

Blake looks at me questioningly while continuing to stare at me like he's trying to see inside of my brain. "People do have to earn trust," he says, "but at some point, you have to take things on faith."

The first thought that comes to mind is that Blake is simply too good-looking to be here which makes me not trust him. But then again, who's to say gorgeous men have an easy time dating? Maybe women throw themselves at him and he isn't finding the quality of person that he's after.

I remain quiet for long enough that Blake breaks the silence by asking, "So, you still want that double gin with a tequila chaser?"

I snort in response. "No, but I wouldn't mind a glass of red wine if they have it."

Blake points to the bar table set up next to the dancing chipmunks. "Let's go see," he says.

I remain quiet on the way to our destination. Blake makes me nervous. He's exactly the kind of guy I could imagine seeing myself with, but he's made it clear I'm not the kind of woman he's looking for. Without thinking, I blurt out, "So what's your ideal woman like?"

"Over three feet tall but under seven feet."

I stop walking and stare him down. "Excuse me?"

He stops moving and says, "She walks on two legs, unless of course she only has one, then I'd have to assume she might hobble a little."

"What in the world are you talking about?"

His smile is enough to set loose a flock of butterflies in my stomach. "I don't know what my ideal woman is like," he says. "I haven't met her yet."

"You mean you don't have a type?" I find it hard to believe that Blake's future mate might be a three-foot, six-inch, peg-legged pirate.

"I've dated a lot of different kinds of women," he says.

I snort loudly in response.

"You don't believe me?"

I suddenly return to the nervous mass of awkwardness that I've always been around him. "It's just that ... well ..."—I point at the top of his head and let my finger slowly move toward his feet —"you're not exactly, you know ..."

"A lumberjack?" he teases.

Oh, he could be a lumberjack all right. Before a trail of drool slides down my mouth, I manage to say, "You're not exactly unattractive."

"Thank you?"

"You're welcome."

He smiles endearingly. "You're not exactly unattractive yourself."

"That's not much of a compliment," I tell him.

"Yeah, I didn't think so either when you said the same about me."

"Sorry about that." *Why can't I act normally around this man?*

He gestures toward the bar. "What do you say we go get you that drink. Then maybe we can wander around the room together looking for our soulmates."

That says it all, doesn't it? As if I needed reminding, Blake does not see me as a potential love interest. And being that we're at a singles' event, if he were even slightly interested in a five-foot, six-inch brunette with blue eyes, he'd certainly let me know, wouldn't he? Either that or he's decided I'm too awkward to catch his fancy. In truth, that's a real possibility.

"I think I'll get that gin after all," I tell him.

When we reach the bar, he tells the bartender, "We'd like two gin martinis, dry, straight up with olives. Make them extra cold, please."

"How do you know that's how I like my martini?" I ask, surprised that he nailed my order.

With a slow grin, he answers, "Because you're clearly not a barbarian."

Laughter erupts out of me. "Only barbarians drink their martinis on the rocks with lemon twists?"

"Obviously," he says with such dry humor I want to throw myself into his arms and beg him to like me. Short of that, I guess I'll just enjoy spending whatever time I can with him.

As soon as we get our drinks, we hear a loud tapping sound before Trina's voice is amplified around the room. She says, "I hope you're all enjoying yourselves. I have a lot of fun things planned for us in the next two weeks. But first things first ..."

She gestures around the room. "Turn to the first person of the opposite sex you see." She waits while we follow orders, then she says, "Now, tell them something about yourself that you've never told a potential suitor." So much for tonight just being a meet and greet.

The room fills with nervous murmurs before the quiet mumbling of confessions fills the air. I look up at Blake before unconsciously fluttering my eyelashes. I mutter, "I've always wanted to date a lumberjack."

His smile is as slow as cold molasses pouring from a jug. Then he leans down and whispers in my ear, "Me too ..."

CHAPTER TWELVE

BLAKE

I can't get Molly and Kyle's story out of my head. They're sure to catch readers' interest. Titles for the piece start to pop into my mind. "Dumped!" "Karma Calling!" Or maybe simply, "Second Chances?"—although Molly doesn't strike me like the type who would ever forgive a betrayal like Kyle's. Even so, there isn't a person alive who wouldn't be invested in seeing how things turn out between these two star-crossed ex-lovers.

My problem is that Molly is so incredibly endearing, all I want to do is talk to her and get to know her better. I come short of admitting that I'd like to date her for myself because I'm sure as heck not going to write about my own social life. In an attempt to break this crazy tension between us, I turn and look around at the attendees of tonight's event and ask her, "Which guy here looks like he's a lumberjack?"

Molly takes a sip of her drink before letting her gaze wander. She finally points across the room at a bearded man wearing a flannel shirt. "Him?"

"That's your type?" I ask, surprised she's not interested in someone more refined looking—someone like me, perhaps.

Her head moves from side to side before she answers, "You didn't tell me to find someone who was my type. You told me to find a lumberjack. Not all lumberjacks are created equal, you know."

I can't help but smile at her wit. "Find a guy you think you might be interested in getting to know better."

She looks up at me from under her long eyelashes before turning toward the assemblage of hopeful singles. Then she points at a man wearing a dark business suit. I inexplicably hate him on sight. "I suppose he looks interesting."

"Interesting. That's it?"

Molly glares at me. "Who do you see me with?"

I look from one group to another before gesturing toward a guy who's probably about five seven. He's wearing glasses and a sweater vest. "What about him?"

Molly's lips curl into something of a sneer. "I don't think so. I like my guys taller."

"But you're only, what? Five-six?"

She slams back the rest of her drink before dropping her glass on the tray of a passing waiter. "Are you only interested in women over six feet?" she asks brusquely.

"I wouldn't have much of a selection, if that was my criteria."

"Nor would I have a big variety if I was determined to date men only an inch taller than me."

"It's not necessarily a height thing," I lie. Pointing to the guy I picked for her, I add, "He looks smart and thoughtful. I bet he'd never cheat on you."

Molly's eyes narrow to the point where only the barest slits remain open. "Fine, I'll go talk to him, but you have to go talk to the woman I pick for you."

Fortunately, I'm not actually looking, and therefore have no problem agreeing. "Go for it."

Scanning the room, Molly settles on a woman I'd guess was a librarian in Victorian times. She's wearing a cardigan sweater over a turtleneck and her skirt is so long it's nearly brushing the top of her shoes. "Her."

"She looks very nice," I tell her. "Dependable."

"You could do worse than dependable," Molly says. "Trust me on that."

"Meet me back here in ten minutes?" I ask. "You know, so we can compare notes."

Molly rolls her beautiful blue eyes. "Fine." Then she wanders off in the direction of the least threatening man in the room. In turn, I head toward her choice for me.

When I arrive at the woman's side, I smile and ask, "Are you having a nice time?"

Her posture jolts upward before she answers, "Not at all. How about you?"

I decide to come clean. "This kind of thing isn't really my bag."

"Then why are you here?"

Playing on a variation of my previous lies, I tell her, "I'm writing a book. The main character is going on one of these dating weekends, so I figured I'd come check it out."

"You're here on false pretenses!" she practically shouts, which causes several people in the near vicinity to turn and stare at me.

"No, not really," I tell her. "I mean, I'm single too."

"If you're not here to meet someone, then you're throwing off the numbers for everyone else."

"But I'm not," I try to explain.

Before I can convince her, she declares, "I'm going to tell Trina. The only people that should be in this room are ones who are sincere about finding love. If you're not serious, you shouldn't be here."

While I'd like nothing more than to get kicked out of this event, I'm guessing Gillian's retribution would be swift and painful. Like she'd put me on the morgue beat or make me the person in charge of covering PTA meetings at elementary schools. I hurry to tell the flustered woman in front of me, "My name is

Blake and while I am writing a book, I'm also a single man looking to find my person."

Her left eye starts to twitch nervously and I'm about to suggest she go lie down when she blurts out, "Olivia. I'm Olivia."

Hoping to establish some normal dialogue, I ask. "What do you do, Olivia?"

"I'm a pet psychic," she answers. *So much for normal.*

"What does that entail?" I valiantly try not to let any judgment show.

"It entails talking to animals and asking them about their feelings. What did you think it meant?"

Suddenly feeling like a three-hundred-pound man walking across a newly frozen lake, I respond, "I didn't really know. You're the first pet psychic I've ever met."

"Do you even have pets?" I'm not sure there's a man alive who would be suited to a woman with this bristly of an attitude.

"Not currently," I tell her, "but I used to have a piranha. I don't suppose you communicate with fish, do you?"

"Why wouldn't I? I'm not prejudiced against fish." I briefly wonder if Olivia didn't just get released from some kind of mental health program. Prematurely.

"I guess I didn't know if fish communicated the same way other animals do."

"Of course they do! They have brains, don't they?" I cannot get away from this woman fast enough.

"I don't know," I tell her honestly. "I don't really know much about fish."

"Then why would you ever share your household with one?"

"I liked the way he looked," I tell her.

"Oh, so you're one of those." At this point, I half expect Olivia to punch me in the throat and be done with it.

"You know what, Olivia?" I ask, but before she can answer, I tell her, "I think that maybe you and I aren't a match."

She has the audacity to look surprised. "Why would you say that?"

"You seem a little hostile," I say. "I get that I'm not everyone's cup of tea, so maybe we should both chat with other people."

Her expression falls to the point where I'm worried she's going to start crying. "Fine, go. I didn't want to talk to you anyway."

A tiny part of me wants to console her, but the bigger part compels me to run for my life. "I hope you meet someone nice," I tell Olivia. I don't wait for her response. Instead, I turn around and hurry back to the spot where Molly and I parted ways. I wait for what must be at least twenty minutes before she finally returns.

"Took you long enough," I accuse.

"Don't get snippy with me," she says. "It turns out you might have a future in matchmaking."

"What?"

"Ronald is very nice."

"You can't be serious." *She can't be serious.*

"Why not? Why would you have picked him for me if you didn't think we would be a good match?"

Because I don't want you to match with him. But I don't say that. Instead, I want to know, "What's his story?"

"Let's see." Molly taps on her chin for a few beats. "Ronald is thirty-four. He's a computer analyst for the FBI." My eyes open wider at that information. I'm not surprised the guy's a computer geek, and the whole working for the feds thing might give him an aura of mystery. I wonder if that's the part Molly likes about him.

"Let me guess, he's a spy and he's here undercover on a mission to save Elk Lake from a communist invasion." I can't seem to keep the sarcasm from dripping out of me.

Molly shakes her head. "No, he's really here looking for a girlfriend."

"And you like him?"

She shrugs. "I don't dislike him. Although, I think the whole," she makes air quotes with her fingers before adding, "'living in his mother's basement' is a bit of a red flag."

"No!" I laugh out loud.

"They have meatloaf every Monday night," Molly says seriously. Her expression turns concerned as she adds, "But last Monday Ronald's mom made roasted potatoes instead of mashed and Ronald isn't quite sure he can forgive her."

"It's no wonder there are so many single people in this world," I say. "Seriously, not shocking at all."

"Did you have better luck?"

A full body shiver overtakes me before I tell her about Olivia. "Mine was a pet psychic with what I'm guessing might be a personality disorder."

"Oh, no."

"Oh, yes," I tell her. "I hate to be that person, but I think she might also be off her meds."

Molly laughs in earnest. "Poor Blake. Coming all this way and not finding anyone decent to date."

Feeling the need to defend my honor, I tell her, "I met a very nice kindergarten teacher earlier."

Easygoing Molly leaves the room. "Really? Then why aren't you talking to her?"

Because I'd rather talk to you. Looking for any sign of jealousy, I announce, "Maybe I'll look for her later."

"Maybe you should go now."

Before I can leave, Trina is back at the microphone. "It's me again!" She signals to the piano player who starts to play an old Frank Sinatra tune. "It's time to hit the dance floor with the man or woman you're currently talking to. Don't ask questions, just open your arms and start moving."

I take a moment to thank my lucky stars I'm not still talking to Olivia. She'd probably put me in a choke hold. But then I realize I'm going to have to dance with Molly, and while I'd truly love nothing more, I'm not sure having her in my arms is for the best.

CHAPTER THIRTEEN

MOLLY

Dance with Blake? Yes, please. But at the same time, I'd better not. Without making eye contact, I tell him, "I … I … I … should go."

He reaches for my hand to stop me. "Where? Why?"

"I think I'll get another drink." Although, it'll probably be water. One martini is my limit if I don't want to do something I'll regret around this guy. Not to mention the difficulty communicating I seem to have when talking to him.

"Trina gave us an order," he says. "And by being here, we've agreed to follow the rules." Blake sounds like a good soldier, which isn't how I would have classified him. I'd peg him as the rebel type.

"You don't want to dance with me." Looking around the room, I add, "Maybe your kindergarten teacher is waiting for you."

"Don't be a party pooper, Molly." Blake pulls me into his arms with enough force that I have no option but to follow. My face lands smack into the crook of his neck. One whiff and I'm done for. From this moment forward, orange and clove, with a hint of bay rum is my new favorite fragrance.

I'm quite literally rendered speechless by this man. His arms, his scent, his overwhelmingly possessive embrace. If he showed any interest in me whatsoever, I'd run away to a deserted island with him and spend the rest of my days eating bananas and beating our clothes against the rocks to keep them clean. I wouldn't even mind all the sand that would surely invade every corner of our beachfront hut. Somehow in my fantasies we're roughing it like castaways.

Blake starts to hum along with the melody of the song, and I feel the vibration to the very core of my being. *Yes, Blake, I'll fly to the moon with you. I'll swing on the stars…*

But of course, this is real life and not a romance novel, so instead, I trip over my own foot which causes Blake's hold on me to become something of a death grip. "Are you okay?" he asks.

I'm mortified is what I am, but I somehow find the nerve to tell him, "That was something I saw on *Dancing with the Stars*. If you hadn't stopped me, I would have hit the floor and started to break dance."

Blake's laughter fills me with joy. "I would have liked to have seen that. Want to try it again?"

I shake my head. "It's a maneuver that requires spontaneity."

"Maybe you'll do it later."

I hope not, but I don't say that. "I never try the same move on the same guy."

"Molly …" Blake's warm breath hits my skin and causes goosebumps to pop up everywhere.

When he doesn't continue talking, I counter with, "Blake …"

"I like …" But again, he doesn't finish his sentence.

"What do you like?" *The feeling of me in your arms? The softness of my hair as it tickles your nose? The promise of a new love?*

"I like pineapple."

"Excuse me?" *Is he likening me to fruit?*

He pulls me closer for the briefest moment before pushing me away to the point where a high school chaperone would not only approve, but she'd also wonder if I had a world-class case of BO. "I'm trying a new line on you. I figure if I'm going to find love while I'm here, I need to up my game. So, what do you think?"

I think I'd like to knee him in the knutz and tell him not to practice his wooing techniques on me unless he's interested in dating *me*. My delicate sensibilities can't handle it. "I think that if it's true love you're after, you should let the woman you're interested in discover the kind of fruit you prefer in a more organic way." I sound like a schoolteacher scolding him for throwing spit wads.

"Like on our honeymoon?" His voice is full of humor which makes me want to jump into his arms.

"Or when you take her out to brunch," I say sourly.

"I have an idea," Blake says. "I think we should buddy up and help each other while we're here."

"Buddy up?" I'm more insulted than I've ever been in my life.

"Yeah, you know, hook up and consult with each other about the people we meet. Help guide each other."

"Hoo ... hoo ... hook up?" My mouth goes completely dry at the very thought.

"You know, have meals together that aren't part of the mixer."

"Oh."

When the song ends and Blake steps away from me, I wind up stumbling forward like I'm trying to get back into his arms. How mortifying. Reaching out to steady me, he says, "So what do you think. Should we be each other's dating pals?"

The words dating and pals should never be used in the same sentence. It's mean. Hurtful. I think of how my mother has always told me to know my worth and not chase after a man, and she's one hundred percent right. There's no better way to show Blake I'm not romantically interested in him than to be his bud.

With that in mind, I tell him, "Sure, let's be *pals*." Now all I have to do is convince myself that's all I want.

"Good," he says. "There's no breakfast get-together tomorrow, so what do you say I pick you up at your room at eight?"

I nearly forgot that Blake and I are practically roommates. We actually might have been had he not told the desk clerk we weren't together. Still, having him right next door to me is sure to cause some sleepless nights. Even though I know I'm only making my life more difficult in the end, I tell him, "Fine. Good. I'll see you then."

"Are you going somewhere now?" He sounds surprised.

Glancing over his shoulder, I say, "We should get out there and mingle if we're going to have anything to talk about over breakfast." Yet, Blake could probably read the menu to me, and I'd totally be riveted.

He bobs his head up and down. "Good plan. I think I'll look for Krista."

"The kindergarten teacher?" My tone is full of disgust. What does she have that I don't? Other than maybe a massive glue stick collection.

"Yeah. How about you? You going to find the guy in the suit?"

"I just might," I tell him. Then without another word, or even a backward glance, I turn and walk away. I'm so butt hurt that Blake doesn't return my interest that I don't pay attention to where I'm going, and I wind up walking right into Kyle. Fun times.

He's carrying two glasses of wine, and nearly spills both before righting himself. "Molly, hey."

"I thought we weren't going to talk," I hiss nastily.

"We weren't but that was before you almost ran me over."

Taking a step back, I say, "Sorry about that."

I'm about to walk away before my ex announces, "I wish there was some way you could forgive me."

I can't seem to stop my eyes from rolling, not that I'm trying too hard. "I suppose if you found a time machine we could go back in time. Then you could *not* cheat on me."

"What do you think our lives would be like now if I hadn't?"

The question causes a deep-rooted angst to bloom inside my belly. I shouldn't answer him, but I'm so caught in the moment that I say, "I suppose we might be married by now. Maybe even be buying a house and expecting a baby."

I should be pleased by the look of longing on Kyle's face, but I'm not. Surprisingly, I almost feel as sorry for him as I do for myself. "That would have been nice," he says. "I'm sorry I messed things up so badly."

"Are you?" I want to know. "Or are you sad that you don't have those things with Amelia?"

He considers his answer for long enough that I know his answer without him saying anything. For the second time tonight, I feel the sharp stab of rejection. "Is there any way we can be friends?" he asks despondently.

"I don't see how," I tell him truthfully. "I don't let men lie to me, and I sure as heck expect better from my friends."

"Can we at least try to not be enemies?"

I think about something my mom always says about forgiveness. She says you don't forgive someone to appease their hearts, you do it to ease your own. And while I plan to be angry at Kyle forever for his blatant disregard of my worth, I don't love him anymore. Being that I truly did like him once upon a time, I decide, "We don't have to be enemies."

"That's a good start."

I shake my head. "Not a start. The end. Full stop. We don't go anywhere from there." And while I should enjoy the look of sorrow my words invoke, I don't.

"I guess I'll see you around then," Kyle says. He pauses long enough that if I stopped him, I'm sure he would stay. But I don't. I simply watch him walk away toward a pretty woman wearing a black cocktail dress and an expression of raw hope.

I instantly know I don't have the intestinal fortitude to continue with this mixer. I know I told Blake I was going to mingle, but the only thing I want to mingle with right now is a hot bath and trash TV. Turning to leave the room, Trina catches my eye. She walks toward me with a pep in her step not often seen by someone who isn't an NFL cheerleader. "You're very popular tonight!"

"Not really," I tell her.

"What about that tall hotty you were dancing with? That looked promising."

"Blake has made me an offer," I tell her. Her expression morphs into one of a child receiving a kitten on Christmas morning. "He's asked me to be his dating buddy. Apparently, he wants someone to talk to about other women." She suddenly looks like her kitty got hit by a car.

"Really? That's not at all how it looked. What about the guy you were just talking to? I just saw the back of his head but that looked decent."

There's no shame quite like public shame and the emotion fills me to the brim. "He and I dated for a year before he left me for someone else."

"No!" It's humbling to know my social life is such a disaster it can surprise a trained professional.

I nod my head. "I know, right? I'm thinking I might be better off just working on your gift shop and avoiding these little get-togethers."

"Don't give up yet," she says. "There are a couple of guys here I think might be great matches for you."

"I'm not sure I can take much more disappointment," I tell her.

"Give me two more mixers, and if you aren't feeling it by then, I won't say another word if you walk away."

If I have two more experiences like tonight's, I might move to the woods and become a hermit. But it turns out I'm something of a glutton for punishment because I hear myself tell her, "Fine. I'll give you two more events."

Leaving the room, I wonder if I should go back into town and see if someone isn't selling a full suit of body armor. I have a feeling I might need it.

CHAPTER FOURTEEN

BLAKE

I had to stop myself from following Molly when she left the mixer. I love how funny and engaging she is. Seriously, when she tried to cover her stumble by claiming she was going to start break dancing, I nearly proposed. While she's clearly not the most graceful woman, she's more entertaining than any I've ever met.

For a moment, I'm almost disappointed that I'm here on false pretenses. Not that I'd ever willingly sign up for something like this, but if I did, I'd certainly have thought I'd struck gold when I met Molly. She's the kind of woman you'd expect to have a line of men beating down her door.

I spend the next two hours introducing myself to women and men alike. I think I might have given a couple of guys the wrong impression by the way they hurried away from me, but so what? I'm here to do a job and I figure I need to talk to everyone that will talk to me.

Walking up to the guy that Molly pointed out as someone she might be interested in, I ask, "Having any luck?"

He shakes his head. "Not yet. It turns out I might not excel at this sort of thing."

"It does kind of feel like attending your own execution, doesn't it?"

He laughs. "Like you're the star of a show that everyone knows is about to be cancelled."

"Why is it that we're not viewing this as a show that's about to be renewed? I think the goal is for us to be filled with optimism."

Continuing the simile, he says, "It might have something to do with our co-stars." He points to Olivia. "That one is particularly scary."

"I didn't last five minutes," I tell him. "It's not that I have anything against pet psychics, but Olivia is truly out there."

"What about the gorgeous brunette you were dancing with earlier?" Ah, so he noticed Molly. I'm not surprised.

I know it's wrong, but I find myself feeling protective, so I tell him, "I think she might still be pining for her ex."

"Really?" He sounds disappointed. Hopefully it will keep him from making a play for her.

"I'm Blake, by the way," I tell him.

"Thor," he answers.

It's clear I have no acting ability because as much as I try to school my expression, I can feel my facial muscles as they contract in horror. "Really?"

He chuckles. "My parents are Swedish. They came to the US after they got married." He adds, "I think they gave their kids intimidating names hoping it would cement our success in America."

"What are your siblings named?"

"My older brother is Odin and my sister is Freya."

"Wow." There's nothing else to say but, "Have you been as successful as they'd hoped?"

"I'm a producer on *Chicago Flame*," he says. "So, I'm not doing too bad. All I need now is a wife and they'll be over the moon."

"You'd think you'd have met a lot of available women, given your field," I tell him.

He cringes. "I'm not interested in actresses."

"I spent the last decade in Los Angeles. I just moved back to Chicago."

Thor grimaces. "I'm sorry."

"About which part?"

"LA," he says.

"It sounds like you know my pain."

"I was there before *Chicago Flame* got picked up. While I never lacked for female companionship, the quality of conversation left something to be desired."

"I wish someone would tell all those women searching for stardom that they don't have to sell their souls to the devil to succeed."

"But they really kind of do, don't they?" he asks. "I mean, the whole business is based on superficiality, so by not being superficial, they wouldn't be playing the right game to succeed."

"That's a depressing thought."

He nods. "Which is why I don't date actresses." Briefly glancing to the left, he adds, "Or pet psychics."

We talk for a few more minutes before I excuse myself. After meeting several other people, it occurs to me that there's a wide spectrum of loneliness out there. I meet two doctors, a lawyer, a couple of schoolteachers and even a woman who owns a chain of car washes. I don't connect with Krista again, but I manage to gather enough information to get back to work on my match-making exposé.

Once I get back to my room, I pull out my laptop and get busy.

What ever happened to meeting people the old-fashioned way? You know, in a bar or at a friend's kid's bar mitzvah? Don't parents set their adult children up with their friends' offspring anymore?

I just spent the last three hours at Trina Rockwell's first mixer at the Elk Lake Lodge and I'm not full of optimism. Rather, I feel sorry for the singles of the world who feel it necessary to put themselves out there in such a blatant way. It's almost like everyone was wearing the same sign around their necks: "I'm sad and lonely and I'm here because nobody else wants me." At least that's how I felt, and I'm not even looking.

That isn't to say the participants were less attractive or accomplished than their non-intending counterparts — other than the fact they're still single.

People from all walks of life are looking for love. The men ranged from blue collar jobs, like plumbers and contractors, to your college-educated careers of system analysts and archi-tects. The women were equally impressive. I met a doctoral candidate who's writing her thesis on black holes, another was a stock trader, and still another who taught martial arts during the day and moonlighted as a bartender at night. There appears to be no foolproof recipe for success in the dating world.

So far, Ms. Rockwell has used an array of interesting tech-niques to get people to talk to each other. She stopped the mixer several times and informed the participants to share secrets, to dance, and even to force them to complement one another. I thought it felt uncomfortably orchestrated, but many seemed to find her machinations positive and unique.
I suppose I might have a different take if I were here to find love for myself, but I inherently believe in fate, not forced communion. Having said that, this was only day one. I'm sure there's more excitement to come, and maybe if people are lucky, some will find a happy ending.

I open another document for stories that I plan to weave in through the various articles. As of tonight, there's only one that comes to mind. I find that I almost don't want to write about it, but I have to because that's my job.

Imagine coming to a dating event two hours away from
your home and running into the man who left you for
another woman. That's what happened to one of the ladies
at Trina Rockwell's first singles get-together. Polly
Anderson thought she was going to meet nice eligible men,
when in fact she wound up running into the man who
broke her heart ...

By the time I get into bed, I feel borderline dirty writing about
Molly. And even though I've changed her name—barely—if she
ever reads my articles, she'll know I was talking about her. While
I'm attempting to be vague, most people probably won't have a
hard time discerning who they are. For instance, I'm making
Olivia an animal massage therapist instead of a psychic. I'm sure
she won't need her sixth sense to decipher that one.

I briefly consider the ethics of what I'm doing, but after firing
off an email to Gillian, she assured me that she'll run everything
through legal before it gets published. While that should bring me
some peace, and it does for most of the folks I'll be talking about,
there's still the small matter of Molly.

What in the world am I going to do about her?

CHAPTER FIFTEEN

MOLLY

When I got back to my room, I checked my phone and found out that I had four messages from Ellen. My sister seriously needs another hobby. Instead of calling her back right away, I take a bubble bath that's so relaxing I nearly fall asleep.

When I finally get out, I wrap myself in the plush bathrobe furnished by the lodge. Then I rub a towel through my hair to soak up the excess moisture, before picking up my phone and climbing onto the bed.

I press the button with my sister's face on it and barely have to wait a second before she excitedly answers. "How was tonight?" She sounds like she knew I was doing something other than eating dinner in my room, which is standard for me when I'm on a job.

"What do you mean, how was tonight?"

She clears her throat and pauses briefly before saying, "Did you go down to the dining room again for supper? Did you get the Beef Wellington?"

"What Beef Wellington?"

"Didn't I tell you about that? It was my favorite meal while I was there."

I have no memory of that but of course, I don't always listen to every word Ellen says. "I thought your favorite meal was the almond-crusted trout."

"That was my second favorite," she says. "So, what did you do tonight and why did it take you so long to call me back?"

It suddenly feels like too much effort to concoct a full-blown lie, so I tell her, "The lodge hosted a cocktail party in the great room for the guests. I went for a bit, hoping to get an idea of the kinds of things they'd like to see in the gift shop."

"All work, huh?" She sounds disappointed.

"That's why I'm here," I remind her.

"You can't blame me for hoping you might meet that lumberjack."

"No lumberjacks, but I did run into somebody we both know and don't love."

"Allison Finch?" she asks.

"Why would Mom and Dad's neighbor be in Elk Lake this time of year?" Before she can answer, I say, "She'd miss out on criticizing everyone's holiday decorations."

"That woman is truly awful," Ellen agrees. "Do you know she told Mom her inflatable snowman looks like a cheater?"

I snort. "Who's he cheating on, the blow-up Santa Claus?"

"Who knows. I swear though, that woman needs to get a life."

"Speaking of cheating and getting a life…" I start to say.

"Yes?"

"The person I ran into was Kyle."

"Your former Kyle? The scum of the Earth Kyle? Kyle, the man I want to run through with a nail file, Kyle?"

Ellen could go on for hours like this, so I tell her, "Yes. That Kyle."

"What in the world is he doing up there?"

If I say he's here for a singles' event, my sister will insist that I throw myself into the mix, so I don't go there. "I didn't bother to ask."

"Was he there with Amelia?"

"I didn't stick around long enough to find out."

"Oh, Molly," Ellen says with such sympathy I feel my eyes start to fill with tears. "What awful, horrible, rotten luck. Do you want me to come up there? I would happily beat him up for you."

The fact that I almost want her to come says a lot about the current condition of my mental state. I forcibly remind myself that it would be a nightmare if Ellen was here. I remind myself that Kyle doesn't mean anything to me and therefore isn't worth the nightmare of Ellen coming head-to-head with him. "Don't come. You need to spend time with Henry and his family."

"*You're* my family," she says, "and if you need me, then you're my priority."

"Henry might be your family soon, too," I tell her.

She grunts. "Maybe, but he's not yet, so just say the word and I'll be on my way."

Ellen may drive me totally insane ninety percent of the time, but the truth is I really do love her and I'm lucky to have her. "I love you, Ellen."

She seems surprised by the declaration. "Seeing that loser really bothered you, didn't it?"

Sliding under the covers, I lean against the pile of pillows behind me. "Yes and no. Part of me is surprised I haven't run into him before now, so I guess it's a relief to have it over with."

"I used to dream about seeing him in a crosswalk and mowing him down."

That sounds like a fantasy I used to have.

She continues, "But then I started watching *Orange is the New Black* and I realized I wouldn't do well in prison."

A burst of laughter erupts out of me. "I don't know, Ellen. I think you'd be running Cell Block C within a week."

"For sure," she says. "But the lack of sunshine would make me depressed and that would cause me to eat twice as much as I already do and before you know it, I'd be too fat to get out of bed."

"That's your worry about going to jail? Getting fat?"

Ellen sighs. "That's my worry about getting up every morning."

I hate that we live in a world where women spend so much time being anxious about their weight. We carry the cross of our appearance like the whole planet would fall out of orbit if we suddenly decided to accept ourselves. "You aren't fat, Ellen."

"Not in the sense that I can't fit through a doorway, but let's face it, I'm no string bean."

"And why would you want to be?" I ask. "Women who starve themselves to be thin have to be totally miserable."

"There are some who are naturally skinny, you know."

"And as much as it pains me to ask this, why aren't we happy for them? Shouldn't we have each other's backs?"

"Molly, is this you? Have you been alien abducted and replaced by a cyborg?"

She's right. I've been known to be critical about some things and one of those has been women who can eat anything they want and not gain weight. But after tonight, I'm feeling a little kinder toward humanity. After all, a lot of the women at the mixer were very thin, and they were at a singles' mixer. "Life is hard for everyone, and I don't want to be a part of tearing people down anymore."

"That's very mature of you," my sister says. "But I'm still disappointed. I've always been able to count on you as my partner to grouse with."

Changing the subject, I ask, "What did you get Mom and Dad for Christmas?"

"Tickets to Bermuda," she says. "Mom claims she doesn't like to travel much anymore but I know she'd do practically anything to get away from a Chicago winter for a couple of weeks. What did you get them?"

"Matching snowsuits so they can get the mail together." Then a thought hits me. "I have a vacation voucher for a resort I worked at in Bermuda. Text me the dates of their airline tickets and I'll see if I can't get their hotel comped."

"Nice! Maybe you and I should plan a sisters' getaway this winter if we can find a time that works for both of us," she suggests.

I wouldn't hate that. Ellen can be intense, but we do share the same family. It's nice to have somebody who knows how you got to be the person you currently are. "Let's sit down with our calendars soon," I tell her.

I hear someone in the hallway and immediately wonder if it's Blake. I don't know why I should care, given his blatant disregard of me, but even so, I get out of bed and hurry to the door. Cracking it open slightly, I peek out and find him standing in front of his door. He turns and says, "Hey."

"Hey."

"Who are you talking to?" Ellen wants to know.

"The maid," I tell her before offering Blake a small wave. Then I close my door again.

"Did she bring by more towels or something?" Ellen asks.

"Who?"

"The maid."

"Oh yeah," I say before adding, "I need to get to bed. I have an early appointment in the morning."

"Okay, Molls, thanks for calling. And I love you, too."

After plugging my phone into the charger, I crawl back into bed. Then I nestle under the covers and wonder what Blake is doing next door. He's probably itemizing a list of women he met that he wants to get to know better. Starting with that kindergarten teacher. Grrr.

So much for my telling Ellen that women should have each other's backs. I currently want nothing to do with the one who's caught Blake's eye. I know I sound petty, but why can't he be interested in me?

But, no. I'm the one he wants to talk about other women to. If that's not bad enough, my ex is here looking for love, too. If this were a movie, it would be a spectacular failure. Just like my social life.

CHAPTER SIXTEEN

BLAKE

I'm standing at Molly's door at seven fifty-eight on the nose. My plan is to wait until eight to knock so I don't appear too eager, but at seven fifty-nine, she opens her door and walks right into me. After a short dance where I worry that she's about to fall over, *again*, she says, "What are you doing here?"

"Picking you up for breakfast?"

"Then why didn't you knock?"

"I was waiting until eight," I tell her. She looks very pretty today in her red cashmere sweater. She's paired it with jeans and heavy winter boots. The white parka over her arm makes me think she's planning on enjoying some outdoor sports after breakfast. At least that's why I brought my coat with me.

Looking me up and down like I'm some kind of creeper, she says, "Well, I'm here. Let's go to eat."

She's clearly in a bad mood. "Did you have a rough night?"

"I slept fine."

We continue to walk down the hall without saying a word. As we pass the family I met yesterday, I call out, "Hey, Ben. You having fun?"

He waves. "So much fun!"

Molly wants to know, "Do you know him?"

"I keep running into him and his parents."

"Trina and her fiancé offer free rooms to families of special needs kids," she says.

"I think I heard something about that. That's pretty cool, huh?"

She nods her head but doesn't say anything else until we're in the elevator. "So, how did your night go with your kindergarten teacher?" She's back to sounding annoyed.

"I didn't talk to her again. I was busy circulating."

Her face crunches up like she just drank spoiled milk. "I bet you were."

"It's why we're here, isn't it?"

"I'm actually here for work," she tells me.

"But you showed up last night, so you're also single and looking for love."

Staring straight ahead, she says, "I'm single. Not sure about the looking for love part."

I feel bad for trying to steer Molly away from Thor last night, and as much as it pains me to say, they might be perfect for one another. While the thought doesn't exactly thrill me, I can't pursue Molly if I'm going to write about her. As such, I probably shouldn't stand in the way of her happiness.

As soon as we get to the dining room, the hostess leads the way to our table. As luck would have it, we walk right by Thor. He's sitting with Krista, the teacher. Stopping in front of them, I greet, "Thor, Krista, how are you both?"

Neither looks particularly happy to see me, so imagine how thrilled they are when I say, "You don't mind if we join you, do you?"

I don't bother to wait for an answer before pulling out a chair and calling to Molly who's still walking behind the hostess. "Molly, over here!"

She turns around and trips over her own foot. I briefly wonder if her lack of grace has something to do with her single status. It's possible not everyone is as charmed by it as I am. When she reaches the table, she awkwardly smiles at Thor and Krista. "I don't think they're looking for company."

"Nonsense," I tell her before practically pushing her down into the chair I've been holding for her.

Once we're both seated, I point to Krista. "Molly, this is Krista. She's a kindergarten teacher." Then I gesture toward Thor. "This is Thor. He produces *Chicago Flame*."

Molly nods her head at them before mumbling, "I'm so sorry. You probably wanted to be alone."

As she moves to push her chair back, I announce, "The more the merrier, am I right?"

Neither Thor nor Krista looks like they agree with my statement, but I'm suddenly married to the idea of matching up Thor and Molly. I know that last night I was against it, but I hate seeing Molly in such a surly mood. Surely, I can't expect to keep her all to myself if I'm not going to make a move on her.

Krista is the first to find her voice. "I didn't see you again last night, Blake. Did you have a nice time?"

"I did, thank you," I tell her. "And I see you've met Thor. Great name, huh?"

Turning to Thor, I tell him, "Molly designs gift shops for hotels. That's why she's here."

Thor nods his head. "So, you're not here for the Midwestern Matchmaker event? I thought I saw you last night."

"Not initially, no," Molly tells him. She's staring at Thor like he's a cheeseburger and she's just spent two weeks on a deserted island with no food. I don't like it, but that's not the point. I have no say in Molly's personal life, and if Thor could make her happy, then that should make me happy.

"There was a cancellation," I announce. "So, they asked Molly if she'd like to join in."

Krista, clearly sensing that she might be losing Thor's interest, announces, "That's too bad." As we all turn to her en masse, she adds, "I mean, it's too bad for whoever had to cancel."

With a wink, I tell the schoolteacher, "It's lucky for me that you didn't cancel." This appears to appease her ego slightly.

Thor glances around the table before asking, "What do you all have planned for the day?"

"I've got nothing," I tell him.

Molly says, "I'm supposed to make use of the various facilities so I can see if there's something the gift shop should carry that they don't already have. I was thinking about zip-lining."

"We should all go together!" Thor suggests. "What do you think, Krista? Does that sound like fun?"

Krista appears uncertain, as though she's trying to discern if Thor's more interested in her or Molly. Either way, she decides, "That does sound like a good time." She asks me, "Have you been zip-lining before, Blake?"

"It's one of my go-to activities," I tell her. "I've been zip-lining over the jungles of Peru and Hawaii."

"I bet that's great fodder for your writing." Oh yeah, that. *Note to self: Don't forget you're writing a novel, Blake.*

Molly interjects, "It's a wonder how you can afford vacations like that on a barista's pay."

"I make great tips," I tell her cockily. When in truth, pouring a cup of coffee is my limit.

"I bet you do." Krista giggles flirtatiously.

When the waiter delivers Thor and Krista's food, he takes Molly's and my order. I get the belgian waffle with chocolate chips and whipped cream. She orders a hard-boiled egg and dry toast. No wonder she's so grumpy; she must be starving.

Thor cuts into his omelet but before taking a bite, he asks Molly, "So how long will you be staying here at the lodge?"

"Two weeks," she tells him.

"That's an odd coincidence," Krista offers. All eyes turn to her, so she explains, "You know, that you'd be here at the same time as the singles' event, and for the same amount of time."

"Life is full of coincidence, isn't it?" I ask. "For instance, what are the chances Molly would be here at the same time as her ex?" Shoot, I didn't mean to say that. I don't want to embarrass Molly.

One look at her though, and I realize she's more annoyed than embarrassed. She explains to our table mates, "Kyle and I used to date a couple of years ago. It's no big deal."

"Is he the same guy that left you for another woman?" Thor wants to know.

Molly glares at me. "You're telling people about that, too?"

Thor grimaces. "I shouldn't have said anything, I'm sorry."

"It's not you who should be sorry," Molly tells him while looking me straight in the eyes.

"I'm sorry, too," I tell her. "I wasn't gossiping about you so much as I was ..." *Gossiping about her.* "Looking out for you," I decide on the fly.

"Looking out for me, how?" she wants to know.

"Thor told me that he thought you were attractive, and I didn't know if you'd be interested."

"After I told you I thought he was someone I could be interested in?" she practically yells. This causes the occupants of nearby tables to turn in our direction.

"You thought you might be interested in me?" Thor sounds pleased.

"Really?" It's clear Krista doesn't share his enthusiasm, so I turn my attention to her. "Tell me about kindergarten."

While not exactly placated, she answers, "I can honestly say that I don't like kids as much as I thought I did before I started teaching."

"How many do you have in your class?" I ask.

"Twenty-nine which is about twenty too many." She elaborates, "People start putting phones into their kids' hands so young to keep them occupied, by the time they start school, children don't have the attention span of a gnat."

"I hadn't thought about that," I tell her. "It kind of makes you nervous for their futures, doesn't it?"

Thor responds, "It makes me more nervous for our futures. The kids today are the people who will be taking care of us in our old age."

Molly shudders. "We're lucky there are people like Krista who are willing to take on the job of training today's youth." And just like that, the women appear to have found common ground and the tension at the table starts to dissipate.

Thor and Krista finish eating before Molly and I get our entrees, so Thor suggests, "Why don't we go and get our gear and then we can meet you both in the lobby for zip-lining?"

"Sounds like a plan," I tell him.

Molly merely smiles. But as soon as they walk away, she drops her fork and insists, "What is your problem?"

"What do you mean?"

"First you told Thor that I was some loser whose ex left her for another woman, and then you invited yourself to join him while he was clearly on a date with Krista. Are you jealous he stole your woman?"

"Krista's not my woman."

"She's all you could talk about last night."

"All I said was that I met a nice kindergarten teacher. I didn't say that I was going to pursue her."

"You intimated as much," she says.

"I figure we'll all need more than one mixer before we know who we're interested in dating."

Molly death glares at me. "And yet you managed to friend-zone me almost immediately. Thanks a lot."

Oh yeah, she's mad. If I'm honest, I'm kind of flattered. I'm willing to bet in other circumstances Molly and I could have been quite a dynamic duo. But I can't tell her that, so I go with, "Don't underestimate the value of a good friend. The women I've dated have come and gone, but my friends are still around."

"Yeah, that makes me feel great, thanks."

I can't seem to help myself from asking, "Are you saying that you'd be interested in dating me?"

CHAPTER SEVENTEEN

MOLLY

My hopeful inner teenager answers Blake's question. *Heck yes, I'd be interested in dating you, you stupid loser.* But outwardly, I counter with, "Why in the world would I be interested in dating you?"

As though defending his honor, Blake says, "Why wouldn't you want to date me? I'm a catch."

Maybe because you don't want to date me? I force myself to swallow my last bite of toast. "You've made it pretty clear I'm not your type, Blake." As such, I can't help but wonder why I think he's my type. I don't make it a habit of liking men who don't like me back. Of course, I haven't liked a guy since Kyle, and that might be the problem. Did I let that bonehead ruin my self-esteem, so I can't crush on someone worthy of me?

Blake doesn't bother denying the truth of my words. "That Thor's pretty cool though, huh?"

"He seems to be. So is Krista."

"Yeah," he says. "She's nice, too." Blake wipes his mouth before pushing his chair back.

After the waiter drops our checks and we both sign for our meals, I stand up and put my coat on. Blake follows suit. He leads the way out of the dining room. Once we get to the lobby, we see Thor and Krista sitting side by side on a sofa, waiting for us. Cozy is the only word that comes to mind.

Blake walks right up to them and puts his hand out to help Krista up. "You kids ready to roll?" he asks.

Thor answers, "We signed up while you were eating. Our group starts in ten minutes." Then he stands up and points toward a sandwich board with an arrow showing us where to go. After walking down two halls, we eventually wind up in a smallish room with several other people.

A man with a clipboard and a beard so full it looks like it could house a hive of bees raises a hand in the air to get our attention. "I'm Kale. I'm going to break you all down into three groups of four." He gestures toward two other guides and adds, "Four of you will go with Kiefer, four of you will go with Shalia, and I'll take the last bunch." He points at Blake, Thor, me, and Krista. "You guys are mine."

After he separates us, he asks, "Who here has never ziplined before?" I'm the only one to raise my hand. The things I'll do for my work surprise even me.

Blake looks surprised. "Why haven't you ziplined?"

I retaliate with, "Have you ever jumped off a skyscraper?"

"No."

"Why not?" I want to know.

"Have you?"

"Obviously not."

"Afraid of heights?" he guesses.

Shaking my head, I assure him, "No, I'm not afraid of heights, I'm afraid of falling from them."

Kale interrupts, "We have you so harnessed up that even if you lost your grip, you wouldn't hit the ground. Also, you aren't really that high up. It's not like we're zipping through the mountains here."

"Which is why I decided this was the perfect place for my

maiden voyage," I tell him. If we were jumping off a rocky cliff, I wouldn't have the courage.

Kale leads us out of the building, down a short path and into a yurt full of gear. After handing out harnesses and helmets, he shows us how to put everything on. Krista leans over and tells me, "Relax, you're going to have a great time. Just don't lie about how much you weigh because the person who catches you at the end of the run will need to know when to slow you down." She blows out a breath before adding, "Otherwise, you could knock them over and really hurt them."

She sounds too knowledgeable for this to be secondhand information, so I ask, "Did you do that?"

Her face reddens. "It was just ten pounds, but apparently that's enough to do some real damage."

I giggle nervously before forcing myself to suppress it. "What happened to him?"

"Her," she says. "I knocked into her with such force, she stumbled backward and fell off the landing. She broke her arm in two places."

"Oh my god, that's terrible!" My giggles return. "You must have been mortified."

"I was hoping to pass it off as clumsiness on her part, but the other instructor knew better. He gave us all a lecture on the importance of being truthful about our weight. He stared at me the whole time."

"I would have died," I tell her honestly.

With her head bobbing up and down, she answers, "That was certainly one of the options I entertained."

"What did you do?"

"I went home and lost fifteen pounds."

Looking at her closely, I say, "You could gain fifteen pounds and still look great."

"That's nice of you to say, but the whole episode scarred me."

"Are you ladies ready to go?" Thor interrupts.

We nod our heads in unison which signals Kale to announce, "I just need your weights and we're off."

"Two hundred," Thor says proudly.

"One ninety-seven," Blake says.

Krista and I share an anxious look. Remembering what I told Ellen last night about being sick of constantly worrying about my weight, I boldly announce, "Two hundred."

Blake snorts loudly. "You are not. You're probably no more than one fifty."

"One fifty? That's a horrible thing to say."

"You're the one who claimed to be two hundred."

With my hands on my hips, I tell him, "My point was simply to make sure that no one gets hurt when they help me stop. I didn't want to broadcast my real weight."

"So, one fifty?" Kale wants to know.

"One forty-two," I tell him louder than I'd planned.

Krista, who is several inches taller than me, says, "I'm one fifty." We share a proud look that the world didn't come to an end by our sharing our weight with other people.

As we tromp through the snowy woods toward the first landing, I'm full of excitement and a small amount of dread. I don't start to have second thoughts until we're all on deck staring at the first run. "It seems pretty high up here."

"We'll send the veterans first so you can see how it's done." Our leader gestures for Thor, who steps forward. Once Kale has all his harness clips attached, Thor holds onto the handlebars and jumps from the platform. He lets out a primal shout as he goes.

Krista steps forward next and while her run is a little less noisy, I'm still nervous. Kale tells me, "The lines are meant to hold up to three hundred and fifty pounds, so if you want, I can double with you on the first run."

My first thought is that if the line holds that much heft, why in the world does everyone have to state their weight up front? But before I can ask that, Blake offers, "Or she can do the run with me."

The thought of being in Blake's arms, flying through the air, fills me with both dread and excitement. For my own peace of mind, I know I should not be that close to him … yet. I consider the possibility for so long that somehow Kale decides this is what I want. He presses the button on his walkie-talkie and tells the guide at the end of the line, "We've got a duo coming in around three forty."

He clips my harness before attaching Blake's behind mine. All the while I'm trying to form the words to tell him I'll be fine on my own. Before I can express this, he instructs, "Hold onto to the handles and Blake will hold onto you."

As soon as I feel Blake behind me, I know I can't go through with this. I try to force my mouth to share this sentiment with Kale, but at the same moment, Blake steps forward and pushes me off my feet.

The feeling of being airborne is both terrifying and exhilarating. I want to shout at the raw sensation of freedom, but I'm too busy trying not to pee my pants. If I let my emotions loose, I might be in real trouble. Maybe next time.

The first run is longer than I thought it would be and I begin to relish the novelty of the experience. But then I focus on the solid wall of Blake behind me. His arms are holding onto me so tightly I almost can't discern where I begin and he ends. It's like we've become one entity flying through the woods, and it's pure magic.

Even so, I'm relieved when I see the next landing come into sight. Blake leans in and shouts, "Keep your feet up and I'll stop for both of us!" This requires more trust in him than I currently have. But what if I don't listen to him and somehow wind up hurting us both? I finally close my eyes, lift my feet, and pray.

Before I know it, Blake is squeezing me tighter, and we come to a jolting stop. The next guide unhooks us and pushes us out of the way so that Kale has a safe place to land.

I'm so hyper-sensitive toward Blake right now that I'm afraid if I talk to him, I'll either declare my undying love or ask him to run away with me. As such, I do my best to ignore him and I walk over to Krista. "That was amazing!" I tell her.

"How was it riding double with Blake?" I can't tell if she's asking out of curiosity or jealousy.

"Oh, him." I turn and give him a passing glance. "That was okay, but the zip-lining was positively thrilling!"

"I told you you'd love it." She smiles at me, but her gaze keeps shifting over my shoulder.

Blake walks up behind me and slips his arm around my waist like it's the most natural thing in the world. "Good job, Molly!" he says. "How do you feel?"

I open my mouth to respond, but nothing but "Uhhhh" comes out. Which is probably a good thing because my instinct is to ask him to keep holding onto me and to never let go.

CHAPTER EIGHTEEN

BLAKE

I ask Molly if she wants to ride doubles with me on all the zip-lining runs. I'm secretly hoping she does, while at the same time I'm relieved when she says no. It turns out she's a natural, which is kind of surprising being that she can't walk across a room without tripping over her own feet.

I'm going to have to work overtime to get her and Thor together because the way things stand, I'm in real jeopardy of declaring my interest in her. Which, I remind myself, is not the reason I'm here. I will not screw up my new job before it starts.

It takes two hours from start to finish before our final run is completed. By the time we turn in our gear, I know I need some space from Molly, so I announce to the rest of the group, "Why don't we go our own way for a while and catch up at the buffet tonight?"

Molly looks relieved, but Krista looks disappointed. This gives me an idea how I might be able to push Thor and Molly together. "Would you like to come with me, Krista?" I ask her. "Maybe we can put our swimming suits on and hit the outdoor jacuzzi."

She looks surprised that I've changed my plans to include her.

"I'd love that!" Taking my arm, she leads me toward the lodge and away from our zip-lining partners, who I'm hoping will pair up as well.

Looking back at Molly I see anger in her eyes, but I can't engage in that. Instead, I turn around and face front. Then I tell Krista, "You're something of a zip-lining pro."

"I've been about a dozen times," she says, "but I'm no pro. Unlike you, I've never done this any place particularly dangerous."

"Life isn't fun without a little danger though, is it?"

I've been in a near sprint to put some distance between me and Molly, so Krista is practically running to match my stride. As I slow my pace, she says, "My motto has more been along the lines of better safe than sorry."

"If you ever get the chance," I tell her, "you should really try the runs in Santa Teresa, Peru. It's like nothing you've ever experienced."

"That's near Machu Picchu, right?" she asks before saying, "You really *are* well-traveled for being a barista. What coffee shop do you work at, anyway?"

I haven't gotten that far in creating my false persona, so I ignore her question and tell her, "You fly right over the Sacred Valley, and I swear it feels like God is right there with you."

"That sounds amazing." As we enter the lodge, Krista announces, "I'm on the third floor, where are you?"

"Second," I tell her. "Why don't we meet in the lobby and go from there?"

She smiles brightly. "I'll be about fifteen minutes." And then she's off.

As I watch her go, I realize that I really do enjoy spending time with her. It's just that there's no electric feeling like I have when I'm around Molly. I sound like I'm likening the experience of spending time with her to scooting across a shag rug in wool socks before touching the refrigerator. *Zap!*

When I get back to my room, I hurry to change into my swimsuit before opening my laptop. On the page I've started for Molly, I write:

Not all trials end in a hanging. *(Note to self: Maybe rethink likening dating to execution?)* At least that appears to be the case for Polly Anderson. Last night I worried she would be defeated by running into her ex at the first mixer, but today she's back on track and spending time with a successful television producer. I have a feeling things may just work out for Polly, and despite my reservations about this event, I'm happy for her.

So far, Trina Rockwell's approach to matchmaking appears to be less intrusive and more about creating ways for people to converse. I'm not sure if that makes her endeavor different from a singles cruise to Puerto Vallarta, but I suppose time will tell …

After putting on the robe that's hanging in the closet, I reach for my phone and keycard before heading out the door. Krista's sitting in front of the fireplace when I get there. "I hope I didn't keep you waiting."

She blushes prettily. "I got ready fast. I'm excited to warm up in the hot tub." The coy look she offers indicates that the person accompanying her—me—might have had something to do with it as well.

As we walk toward the elevator that will take us down to the spa area and subsequently outside to the jacuzzi, I ask, "So, what are you looking for in a man?"

She answers easily. "I want someone that I enjoy spending time with. You know, a man who can zipline as well as carry on an interesting conversation." Oh yeah, she's talking about me.

Hoping to lessen her interest, I ask, "Is his career important to you?"

She looks thoughtful. "I hadn't really considered that. I

suppose if he makes enough money to pay for his life, that's all that matters."

"Yeah, but you want to make sure he's going to be capable of more than mere survival, don't you?"

"I guess. But dreams are important, too." She takes hold of my arm and squeezes it. "Like your dream of being a novelist. I think that's cool."

"*If* it happens," I tell her. "What if I'm destined to do nothing more than make coffee for the rest of my life?" I hated this assignment when I got it, but I'm starting to really resent Gillian. I don't want to give women the wrong impression as to why I'm here. Yet the long and short of it is, that's the only impression I can give them if I'm to maintain anonymity so I can write about them.

Unaware of the conflict coursing through me, Krista suggests, "You could always start your own business and become the boss." Releasing my arm, she adds, "I just teach kindergarten. It's not like I'm destined to be the head of a Fortune 500 company."

"That's a refreshing attitude," I tell her while turning left and walking out the double doors that lead to the outside spa area. The jacuzzi has been built against a rugged rock backdrop that gives the illusion it's a natural hot spring in the mountains.

After dropping my robe on a nearby chair, I follow the narrow path that leads toward the entrance. Krista does the same. With her arms wrapped around herself, she shivers. "It's freezing out here!"

"Which is part of the fun. Have you ever done the ice dunk?"

"A hot tub dunk is more my speed."

"Let's do this," I say while submerging myself in water that feels like it's practically boiling. The frigid outside air has a way of making the heat feel much more intense than it really is.

By the time Krista gets in, I spot two other couples approaching who had the same idea we did. One of them is Molly's ex, Kyle. He's with a woman I haven't met yet. The other duo is Olivia, of all people, along with the guy I teased Molly about getting together with. I think his name was Ronald.

As soon as they're within greeting distance, I call out, "Welcome!" Krista looks less than pleased by the interruption.

Kyle says, "Hey, Blake." He gestures toward the woman with him. "This is Heather." That signals the start of introductions being made all around.

Everyone seems nice enough except for Olivia who appears to have taken offense at my very existence. "It's you." Her tone is full of loathing. Glancing at Krista, she adds, "I see you've met someone more to your liking."

Olivia doesn't seem to possess a governor in her brain that keeps unpleasant thoughts from pouring out of her mouth. Krista looks nervous, as I think we all are, so I tell Krista, "Olivia is a pet psychic. Isn't that interesting?"

"It is!" Krista sounds genuinely intrigued. Turning to Olivia, she adds, "What a fascinating job." Olivia grunts in response.

Turning my attention to Kyle, I say, "It looks like you're enjoying yourself." The woman he's with is average height with dark hair and blue eyes. It occurs to me that Kyle might have a type.

While the rest of the group gets to know each other, Kyle leans toward me and asks, "Have you seen Molly?"

"We went zip-lining today," I tell him.

"Did she talk about me?"

"Um, no. Were you expecting her to?"

He shrugs. "I guess not. I just can't stop thinking about her."

"Kyle." I say his name with a cautionary tone. "It might be best if you did."

"You don't think it's possible she'll give me a second chance?"

"You left her for another woman. What do you think?"

He hems and haws for a moment, before saying, "It's just that we already know each other and we get along ..."

"You left her," I remind him.

"Are you interested in her for yourself?" he wants to know.

Yes. "No."

"Then do you think you might help me?"

No. "Maybe." I don't for one minute think that Molly is stupid enough to give Kyle a second chance, but what I do think is that this scenario might be interesting for my readers. Empowering even, when they see how Molly shuts Kyle down. Suddenly, I'm kind of looking forward to seeing that for myself.

CHAPTER NINETEEN

MOLLY

I can't believe Blake asked Krista to go to the hot tub with him. It's almost cruel how *not* into me he is. I can't seem to stop thinking about his arms around me, his requests to double on the zipline, and then dumping me to hot tub with Krista. First Kyle, then Blake. I should seek professional help because my man-picker is definitely broken, and I deserve better than both of them.

After Blake and Krista left, I thought Thor would ask me if I wanted to do something. That would almost be expected, right? Except he didn't. Instead, after we walked back to the lodge together, he awkwardly announced, "I guess I'll see you tonight." And then he walked away.

I stood there with my mouth hanging open like a mounted fish. What's wrong with me? Not to be conceited, but I'm not hideous. I'm accomplished and possess the ability to hold an intelligent conversation. You'd think that would be enough to attract moderate interest from the opposite sex.

I hurry up to my room and peel off my outerwear. Then I stand in front of the mirror and give myself a once-over. Helmet head aside, I decide I'm practically gorgeous. Curvy in all the right places, with icy blue eyes that aren't at all common in women who have nearly black hair.

Picking up the phone on the nightstand, I call downstairs and ask the front desk, "Is there a shuttle going into town soon?"

"There's one in twenty minutes," the woman tells me.

That's it, I'm going to go back into Elk Lake to see if Bride's Paradise carries dresses sexier than the ones I already bought. After all, desperate times call for desperate measures. And after today's trouncing of my self-esteem, I feel borderline frantic to find someone worthy of me.

After changing into a dry pair of jeans, I get my purse and head to the lobby. I expect to see Paul waiting, but there's a younger guy driving today. "Hello," I say. "Are you going into town?"

He nods once. "Yup. You ready to go?"

"Yup." Getting into the car, I ask, "I'm the only one?"

"Looks that way."

Ah, a man of few words. I can work with that. "I'm Molly, by the way."

"Hey." That's it. I covertly lean down and sniff my armpit. Nope, I'm fine. Then why is it this guy won't even tell me his name?

I remain silent until I reach my destination, then I get out of the car without saying goodbye. As I walk into Bride's Paradise, I realize I might be taking the driver's silence too much to heart, but honestly, I'm really starting to wonder if the world perceives me way differently than I imagine they do. I thought I hadn't been dating because I wasn't interested in dating, but maybe it's because no one wants to go out with me. How depressing.

The bell over the door rings as I walk through it, and Melissa looks up from what she's doing. "Molly, hi!" she greets enthusiastically. "How did the mixer go last night?"

Taking off my coat, I tell her, "Not well. Not only did I run into my ex, but the guy I thought I could be interested in friend-zoned me immediately. There was one other guy who seemed like a decent prospect, but I think he's interested in the same woman the guy I'm interested in is."

"Yikes." Melissa shakes her head sadly. "I'm so sorry."

"Me, too," I tell her. "So much so I've come back looking for a real showstopper."

Melissa absentmindedly rubs her pregnant belly. "How do you feel about going backless?" she asks.

"Cold," I respond. "But if that's the sexiest you've got, I'm willing to give it a try."

Walking across the room, she pulls out a silvery blue silk dress that looks more like a nightgown than real clothes. "This isn't for everyone, but I think you can pull it off."

I'm not sure why she thinks that, but I'm desperate enough to try anything. "I'll need a size ten," I tell her.

Rifling through the rack, she says, "I've got an eight and a twelve. Let's try them both."

Following her into the dressing room, I decide that if either of them is going to work, it's going to be the twelve. I haven't worn a size eight since high school. After Melissa hangs the dresses on a hook in my cubicle, she says, "I'll go out and see if I can find some other options."

I take off my clothes before putting on the larger of the two dresses. It's so big I look like I'm wearing a fancy potato sack. Taking it off, I try on the size eight. In a word, it's snug, but not unattractively so.

When Melissa comes back to inquire how I'm doing, I ask her, "Do you carry any shapeware?"

"That sounds promising," she says. "Let me see you and then I'll try to find something that will work."

I open the door, and the shopkeeper lets out a low whistle. "Girl, you're on fire!"

While I appreciate the props, I tell her, "I'm about an inch and a half away from being on fire. That's why I need some help."

Melissa eyes me closely. "The problem is the back dips so low if you wear a support garment, the waistline will show. In fact," she adds, "this is really a no underwear kind of dress."

I stare at her like she just suggested I walk into tonight's event stark naked. "That's not an option."

"Why not?"

"Because I don't fly commando," I tell her prudishly.

She laughs. "The dress is long enough that you won't flash anyone."

"That's not the point. I like underwear."

"Molly," she says. "This dress fits you like a glove. As such, you can't wear underwear, or you'll have lines."

"Then I'll find another dress."

"Or," she suggests, "you can put your fears aside and wear this one. You're a total smoke show in it."

Turning back toward the mirror, I move from side to side. I suppose if I suck my stomach in like I'm preparing to take a punch, it might work. "I'm not sure I can sit in it."

"Let's try." She leads the way out of the dressing room and gestures to a pin cushion stool. "That's pretty low so if you can sit on that, you should be fine with any kind of chair."

Walking over to the stool, I turn my knees to the side before lowering myself. So far, so good. Once I'm settled, I tell Melissa, "If the seams didn't rip doing that, I might just be okay."

She points to the mirror in front of me. "Look at yourself."

I follow the direction of her finger and gasp. If that's me, and I'm having a hard time believing that it is, I *am* a smoke show! "Wow."

"Right? You look amazing!"

I wiggle around a little and check for signs of anything inappropriate hanging out, but she's right, this dress looks like it was sewn right onto me. It's perfect. "No underwear, huh?"

She shakes her head. "No way."

Standing up, I approach the three-way mirror to get a look at the back. I'd whistle at myself if I didn't think it would be conceited. "And a size eight to boot." Running my hands down the sides of the material, I tell her, "It feels amazing on."

"It looks stunning. Listen, Molly, I'm not just saying this, but you look like a sexy queen in this dress."

"I'll take it," I tell her before asking, "Is there someplace in town where I can get my hair styled?"

"You bet there is!" she says with a huge smile on her face. "In fact, I'll make a call and see if I can get you in right away."

She hurries over to the counter while I take another minute to enjoy the view. I feel so confident in this dress, I decide to be brave and trust that I'll survive a night without undies.

Once I'm back in my street clothes, I meet Melissa at the cash register. "My friend, Fernando, made a call and moved his next appointment. He can see you right away."

"Fernando, huh? That sounds exotic for a small town in Wisconsin."

"You think his name sounds exotic, wait until you meet him." Her tone suggests I'm in for a real treat. "Leave your dress here and pick it up after your hair is done," she says. "I want to see what he does to you." Pointing out the window, she adds, "He's three doors down in a shop called Caliente."

Giving Melissa my credit card, I nervously ask, "He's good though, right?"

"He's great!" Then she says, "You have nothing to lose, Molly, and everything to gain. Just let yourself go."

Her words sear into my brain like my new mantra. I've already lost the guy and can't seem to interest anyone else. Why not let Fernando loose to see if he can unearth my inner goddess?

Walking into Caliente feels like walking into an elegant nightclub. The walls are painted black. The only relief from the darkness comes from the gold frames around the mirrors and the pristinely white styling chairs. Crystal clear chandeliers hang at various levels around the room.

"Molly, is that you?" An extremely short man with spiky hot pink hair claps his hands together enthusiastically while pushing people out of the way to get to me.

"Fernando?" I guess.

"Girl, yes! Melissa said this was an emergency and she wasn't kidding!" *Says the man with hot pink hair.*

Ignoring the obvious insult, I tell him, "I need a style for a dinner tonight."

He walks around me like he's a carousel and I'm the center island holding the ride together. "Honey, no. You also need some shape." Reaching out to touch the ends of my hair, he adds, "And a serious deep conditioning." And I thought my self-esteem was lagging before coming in here.

"I don't want to lose a lot of length," I tell him.

He ignores my comment. "Shake your head from side to side." As I follow orders, he looks even more aghast. "It doesn't move."

Reaching out to take my hand, he leads me across the room to his station. I'm a little nervous sitting down, but then I remind myself that Melissa recommended this guy and she looks normal.

Fernando takes a cape out of the cabinet beneath the vanity and proceeds to shake it out like he's a bullfighter and I'm the bull. Then with great flare, he wraps it around my neck. "Would you like a glass of wine?" he asks.

In lieu of answering, I shake my head. I think I'd better be stone cold sober in case he decides to go rogue on my head. Fernando twirls the chair around so it's facing away from the mirror, before telling me, "Close your eyes."

"Fernando …"

"I know what I'm doing, Molly. I promise you won't be disappointed." For some reason, his confidence soothes me, so I do as I'm told.

Instead of carrying on a conversation like most hairstylists do, Fernando concentrates solely on my hair. He snips for a solid thirty minutes before he's satisfied. But even then, he won't let me look in the mirror. I have to keep my eyes closed while he leads me to the hair washing station. My head is wrapped in a towel on the way back.

I'm beyond anxious by the time he's done blowing it dry and making the final snips. Then he twirls my chair back around to the mirror and declares, "Tada!"

I tentatively take in my reflection. I can't help but wonder, who in the heck is staring back at me?

CHAPTER TWENTY

BLAKE

By the time I get out of the jacuzzi, I'm so sick of single people I consider skipping the mixer tonight. I suppose if I were here in another capacity, I might feel differently, but it's exhausting trying to ward off female attention, all the while looking for angles for my articles.

The more time I spend with Krista, the more I feel her desperation to get my attention. I hope that Thor and Molly sealed their interest in each other today so I can cut Krista loose before she gets too invested in me.

Once I get to my room, I order a late lunch before setting up my laptop.

I spent the morning zip-lining with several other singles and had a great time. I mean, how can you screw up zip-lining? We were too busy enjoying the sport to do much else, but then came an hour in the jacuzzi. The banter, the flirting, the nervous giggling. It was a lot.

We're only on day two here, but it feels like day ten. There's a desperation in the air to find your person and claim them for your own before the competition moves in, and it's borderline painful.

You can't force a connection with people. I originally thought two weeks was an excessive amount of time when I first heard about Trina Rockwell's new endeavor, but I now feel like it might not be long enough. The pressure to win a partner's attention is real.

I eat my cheeseburger as soon as it arrives and then rent a movie to watch. While I'd love to go snowmobiling, I really don't want to run into anyone else before I have to. Tonight will come soon enough.

I wind up nodding off during my favorite Christmas movie of all time, *Die Hard*. Then I uncharacteristically nap for the better part of three hours. By the time I wake up, I only have thirty minutes to shower and shave in order to get downstairs in time for the next group get-together.

Being that tonight is more than cocktails—it's a full-on dinner —I pull out all the stops and wear a suit. I do this with some hesitation though, because I cut a fine figure in my Hugo Boss, and I don't want to elicit too much attention.

By the looks of the crowd in the ballroom, I'm one of the last people to show up.

It's clear by just glancing around that the machinations have already begun. Excitement hovers in the atmosphere like a cloud of mustard gas. Comparing these events to an act of war might be a bit extreme, but after this afternoon, there's a real feeling of do or die in the air.

Krista spots me almost immediately and hurries to my side. "Blake, you look very handsome!" She boldly leans forward and kisses me somewhere between the cheek and the mouth.

"Krista, how are you?" I step back, ostensibly to admire her dress, but I really just want some space.

"Good, now that you're here," she purrs.

I try to remember at what point she became so forward. I think it might have been when Kyle's companion said she thought she knew me from somewhere. At any rate, Krista changed, and not for the better.

"Have you seen Thor?" I ask her.

"I haven't looked for him. I was waiting for you."

"Why don't we look for him together," I suggest. *Maybe Krista will think I'm interested in Thor and back off.*

As we walk around the ballroom, I nod to several people I've already met. Kyle is talking to a new woman, Olivia and Ronald are cozying up together, but Thor is nowhere to be found. A weird hush momentarily takes over the room, and then I hear Krista say, "Is that Molly?"

Turning around, I follow the gaze of the masses and nearly swallow my tongue. What in the world happened to her? Molly looks like another woman entirely. Not that she wasn't beautiful before, because she most definitely was, but this version of her is positively mind blowing.

I feel a pull toward her like we're opposite sides of a magnet and the only scientific possibility is for us to come together. Krista follows closely beside me. When we reach Molly, Krista says, "What have you done?"

Molly inexplicably asks, "Is it horrible?"

"Not at all!" Krista seems disappointed when she says, "You look stunning!"

Molly's shoulders relax slightly. "I got my hair done this afternoon."

And while it's clear her hair looks great, it's the dress that's caught my eye. Or the lack of dress if you're looking at it from behind. There's so much bare skin I can count the vertebrae on Molly's back.

"That dress is to die for," Krista tells her, sounding sincere.

Molly glances at me briefly before leaning in and whispering something in Krista's ear. Krista's eyes widen before she says, "That takes guts."

Inserting myself into the conversation, I announce, "You look very nice, Molly." I sound like I'm complimenting her yard maintenance or something equally mundane.

She offers a pained smile in return. Then we all stand there like we have no idea what to say next. Luckily, that's when Thor finds us. He's with two new women. *Boy, this guy really gets around.* He says, "I'd like you all to meet Brooklyn and Emily."

I shake their hands before introducing Krista and Molly. Meanwhile, Thor nods his head at Molly in a friendly manner and tells her, "I like your dress." He doesn't appear to be nearly as dazzled as I am.

Molly barely makes eye contact with him while mumbling, "Thank you."

The air between them is weird. It makes me wonder if things didn't go well for them after Krista and I left. Turning to Thor, I ask, "What did you do this afternoon?"

"I worked out in the gym and then went for a long walk."

"Alone?"

Emily, one of the women he brought over, announces, "I went with him. We met at the gym." I can't for the life of me figure out why he and Molly didn't spend more time together, but I clearly can't ask him here.

Before things get weirder, Trina taps on a microphone at the front of the room. "Welcome to our second event! I'm guessing some of you might have already found some interesting prospects, but it's early days, so I'm going to continue to make suggestions. Ladies, take the hand of the man who's standing at your right side and lead him out on the dance floor. Don't hesitate, just do it."

Despite the fact that I'm on Molly's left, she reaches out for my hand. She practically pulls me away from our little group before demanding, "What's wrong with me?"

Absolutely nothing. "What do you mean?"

"I mean, what's wrong with me?" she repeats. Luckily, she doesn't ask why I didn't invite her to join me in the hot tub, but it's clear that's what she's thinking,

The music starts to play, so I open my arms to her. The problem is that I'm not quite sure what to do with my hands. Molly's entire back is bare, and as much as I want to, I should not touch her like that. I quickly readjust my position and take her hands before answering, "There's nothing wrong with you. He just wanted to work out." Then I slowly try to lead our dance which is not easy while also trying to keep her at a distance.

"Why didn't Thor ask me to work out with him. I can work out," she says heatedly.

"I don't know why he didn't ask you," I tell her. "You're quite lovely."

"You didn't ask me either," she accuses. *Oh, but I wanted to, Molly.*

"I thought you and I were friends," I say, all the while not feeling in the least friendly toward her. "I didn't want to hog your time and keep you from finding a real prospect." Her posture slags, so I know I've just hurt her feelings again. But in the long run, this is a much better scenario than dating her for real and then writing about it for all of Chicago to read. She'd never forgive me for that.

"Why did you friend-zone me so quickly?" she wants to know.

I can't tell her the truth, so I lie. "I guess I just felt like we had a strong friend chemistry. I figured we could both use a pal of the opposite sex while we're here."

"I'm not sure I'm going to keep coming to these things."

"Really, why?" *Also, yay!* Not only will I not have to write about her, but maybe then I can be honest with her and let her know I'd be interested in dating her. I'm tempted to tell her that either way, but if she gets mad and outs me to the other people at the event then my job might be in jeopardy.

"I'm not sure this is my kind of thing." She sounds dejected.

"You might be right." She widens the distance between us, and

I belatedly realize she thinks I'm rejecting her again. The rest of our dance is spent in painful silence.

As the music ends, Trina approaches us. She's with Kyle. "Molly, I'd like to introduce you to Kyle. I think the two of you might have a lot in common."

Molly rolls her eyes. "Kyle was the ex I was telling you about."

"Oh dear," Trina mutters. Then she looks at Kyle and accuses, "You left *Molly* for another woman?" She says this like it's the most unbelievable thing she's ever heard. I agree.

Kyle's face flushes a deep red. "To my great shame." I'm guessing he says this to try to lessen the horror of his crime. To my surprise, Molly appears to be buying it.

"Contrition looks good on you, Kyle," she tells him.

"Can we go somewhere and talk?" he asks her.

No, you can't. But before I say that out loud, Molly side-eyes me and asks him, "Why not?"

While I like Kyle well enough as a human being, and only earlier today determined to put him in Molly's path for the entertainment of *Chicago Wind*'s readers, he's nowhere near good enough for her. I thought she was smart enough to know that.

CHAPTER TWENTY-ONE

MOLLY

"You really do look beautiful tonight," Kyle repeats appreciatively as we walk to the outskirts of the ballroom together.

I know I do. Melissa's friend Fernando, while wildly eccentric—I mean, the man wore harem pants like he was starring in *Aladdin*—definitely knows what he's doing with hair. He only took off about two inches, but he spent ages cutting layers that make it look like my hair is in constant motion.

I don't know why I agreed to talk privately with Kyle, except I knew I couldn't stay near Blake for another minute. Against my better judgment, I want him for more than a friend. He's nice, intelligent, kind to others, sweet, and extremely good looking. The fact that he's determined for us to be nothing more than pals is really making me mad.

"What did you want to talk about?" I ask Kyle.

"I wanted to tell you again how very sorry I am about the way things ended between us. I've thought a lot about it and in retrospect I realize that we might have really been perfect together."

"Forgive me for finding that hard to believe, Kyle. You did cheat on me."

"Which was a horrible thing to do. I think that things would have been different had we been living together. We would have seen each other more, and I would have been always thinking of us as a unit, not separate entities."

"A unit, huh?" That's probably the least romantic thing he could have said to me.

"You know what I mean. You were only in town for a couple weeks out of every month. It was hard to settle in with such limited time."

"You're an all-or-nothing kind of guy, huh?"

He shakes his head. "Not anymore. We really worked when we worked, Molly. I know I ruined that, yet I can't help but wonder what would happen if we tried again."

I glance over Kyle's shoulder and see Blake striding determinedly in our direction. I suddenly wonder if I could make Blake view me differently if he thought Kyle and I were getting back together. I know it's wrong to use Kyle as bait, but the man has some retribution due him, and I'm not opposed to helping the karmic wheel turn.

So as soon as Blake is right behind Kyle, I ask, "What did you have in mind?"

Kyle, who is unaware that we have company, answers, "I thought you might let me court you while we are here in Wisconsin together."

Court? Did my ex become a knight of the realm in the last few years? "Are you planning on *courting* other women, as well?" I ask.

That's when Blake decides to insert himself into the conversation. "Molly, I need to talk to you."

"What about?" *Other women?*

He nods to Kyle before answering, "It's a private matter."

Blake and I don't know each other well enough to have any private matters that need discussing so I can only assume my attempt to make him jealous is working. I tell Kyle, "I'll think about your suggestion and get back to you. In the meantime, my *buddy* here needs a word."

Kyle walks away sheepishly like a dog who's chewed up one too many slippers. And while I should appreciate his defeated posture, I find that I'm more interested in whatever brought Blake over to me. "What?"

"What do you mean, what?" he wants to know.

"What did you want to talk to me about?"

"Oh, that." Blake inhales deeply before saying, "I don't think you should spend time with Kyle."

"Why is that?" I cannot *wait* to hear how he answers.

"Once a cheater always a cheater," he says. "You'd never ever be able to trust him."

"What does it matter to you if I give Kyle another chance?" *Come on, Blake, say it. Tell me that you want to date me. Tell me you want me for yourself so I can not be interested.* As contrary as that sounds its' the only way I can think of to regain my lagging self-esteem.

His nostrils flare slightly before answering, "It doesn't matter except for the fact that you're my friend, and I'd hate to see you hurt."

"Why do you care? You don't even know me," I hiss.

"I know you're not a lumberjack," he jokes before adding, "I might not know you well, but you're the first person I met here. As such, I feel a certain investment."

I'm tempted to stick my finger down my throat and pretend to gag myself. But I don't. Instead, I ask, "Where's Krista?"

"I left her with Thor and his two lady friends."

"What's up with him tonight?" I ask.

"What do you mean?" Blake asks.

Stating the obvious, I tell him, "He barely even looked at me."

"Maybe you intimidate him."

"Oh yeah, I can see how all five-six of me might seem threatening to a man well over six feet tall." Sarcasm is my go-to at times like this.

"Not your height," Blake says. "More your ..." he gestures in front of me like he's spokesmodeling a microwave, "... presence."

"My presence?"

"You're stunning. Some men are intimidated by that."

"He's used to being around actresses, Blake."

"Let's go get dinner and we can talk about it there."

"You want to eat with me?" I find this hard to believe. "I thought you had ladies to impress."

"Obviously," he drawls. "But I'd like to work out my game plan with you first. After all, you're a woman so you might be able to give me some advice."

"Yes, but I'm a single woman who's here hoping to meet single men," I tell him. "Why would I give up valuable time to help you?"

"Because I can give you some good tips," he says. "You know, like stay away from cheaters."

As annoyed as I am with Blake, I'm hard-pressed to walk away from an offer to spend time with him. Even though I don't believe in insta-love, I can't deny that I'm overwhelmingly attracted to the guy.

It's not only that he's handsome, either. I'm not quite that shallow. I like his energy, his smile, his ... fine, I like how his butt looks in his jeans. "Let's go get our supper and have a talk," I tell him.

Blake leads the way toward the buffet, and I follow behind. Once we get our plates, we choose our food and then find an empty table to sit at. As soon as my napkin is in my lap, Blake looks down at my plate. "The first tip I'd give you is to avoid garlicky foods. You don't want to kiss someone with garlic on your breath."

I pick up the piece of garlic bread on my plate and take a giant bite. Then I glare at him the whole time I'm chewing. Once I swallow it, I inform him, "Good thing I'm not going to be kissing anyone tonight."

He eyes my bread longingly, so I offer it to him. After taking a bite of his own, he groans and then says, "That has to be at least as good as kissing. I'll go back and get us some more if we still have room after we're done eating." His easy sense of humor catches me off guard.

"What's your story, Blake?"

He shrugs. "Not much of a story. I'm just a single guy of a certain age wondering where my person is."

"You'd think you'd meet a lot of women at whatever coffee shop you work at." My left eyebrow quirks into a question mark.

"You'd be surprised how many women don't want to date the guy making their coffee," he says.

"There are a lot of women who don't judge a book by its cover." Also, if he was making their *morning* coffee at home, I'm sure there would be zero complaints.

"Do you judge a book by its cover?" he asks before stabbing a piece of chicken with his fork.

"I don't care what someone does so long as they're not breaking the law." I didn't mean to come off as quite such a goody two-shoes, but there it is.

"Darn it!" Blakes smacks the tabletop playfully. "I guess I shouldn't have been smuggling drugs for the Nicaraguans then."

"Ah, but you're not interested in me in that way," I remind him. Then I take my garlic bread back and practically shove the rest of it down my throat.

"You're not interested in me, either," he responds quickly. Then he gives me a challenging look as though his statement mandates an answer.

"No, I guess I'm not." *Liar.*

"So," he says, "Thor doesn't appear to be the guy for you, and clearly Kyle isn't. Who else are you interested in? Should we steal Ronald back from Olivia?"

"I think I'll let Olivia have that prize." I turn and look around the room, setting my sights on the first good-looking man that crosses my path. He's tallish and he has a short beard that hints at an air of mystery. "That one looks like a possibility. Maybe I'll go talk to him."

As I push out my chair to stand up, Blake does the same. "I'll go with you."

"What? Why?"

"I can ask some questions that you might be uncomfortable asking and then we'll have a better idea if he might be the one."

"I don't need you to interview my potential dates," I tell him.

Blake takes my hand in his and pulls me along. "You might not need me, but I could save you a lot of time, so let's go."

As I trip along after Blake, I can't help but wonder what he's really up to. If he isn't interested in dating me, which he lets me know often, then why in the world does he care who I set my sights on? Unless of course, he really does think of me as a friend and he's protecting me.

How depressing.

CHAPTER TWENTY-TWO

BLAKE

I really need to walk away from Molly and talk to other people. If not for my article, then for my sanity. Yet for obvious reasons, I don't want to leave her side. She's so darn lovely that I can't stand the thought of other guys hitting on her—ones who aren't good enough for her. As such, I decide to help her find the perfect guy. Then I'll be free to do my job.

As we approach the man she expressed interest in, I can't help but say, "He's short."

"Last night you suggested a man closer to my own height was the way to go." She sounds mad and I don't blame her.

"That was just Ronald. But now that I see how ill-suited the two of you are, I think you should set your sights higher. Literally."

Reaching the target, I announce a touch too loudly, "Hello! What's your name?"

The man takes a cautious step backward before answering, "Brian. What's yours?"

"I'm Blake," I tell him. "And this is my friend Molly."

Molly rips her hand out of mine and extends it toward Brian. "Hi there."

His eyes shift nervously from me to her. "Um, hello?"

"What do you do, Brian?" I ask.

"I'm an engineer. What do you do?" Again, he looks at me and then Molly like he's not sure who he's talking to."

"I design hotel gift shops," Molly tells him at the same time I announce, "I'm a barista/ novelist."

Brian's eyebrows furrow before he asks, "Are you two a couple?"

"No!" Molly screams.

"We're good friends," I tell him.

"And you're here together?" he wants to know.

"No!" Again, from Molly.

"We met here," I tell him.

Molly steps in front of me as though trying to pretend that I'm not even here. "What kind of engineer are you?" she asks Brian. "Mechanical? Civil? Chemical?"

Brian responds, "Train."

"You design trains?" Molly asks.

"I drive them," Brian says.

I don't even try not to laugh at that and both Molly and Brian stare at me in horror. "I'm sorry," I tell him. "I didn't mean any offense. It's just that you don't meet many train drivers, do you?"

"I do." *I bet you do, Brian.*

Molly shakes her head and demands, "What is wrong with you, Blake?"

"I honestly don't know," I tell her. "I really didn't mean to be rude."

She shoos me away with her hand. "Go. Now."

I don't want to leave her here on her own, but I don't have any choice. "I'll meet you at the bar in thirty minutes," I tell her.

"No." She turns her back on me to talk to Brian. Meanwhile, I stand there like an extra pair of shoes until Trina comes over.

"Come with me, Blake," she says like she's going to personally escort me off the property. When we're several yards away, she stops and asks me, "What are you doing here, Blake?"

Oh, no. Did she find out who I am? I open and close my mouth repeatedly before answering, "Looking for love?"

"Are you, though?"

"Yes?"

"You don't sound very certain," she says. "You also appear to have a hard time leaving Molly alone."

"What if I'm interested in her?" I ask.

"Are you?"

Yes. "I like her."

Trina's eyes narrow. "Molly said you liked her as a friend and nothing else. And while I'm all for people making friends, that's not what this event is about."

"Are you telling me to stay away from Molly? Because I'm not sure that's your place." I sound like I'm gearing up for a fight.

Trina's dark hair swings back and forth as she shakes her head. "I'm not telling you to stay away from her. I'm suggesting that you let me introduce you to some nice women whom you might be interested in being more than friends with."

I can hardly say no to Trina offering me content for my articles, so I tell her, "That would be nice, thank you."

With a smile, she says, "It appears that you and Krista might already be making a connection."

"I think the connection is greater on her part than mine," I tell her.

"Oh?" I'm not surprised she's having a hard time believing this. After all, Krista is one of the more beautiful women in the room.

"What do you like in women, Blake?" Trina asks. "Do you have a physical type?"

"I like all kinds of women," I tell her honestly.

"But you don't go for the obviously beautiful ones," she decides.

"Why would you say that?"

Raising one finger in the air, she says, "Molly." Then she adds another. "Krista. They are both quite beautiful." She's got me there.

Before I can set her straight, not that I'm sure how I'd go about doing that, Trina takes my hand and leads me to the front of the ballroom. Once she's at the microphone, she announces, "I have a new game I'd like you all to play."

The chatter quiets as she continues, "I'd like you to walk away from the person you're talking to and tell the first member of the opposite sex that you see what kind of car you think they'd be."

She gestures to me and adds, "I'll go first. This is Blake and I think Blake would be a black sports car with a faulty starter."

Wait, what? Did she intend to be insulting? But before I can ask, she asks me, "What kind of car do you think I'd be, Blake?"

"A semi-truck speeding down the freeway about to run over a black sports car."

She snorts before telling the room, "You see how much fun this can be? Don't stop to talk to anyone until you've told ten people what kind of car you think they'd be."

When everyone gets busy doing what they were told to do, I ask Trina, "A faulty starter?"

"Definitely. The good news is that starters can be fixed. Now go. I want to see you talking to ten different women and they can't include Krista or Molly."

The first woman I see after Trina leaves my side is a short, no-nonsense-looking blonde. I stop in front of her and announce, "Volvo."

She tips her head to the side before saying, "Cadillac SUV."

I'm called a pickup, a Hummer, an Audi, and a Jeep before I find myself standing at the bar. "I need something strong," I tell the bartender.

He hands me a shot glass and a mug of beer. I watched my grandfather drink boilermakers for years, so I do it the same way he did. I drop the shot glass directly into the beer before taking a gulp. Then I tell the bartender, "Thank you."

I decide to finish my drink and then seek refuge until this stupid game is over. But before I can, Molly walks over to me and laughs. "A faulty starter …"

"I've been instructed not to talk to you," I tell her.

"By whom?" she wants to know.

"By Trina. She doesn't want me talking to you or Krista."

"Really, why?" Molly seems truly perplexed.

"Because you told her that I only wanted to be your friend, and she says that's not why we're here."

Molly nods her head in agreement. "She's right."

Before I can say anything else, a guy in a suit walks over to Molly and says, "Aston Martin DBS Superleggera—in red."

"Don't be pretentious," I hiss at him.

His face contorts in disgust like he just ate a bad clam. "Dude, I'm not talking to you. I'm talking to the lady."

"You're being sleazy," I tell him.

"I was complimenting her."

"You were insulting her. Molly isn't a sports car."

"Really?" Molly has decided to join in, and she doesn't sound pleased.

"You're a Rolls Royce," I tell her. "You're a classic beauty that will look as beautiful in fifty years as you do now." That sounded way more seductive than I was going for, but it's the truth. Molly is pure class.

"Thank you, I guess," she decides.

I wait for her to tell me what kind of car I'd be, but she doesn't. Instead, she looks confused as she turns and walks away from me, leaving me feeling like a Tesla without its charger.

CHAPTER TWENTY-THREE

MOLLY

Blake said I was a Rolls Royce. While I'm totally flattered by the comparison, I'm equally confused by it. I would have thought he would have called me a VW Bug or a Mini Cooper. You know, cute enough but nothing special. That's how he treats me, anyway.

After walking away from him, I keep going until I'm out of the ballroom. I'm not sure I'm the right kind of person for an event like this. Not only do I not like advertising my single status to the free world, but it all feels so desperate. Which I guess I am. As in, who goes out and buys a fourth new dress when there are two that still have their tags on?

It's just that I know beyond a shadow of a doubt that if I can capture his attention and not mess up my words, he'd finally see how compatible we are in all areas.

Once I reach the great room, I sit in an overstuffed chair next to the fire. I pull my phone out of my purse and call Ellen. "Hey, sis," I say as soon as she answers.

"Molly! Are you okay?" *She* doesn't sound okay. In fact, she sounds like she's been crying.

Instead of asking her, I say, "I'm good. You sound surprised to hear from me."

"I am," she says. "I mean, I'm lucky to talk to you once a week. Three days in a row isn't exactly normal for us."

She's right. I'm not the greatest communicator, but that mostly has to do with the fact that Ellen thinks she knows everything and she's often too free with her advice. The thing is, I kind of want her guidance now. "I have a question," I start to say but then stop.

Ellen is uncharacteristically quiet. For once, she appears to be waiting for me.

I ask, "How are things going with Henry?" She doesn't speak right away. Instead, I hear what sounds like soft sobs. "Ellie?" I only use her childhood nickname for her when I'm worried, which I currently am.

"I'm here." She inhales deeply before saying, "Henry and I broke up tonight."

"What? I thought he was going to propose soon."

"He did."

"Start at the beginning," I tell my sister.

"Henry picked me up for supper tonight. He said he had something important to ask me."

"And?"

"He asked me to marry him."

"I'm so confused right now, Ellen. If Henry asked you to marry him, why did you break up?"

"He didn't like the way I answered."

"You said no?" I exclaim so loudly an old lady across the room stares at me like she's trying to decide if she needs to call 911.

"No. I said, 'Why not?'"

"Henry asked you to marry him and you answered, 'Why not?'"

"Yes."

"Oh Ellen, why didn't you shout out yes? Why didn't you tell him that you'd love to marry him?"

"Because I'm not sure I want to be married." She says this so quietly it takes a minute for it to soak in.

"I thought that was always the plan," I tell her. "I know Don did a number on you, but you've always seemed like the marrying type."

"What's the marrying type?" she wants to know.

"Conservative. Steady. Normal," I tell her.

"It's perfectly normal not to tie yourself to another human being, Molly."

"Who is this and what have you done with my sister?"

"Ha, ha. I'm just saying that I'm a full person in my own right without needing a man to define me."

"Ellen, did you have a stroke? You are constantly on me to meet a nice guy so I can get married and live the American dream."

"I don't want to be the only person taking care of you. I want to know that someone else has your back."

"Why do I need taking care of? I think I'm doing a pretty good job of that for myself," I insist.

"I want you to have everything, Molly. That's all."

Shifting in my seat, I ask, "Don't you deserve everything, too?"

"It's too late for me," she says dejectedly.

"How do you figure?"

Sounding sadder than I've ever heard her, Ellen explains, "I'm not lovable like you are. I'm broken."

"Because of Don?" I never did like that guy. I thought he was a loser from the start but still, I can't believe my strong-willed sister is giving her ex this kind of power over her.

"Partially because of Don, I guess. But partly because of me. I'm not the kind of woman men put first."

"Henry loves you," I tell her. "It's obvious to everyone that he adores you."

"But I'm not first," she says. "I'm not even a close second."

"How do you figure?"

"His kids are first, second, and third. He would put each one of them before me in a heartbeat."

"But isn't that one of the reasons you love the guy?" I ask. "The fact that he's such a good dad makes him a winner in my book."

"That's *one* of the things I love about him," she says. "But that doesn't change the fact that I'm not on the top of his list of priorities."

"Why can't you all be at the top?" I ask. "I'm sure if something was important to you, Henry would make it a priority."

"Not if one of his kids needed him."

"Ellen, I have no idea where this is all coming from."

"Good," she says. "That means you haven't been broken yet. I don't ever want you to be broken, Molly."

I want to cry for my sister right now. She's always been the strongest and fiercest woman I know, which makes it hard to reconcile how she's acting right now. "Do you want me to come home?" I ask. I'm fully prepared to get the next train out of here, even if it means leaving my job unfinished. Even if it means never seeing Blake again. My sister is that important to me.

"Don't," she says. "I'm fine. In fact, I'm going to go home early and see the folks. I can help Mom bake cookies and convince Dad that if he keeps adding outdoor lights the neighbors are going to start a petition."

"Are you sure, Ellen?"

"I'm sure. I just need some time to think. But more than that, I need time not to think."

"Call me if you need anything," I tell her. "I'm always here for you."

"Thanks, Molly. I love you."

"I love you, too." She hangs up before I can say anything else. I have never heard my sister sound so sad and unsure of herself. I have never known her to give up on anyone or anything. In fact, she was so certain she could change her first husband that she begged him to go to marriage counseling. He's the one who walked.

Still clutching my telephone like it's a lifeline, I stare at the flames in the fireplace. As I watch them leap and jump in unexpected patterns, an unfamiliar feeling of unease consumes me.

Ellen has always been love's biggest advocate. She's always been its loudest cheerleader. Even though she didn't sound excited about Henry proposing when we talked the day I left for Elk Lake, I thought she was just being cautious. I had no idea she felt like she played second fiddle in his life.

Thoughts swirl through my head when I hear Blake say, "Are you leaving the mixer?" I didn't know he followed me out here.

Looking into his green eyes, I wonder who this man really is. He doesn't act like a guy looking for love at all.

"Sit down, Blake," I order sternly. He looks nervous as he takes the seat next to mine. "Why are you here?" I ask.

"To find my person?"

"I don't think so," I tell him. "You don't act like a man looking for love."

His Adam's apple bobs perceptibly before he asks, "How does a man like that act?"

"First of all," I tell him, "he doesn't find himself a female friend to harass."

"I never once harassed you," he says. "I was trying to help you."

"A man looking for love doesn't worry about helping a random woman find a man unless he wants to be that man. Which you've made perfectly clear is not the case with us." I repeat my question, "So why are you here?"

Instead of answering, he says, "I guess I'm just nervous."

"Are you?"

He shrugs "Maybe."

I abruptly stand up. Once I'm staring down at him, I announce, "I don't think we should hang out anymore."

"Why?"

"Because I actually want to meet someone and you're getting in my way."

I know I've hurt his feelings, but I don't care. He's confused me royally and unless he's going to throw his hat into the ring for my affection, I don't want anything to do with him.

I don't know what's going on with my sister right now, but I do know one thing: I don't want to be all work and no play anymore, even if some of my research for my job looks like play. I want to meet someone and have a life with them. I also want to feel adored by that person.

I suddenly understand what Ellen was saying about wanting to feel like she's first because that's exactly what I want.

I want to be the first person the man I love thinks of when he has good news to share or needs consoling. I want to be the most important person in his world, and I don't need someone like Blake getting in my way.

I'm not sure if I'm going to keep going to Trina's mixers, but I know that I'm done wasting my time pining after someone who is clearly not interested in me.

CHAPTER TWENTY-FOUR

BLAKE

It's been two days since Molly and I talked. Two full days. I haven't heard her coming and going next door, she won't speak to me at the mixers, and if I get too close to her—which appears to be anywhere near fifty feet—she runs in the opposite direction.

So instead of enjoying myself with her and helping to steady her when she trips—which she does all the time—I've chatted up as many of the singles as I can. Krista's finally taken the hint that I'm not interested in dating her, and she's started to ignore me with a vigorous sort of anger. I overheard her tell another woman not to waste her time with me because I was nothing but an emotionally unavailable tease. That couldn't be farther from the truth, but as I haven't been telling the truth here, I can see how she might not see it that way.

Instead of going down to breakfast this morning and facing whatever drama is destined to occur, I hide out in my room and order room service. After that, I call the office and ask for Gillian.

"I'm sorry, she's in a meeting," her secretary tells me.

"Please ask her to call me as soon as she can," I say before hanging up.

I really don't want to be here anymore. I feel like I've gotten enough information to write about this event without having to see it through until the bitter end, and believe me, at the rate I'm going, the end will definitely be bitter.

While I wait for my food to arrive, I open my laptop and get back to work.

> If you have any desire to maintain your sanity, you should not sign up for a dating getaway at the Elk Lake Lodge. This process has been humbling and borderline humiliating. It is not for the faint of heart. The truth is that you probably stand a better chance of meeting your future life partner at a bar, a dog park, or a red-eye flight to Antarctica. At least in those places you'll be able to trust that you're actually attracted to someone and you're not just trying to beat a competitor to the punch. Because let's face it, this is a competition. It's a contest that will have winners and losers, and I do not like the odds of success.

I take a break to think about last night's encounter with a woman Trina introduced me to. Her name was Harlow, and she's a flight attendant. She travels a lot, but she's based in Chicago. I have no idea why the Midwestern Matchmaker thought we'd hit it off unless she assumed the only person who wouldn't mind dating me was one who didn't have to see me very often. I sense that Trina is not my biggest fan.

Harlow and I didn't have a chance to talk for long before two other men, whom she'd previously been getting to know, joined us. They nearly came to blows over who was going to walk Harlow to supper. That was my cue to skedaddle.

I did talk to Thor, and I asked him what was going on between him and Molly. He assured me that nothing was going on, and when I asked why, he said, "It's obvious that you have a thing for her, Blake. I didn't want to get in the way of that." I thought I'd been better about hiding my feelings. Also, I'm surprised Thor would be so cool about letting Molly go. If I was in this for real, I would be way more aggressive than that.

"I don't have a thing for her," I told him. He merely rolled his eyes and said it was also clear that Molly also has a thing for me, which is why he didn't waste his time pursuing her. I've been thinking about that since last night.

Molly does give off the vibes that she's attracted to me. And while it's true that I'm also interested, I've been ordered not to tell anyone why I'm here. Therefore, I can't ask Molly out for real without breaking the terms of my assignment. My first assignment, and if I'm not careful, maybe my last.

There's a noise in the hallway which I assume is my breakfast. Getting off the bed, I quickly cross the room and open the door. But it's not my food, it's Molly. Her eyes pop open so wide when she sees me, I'm afraid she's going to run again. "Molly," I say.

Her gaze shifts nervously from the left to the right before she replies, "Blake."

"How are you?" I ask. She's wearing leggings and an oversized sweater. She looks so cuddly, I want to take her into my arms and hold her.

"I'm fine." She doesn't say anything else.

"I miss talking to you," I tell her.

She shrugs her shoulders like she couldn't care less.

"Are you on your way to the dining room?" I ask.

"Maybe."

I spot a waiter walking down the hall in our direction. He's pushing a cart that I hope is carrying my breakfast. I was so hungry this morning I ordered three different things. I figured if I had to be here against my will, the least the newspaper could do is make sure my stomach is happy. It may seem petty, but I want to make them pay in some way, other than just my paycheck.

Stopping at my door, the waiter announces, "I have your family's food."

Molly's eyes narrow like she's decided that means I have company. "Your family, huh?"

"Would you like to come in and join us?" I ask her.

Unable to resist the temptation, she pushes me to the side before storming into my inner sanctum. While she looks around for whoever she thinks is there, I sign the check and walk the waiter out.

When I come back into the room, Molly is bent over at the waist looking under the bed. "There's no one there," I tell her.

She stands up so quickly she nearly tips over. Leaning into the mattress, she asks, "Is she in the bathroom?"

"I'm the only one here."

"So, she's already left?" She says this like I didn't show my fake date a good enough time to warrant her staying.

"I'm all alone, Molly."

Staring at the food cart, she charges, "You're eating french toast, an omelet, and oatmeal all by yourself?"

"Everything sounded so good this morning, I couldn't decide what I wanted." Her stomach growls with such intensity I ask, "Would you like to join me? You can have whatever you want."

"I shouldn't …" she says petulantly.

"I won't take it as a compliment," I assure her. "I'll just assume you're so hungry you don't want to wait another forty-five minutes that going to the dining room would entail." Her stomach rumbles again as if she couldn't possibly make it that long.

"Fine," she says, before crossing the room and sitting down at the table by the window. "But I get the french toast."

Pushing the cart toward her, I agree. "That's okay with me." Then I ask, "Would you like me to make you a cup of coffee?"

She shakes her head while reaching out to take my glass of orange juice off the tray. "I'll just drink this." I love how sassy she is. I really have missed talking to her.

Sitting down across from her, I ask, "Have you been enjoying yourself?"

She looks up from her plate sheepishly. "I guess."

"Have you met any nice men?"

"I've been talking to Kyle a little bit."

"I hope you told him to hit the bricks," I tell her.

"I'm not taking him back, but it's nice to spend time with someone who knows me. Someone who's interested in me." That jab meets its target—me.

"I'm interested in you, Molly."

She nearly spits out her orange juice. "As a friend."

I barely resist the temptation to tell her what's going on in my head. "I have an interesting story for you."

I don't elaborate quickly enough because she drops her fork and commands, "Go on."

"My mom and dad used to be best friends."

"You mean they aren't anymore?"

"I mean," I tell her, "my mom dated my dad's roommate in college. They were together for a full year until one day Mom realized she didn't like talking to her boyfriend nearly as much as she enjoyed talking to my dad."

"Oh?"

Nodding my head, I tell her, "Yup. Mom told Jake that she wanted the two of them to go away for a weekend so they could really get to know each other."

Molly is intrigued. "What happened?"

"They went to the Wisconsin Dells and spent two days and two nights."

"And?"

"When they returned, they were no longer a couple."

"Wow, okay. Why are you telling me this?"

I open one of the cloth napkins and situate it on my lap, before saying, "I'm telling you this so that you understand how seriously I take friendship."

Molly blushes charmingly. "Are you saying that you're always friends with someone before you date them?"

"Not always, no." Her eyes begin to water, and she blinks rapidly to keep excess moisture from leaking out. She's breaking my heart. "I'm saying that friendship is very important to me.

Friendship can always lead to something more, and if it does then that something more would be very special. Don't you think?"

She opens her mouth like she's going to answer, but then she simultaneously picks up her fork and knocks the glass of orange juice over. Molly jumps up and lets out a shout as the cold liquid rolls down the table onto her legs.

In the past, I would have never thought this to be the case, but it turns out my perfect woman might just be a world class klutz.

CHAPTER TWENTY-FIVE

MOLLY

Of course, I just spilled my orange juice all over myself. What's wrong with me? Why can't I act like a normal person in front of Blake? Running into his bathroom, I use a clean towel to wipe myself up before grabbing another one to soak up the wetness from the carpet.

Hurrying back into the room, I tell him, "I'm so sorry. I know you're not going to believe this, but I've never been this clumsy."

The smirk on his face indicates that he doesn't believe me. And why should he? Not only do I trip nearly every time I seen him, but I jabber on like a lunatic. It all started when I told him I wasn't a lumberjack, and then escalated from there like I've been trying to outdo myself at every turn.

While I clean up my mess, Blake removes my french toast plate. It's swimming in orange juice as well. He replaces it with his omelet. "You can have my eggs."

"Why are you being so nice to me?" I ask. "I stormed in here like some jealous girlfriend, and then I ruined your breakfast. You shouldn't even be talking to me."

"I'm nice to you because I like you, Molly."

"Because we're friends?" I say this as though I mean the exact opposite—*mortal enemies.*

"Aren't we friends?" Chills erupt at the base of my neck and shoot across the expanse of my head.

"I guess." But I didn't agree to come to these singles gatherings because I was looking for another friend. I came because Blake caught my eye in a big way, and I was hoping he might be open to something more.

Although, the story about his parents was kind of interesting. Maybe Blake wants to start out his next relationship as friends. Maybe he thinks that way it might lead to something permanent.

His phone rings which causes him to jump up and run across the room. Blake looks at the screen before saying, "I need to take this." Then he literally sprints toward the bathroom.

I'm not an eavesdropper by nature, but I'd be lying if I didn't confess to being curious about who Blake's so excited to talk to. Standing up, I walk over to the dresser before looking into the mirror like I'm checking my makeup. Then I lean in so that I'm closer to the bathroom door.

"I don't care what you want, Gillian," I hear him say. "This is no longer working for me."

Gillian? Does Blake have a girlfriend? And if he does, then why is he here? I know he said that whatever is going on between them isn't working, but that doesn't sound like they've already broken up. In which case, he's not free to look for her replacement.

Giving up the pretense of being interested in my reflection, I move so that I'm standing right outside the bathroom door. Then I press my ear to it.

Blake says, "Look, I was clear what I wanted, and you aren't giving that to me. I'm not the one who's reneging on our deal."

Their deal? That doesn't sound like a romantic relationship.

Then he adds, "What's the point of giving you more time? You could change your mind again, and then I'm stuck."

I'm so confused right now. Is she trying to talk him out of leaving her?

"*If* I come back, and that's a big if, I want it in writing that I will never have to do anything like this again." I have no idea what her response is, but his tone softens. "I came all the way to Chicago from LA. I did not do that lightly and I don't appreciate your lying to me."

What is she lying about? And again, what is Blake doing at a singles' event if he has a girlfriend?

I'm no closer to figuring out what's going on when the bathroom door bursts open and hits me square on the nose. I cry out as I clutch my face while stumbling backward. I nearly fall to the floor, but the bed stops me.

I thought bathroom doors were supposed to open in, not out. I wonder if it has to do with them being handicap accessible and needing all the space in the bathroom.

When I reach back to steady myself, I realize my hands are covered in blood.

"What were you doing there?" Blake entreats before going back into the bathroom to get another towel. At this rate, he isn't going to have any left.

Tipping my head back to lessen the blood flow, I tell him, "I had to use the bathroom. I was about to knock on the door." I'm not sure if he believes me or not, but he doesn't question me further.

Dabbing the towel to my face, he says, "Let's get you sitting down and then I'll fetch some ice." He helps me across the room back to my chair before grabbing the ice bucket.

Blake comes back a couple of minutes later. He fills the plastic laundry bag and hands it to me. "You're very accident prone, aren't you?"

"I'm really not." *Says the woman covered in orange juice and blood.* Looking down at the table is like witnessing a particularly grizzly crime scene. "I've never even had stitches before," I boldly declare.

Blake rolls his eyes. "I find that hard to believe." Then he goes into the bathroom for another towel. I hear him grumble, "The maid is going to think I killed someone in here."

As soon as he comes back, I ask, "Who were you talking to on the phone?"

He freezes like he's playing that old childhood game, statue maker. "Who? You mean just now?"

I nod my head.

"That was my ... mom. She was checking in to see how things are going. You know how invested moms are in their children's social lives."

His mom? I highly doubt that, but on the off chance he calls his mom by her first name, I ask, "What are your parents' names?"

Furrowing his brow, he answers, "Beth and John."

Beth sounds nothing like Gillian, so I know he's a big fat liar. I'm about to call him on it when he adds, "Now you understand why I think friendship is so important, right?"

No, but I do know why Blake hasn't made a single move on me. He's already seeing someone. What I don't understand is why he's at a dating getaway. It almost sounded like his girlfriend knew he was here, too. Which makes things even more confusing.

"Friendship is the key to all good relationships," Blake reiterates.

"Are you and your girlfriend good friends?" I want to know.

His eyes shift around the room like he's looking for a hidden camera. "What girlfriend? I don't have a girlfriend."

"Uh-huh."

"If I had a girlfriend, why would I be here?"

"I don't know, Blake, why would you?" My voice sounds muffled from the ice bag currently sitting on my face. I continue, "You seem more interested in asking people questions than you are in romance."

I can almost see the hamster wheel turning in his head. "How will I know if I want to be romantic with someone if I don't ask them questions?"

Removing the towel full of ice, I lower my chin and stare directly into his eyes. "You ask Thor and Kyle a lot of questions. Do you think you've ruled out wanting to date them?"

"I'm not gay, Molly," he tells me, "I just like getting to know people."

"I don't believe you."

"That I'm not gay?" He sounds borderline offended.

"I don't believe you're here looking for a girlfriend."

A dozen different emotions cross his face before he settles on what I'm sure he thinks is a look of innocence. "Think what you want."

"Oh, I will," I tell him, "and I think you're lying to me and everyone else here."

He shrugs in such a way that I know I've hit the nail on the head.

At this point, I have nothing to lose, so I ask, "Who's Gillian, Blake?"

His shocked expression tells me all I need to know. Blake is otherwise engaged.

CHAPTER TWENTY-SIX

BLAKE

Thor was right, I do have feelings for Molly, and I would like to ask her out. I just can't do that while I'm pretending to be just another single person on the prowl. I will not start something with her based on a lie.

After several long moments where I try to figure out the best way to proceed given my need for anonymity, I finally sit down in the chair next to Molly and blurt out the truth—or a portion of it anyway. "Gillian is my boss."

"Your boss," she repeats like I just declared that she was my pet iguana. Talk about irony. I finally come clean about something, and she doesn't believe me.

"Yes," I tell her. "Gillian is my boss. She's the reason I moved home to Chicago."

"Because you're dating her ..."

Shaking my head, I say, "She recruited me."

"To make coffee."

"I do more than make coffee," I tell Molly. *Borderline truth.*

"What, you make the scones, too?" Her tone is heavily laden with disdain.

"I ... um ... rather ..."

"Just tell me, Blake."

I cross my fingers behind my back like I did in grade school before I was about to tell a whopper. I know there's no scientific evidence this will have a positive effect, but at the moment I'm willing to try anything to lessen the reverberations of telling so many lies. "I'm going to spearhead some singles' get-togethers at the coffee shop and Gillian wanted me to come up here and get some ideas."

Molly rolls her eyes. "Your boss paid for you to come here to discover what you could learn from watching any romcom on Netflix?"

"I don't think she wants the Hollywood version of what dating events are like," I tell her. "She wants firsthand knowledge about what's going on in people's heads. That's why I'm talking to everyone."

"So, you really aren't here looking for yourself," she accuses.

"Correct. I'm on assignment."

"Are you the coffee shop manager or something?" she wants to know. "I mean, what are you so good at that Gillian would hire you away from wherever you were working in LA?"

The thing about lying is that once you start, there really is no end to it. But even so, that's the sinking ship I'm currently on. "Gillian is a friend of my family's," I tell her. "She partially hired me because my mom wanted me to come home, but also, because I'm really good at my job."

"Making coffee ..."

"I also come up with ways for the businesses I work at to make extra money."

This seems to make more sense to her, because she says, "That's what I do with hotel gift shops. I come in and find ways for them to serve their clientele while still lining their pockets."

I reach for my coffee cup which is now cold. Undeterred, I take a giant swig before embellishing my story even further. "Everything has gotten so expensive, even a cup of coffee." I raise my mug for effect. "People can't even afford their daily latte anymore. And being that dating is so expensive, I figure that instead of dropping a hundred bucks on dinner, we could encourage people to get to know one another over coffee."

Molly ignores my genius and asks, "What's the name of Gillian's shop?"

Stumbling to make up a name on the fly, I tell her, "P... P ... Perky Cups."

"Are you serious?" The look she gives me is enough to wither a cactus. "That sounds like the name of a store that specializes in bras for grandmothers."

She's not wrong, but I can't change the name now. Plodding forth, I say, "So, now that you know why I'm here, will you please do me a favor and not tell anyone?"

"You realize you're throwing off the numbers by not being interested in meeting someone for yourself," she says. "There are thirty women and thirty men for a reason." When I don't respond soon enough, she adds, "That's potentially thirty couples, Blake."

She and Olivia are clearly of like mind. "Maybe so, but at least I'm not purposely trying to mislead anyone."

"That's a lie," she hisses. "Every woman you talk to thinks there's a chance for her. You're taking time away from her potentially meeting the one."

I absolutely see her point but what are the chances of thirty couples pairing off by the end of this thing? Not high at all, if you ask me. "I'm not letting it go anywhere, though," I maintain.

Molly suddenly stands up in a huff. She sways slightly on her feet, probably due to the excessive blood loss, and then declares, "I will not promise to help you lie to these women, Blake. I think it's unethical, and borderline cruel."

I take a step toward her. "Please, Molly. I'm not hurting anyone, and I really need my job. I moved all the way from LA for it." At least I'm back to telling some version of the truth.

The look on her face makes me think I might have convinced her, but I don't want to push too hard. "Please ..."

Flinging both her hands in front of her like she's shooing away a swarm of flies, she says, "Just stay away from me, okay?" I step aside as she teeters toward the door—she really isn't stable on her feet.

It's clear that if I decided to come clean and tell Molly the whole truth, she'd most likely be so mad that she'd tell Trina. Then my whole mission would be compromised, along with my employment status.

After leaving the room, Molly slams the door with enough force to cause a picture on the wall to tilt. Ignoring the food that's still sitting on the table, I pick up my laptop and find a place to sit and work.

If the future of humanity hinges on the success of match-making events, I fear for our species. People, I implore you to introduce your single friends to each other. Moms and dads, get moving! Surely you know someone whose child needs a mate.

In addition to old-fashioned intervention, we desperately need to allow courtship back into the workplace. While I understand sexual harassment has been a big problem in the past, we're not currently living in the *Mad Men* generation. People should be allowed to flirt at the office. Co-workers should be free to co-mingle. If we continue to impede people's access to organic coupling, then our civilization could be in real jeopardy!

I know I sound dramatic, but other than Olivia and Ronald, I have not seen one successful match that has been made, and it's too soon to say whether theirs stands a snowman's chance in Bermuda of making it.

Releasing a giant sigh, I close my laptop and try to figure out how I'm going to spend my day. There's a group going cross-country skiing, and another snowmobiling, but I'm not in the mood to put on a happy face and pretend.

Turning on the television, I search for one of those movies Molly was talking about on Netflix, when out of nowhere I suddenly get inspired. What if I put my time to good use? I've met nearly every person here, so why not play matchmaker myself and introduce people I think would be a good fit. It's not like I'd be anything like Trina. In fact, I'd be the anti-Trina. I'm not profiting from getting people together. I'm helping them the old-fashioned way—friend to friend.

With a renewed interest in the day, I put on my coat and head out the door. My first stop is the breakfast buffet that has been set up for our group. After the first night, there's been one shared meal a day along with a group activity and a morning coffee or evening mixer, depending on which meal we have. For instance, if the meal is breakfast, then it's an evening cocktail mixer.

On my way to the elevator, I run into the mom of the family that I keep seeing. "How's Ben?" I ask her.

She looks tired, so I'm not surprised when she says, "He had a long night."

"Having too much fun, huh?"

She smiles like the action takes all her energy. "He's a little overstimulated. Life at home is nowhere near this exciting."

I don't want to be nosy, but I am curious, so I ask, "I hope you don't mind me asking, but is there something physically wrong with Ben?" Her eyes immediately become watery, which leads me to believe that there is. I should have kept my mouth shut.

"Ben has leukemia."

I'm not a doctor, but I've noticed his greying pallor. That leads me to guess he might not be doing well. "I'm so sorry," I tell her before offering a platitude I'm sure she hears all the time. "I'm sure he'll get better soon."

Tears silently start to fall down the woman's face. "He won't be fine," she says. "In fact, if we had any hope that would be the outcome, we would have never brought him here and risked him getting sick with something else." She adds, "His immune system is shot from all the chemo."

I say a silent prayer—actually, more of a plea—that God helps this family. "I'm so sorry. I wish there was something I could do."

Her shoulders sag wearily. "Thank you." Reaching out her hand to mine, she says, "I'm Francie, by the way. You know Ben, and my husband is Ward."

Taking her hand, I ask, "Is there anything I can do?" I can't imagine what that would be but honestly, I'd do anything I could to help this kid have a great vacation.

"Not unless you can get him courtside tickets to a Bulls game. The Make-A-Wish Foundation is working on it for him, but you wouldn't believe the number of dying kids who want to score dream tickets like that."

Dying. Just hearing the word causes my nervous system to backfire. Pulling out my wallet, I take out a business card and hand it to her. "I'm the new sportswriter at *Chicago Wind*," I tell her. "I don't start until the current guy retires, but I would be happy to contact my boss and see if there's anything we can do."

Francie takes the card like it's the answer to her prayers, which it probably isn't because I don't really have any pull yet. And I'm currently not Gillian's favorite employee. "Thank you, Blake. That would be amazing."

Francie grimaces when she sees the look on my face, which I'm sure conveys the doubt I'm feeling that I can come through for her. "Don't worry, I won't say anything to Ben. I know this is a huge ask."

I decide then and there to do everything in my power to help this kid. I can't imagine anything would be too big to ask if it would bring some joy to a dying child.

I'm reminded of the last weeks of my brother's life. My sister and I were so young we couldn't sort out what was happening to him. All we knew was that he wasn't going to get better and that he was going to live in heaven with Jesus. We had no basis for processing the reality of that concept.

I assure Francie, "I promise you, I'm going to do everything I can." And while I'm at it, I'm going to try to sweeten the pot in any way possible.

Looking as though she's carrying the weight of the world on her shoulders, Francie says, "Thank you, Blake. I'd better get back to Ben now."

My heart nearly breaks in two as I watch her walk away. Instead of going down to the mixer, I go back to my room and call Gillian again. I'm transferred straight through this time.

Her first word is, "What?"

"I need a favor," I tell her. "A big one."

CHAPTER TWENTY-SEVEN

MOLLY

The fact that Blake is here under false pretenses really ticks me off, and I didn't even come to the lodge with hopes of meeting anyone. I'm here to work. So after going back to my room and changing into some dry and non-bloodied clothes, I head down to the gift shop.

Lorelai takes one look at me and gasps, "Have you been in an accident?"

I knew it was only a matter of time before I started to bruise. I should have put an extra layer of foundation on. "I walked into a door," I tell her.

Concerned, she asks, "How is that even possible?"

I'm not trying to protect Blake as much as myself when I tell her, "I tripped."

"Do you need to see a doctor?" She doesn't appear convinced that I'm okay.

Shaking my head, I say, "I don't think I broke anything." Then I hurry to change the subject. "Have you had any requests for things you don't already carry?"

Reaching under the counter, she pulls out a small notepad.

"I've been keeping track. So far, I've had three people ask for protein bars, two for holiday-themed press-on nails, and one for inexpensive festive earrings." She smiles before telling me that twin seven-year-old girls wanted the press-on nails so they could get fancy for supper in the dining room, and a teenage girl asked for the earrings.

I smile as I write this down. Being that the lodge caters to families, I like the idea of them carrying things like nails and cheap earrings. Big girls and little girls alike love that stuff. And being that Trista and her fiancé don't care if they make money from the shop, these two items would be a great addition.

"Why don't you already sell protein bars?" I ask. I assume it has to do with wanting people to eat in the dining room, but with so many outdoor activities it would make sense that people get hungry at non-mealtimes.

"We have granola bars and cookies," she says, "but I think people want more if they're doing sports."

"Okay, Lorelai, thanks." Then I tell her, "I think I'll spend the day talking to guests and try to get some other ideas."

As luck would have it, as I turn to leave the gift shop, I walk right into Kyle.

"Molly." By the look on his face, he's obviously wondering what happened to me. I'm relieved when he doesn't comment.

I talked to Kyle for a little bit last night. He asked to have breakfast with me, but I declined. In retrospect, I might have been better off had I eaten with him. Chances are my nose wouldn't be so sore.

That's when I realize I still haven't had my breakfast. I spilled Blake's juice on the french toast and beat it out of his room before I could eat the omelet. "Hi, Kyle. Have you eaten?"

He looks surprised. "No."

"Would you like to join me?"

"But you said no when I asked you last night." He hurriedly adds, "I'd love to eat with you." As we walk toward the banquet hall, he asks, "How did you hurt yourself?"

"I tripped. But it looks worse than it is." As we cross the lobby, he tells me, "I'm really glad you've decided to spend some time with me. I've felt just awful about everything ever since I saw you here."

I shoot him a look that has him rushing to add, "I've obviously felt awful for longer than that."

Thinking about my situation with Blake somehow makes me feel compassion for Kyle. "You can't choose who you love."

"But you can choose how you proceed."

"That's the truth, Kyle." That's when I realize I need to quit telling myself to stay away from Blake and just do it. What was I thinking, having breakfast in his room today? And now that I know he's here under false pretenses, I *really* need to keep my distance.

As we near the room that's been set up for our group's breakfast, Kyle asks, "What do you say we skip the circus and eat in the dining room? You know, away from curious eyes."

"That sounds like a great idea," I tell him. Also, that way, there will be no chance of running into Blake if he decides to come down.

Once we're seated and we've ordered, Kyle asks, "So, have you thought more about giving us another go?"

I shake my head. "I'm sorry, but I can't forgive being cheated on. Distrust is no way to start over again." Truthfully, I'm surprised I even agreed to have a meal with him. I blame Blake for throwing me off my game so badly.

"I don't blame you," Kyle says. "I was horrible to you."

I don't know what comes over me, but I tell my ex, "It's done. You can't keep beating yourself up about it. You just need to move on and do better the next time."

"I thought I'd done better with Amelia," he says. "Not that you want to hear about that …"

I'm so over Kyle that I find I don't mind listening to him. "You can talk about her if you want. I know how you must be feeling."

"Because of me." Even though I'm glad he's experiencing remorse, I also feel sorry for him.

"You know that old saying." His blank stare prompts me to tell him the same thing I told Blake at the beginning of this. "All's fair in love and war." With a shrug I add, "There's truth to that. No one should settle for someone they don't wholeheartedly adore. Life is too uncertain not to be totally committed to the one you're with. And you should do everything you can to be with that person."

Kyle picks up the glass of ice water in front of him and takes a slow sip. "Yeah, but what if you're sure the one you're meant to be with doesn't feel the same way about you?"

I know he's not talking about me. "Then you find something to distract yourself with until your heart doesn't hurt so badly."

He looks at me sheepishly. "Is that what you did?"

It's time to stop being sympathetic and regain some self-respect. "I was sad when you left, Kyle, but I wasn't devastated. I took time to reevaluate my life, and then I started going out again." I don't mention that was with my girlfriends, not with potential love interests.

Looking mildly hurt, he decides, "I didn't mean that much to you, then."

This conversation is exactly what I've needed. I don't want Kyle to remember me as the loser he dumped. And while there's some truth to that, there's also the knowledge that he and I would have never been happy together. "Our feelings for each other were similar," I tell him.

He surprises me by saying, "I'm glad for that. I've been worried I was the reason you're still single."

Oh, he is. But not in the way he thinks. Even though Kyle and I wouldn't have been good together, he is responsible for making me afraid to trust other men. I have to force myself to remember that not all men are liars and cheats. I just need to figure out how not to be attracted to the bad boys who are destined to break my heart.

The waiter brings our coffees and Kyle's orange juice—note to self: stay away from the juice. Leaning out of harm's way, I ask Kyle, "Have you met anyone you might be interested in dating here?"

He shakes his head. "Honestly, I think it's too soon." Then he sheepishly adds, "When I saw you, I thought the universe was trying to help me fix a past mistake, but now I see it for what it really is."

"Which is?"

"A warning that you can't blow through life only looking out for yourself."

"You know what I think?" I ask him. He shakes his head. "I think it's a good thing that we saw each other here. It's closure we both needed to carry on."

"It's going to be awhile before I carry on," he says, "but I really am glad that you're here." After a beat, he asks, "How are Ellen and Henry doing?"

"They broke up," I tell him.

He's as surprised as I was hearing this, and he only knew them at the very beginning of their relationship. "But they were perfect together!"

"I thought so too, but Ellen feels like she plays second fiddle to Henry's kids. As such, she was less than receptive when he proposed."

The waiter arrives and places our meals in front of us. The french toast I ruined up in Blake's room looked so good that I got it again. Picking up my knife and fork, I change the subject and ask Kyle, "Is there anything that you think the gift shop should carry that they don't have?"

He smiles. "Watch out, Molly; all work and no play isn't good for you."

"Don't worry about that," I tell him. "Researching for the resort has been about ninety percent play." Once again, I wonder why I was booked for two full weeks. My normal jobs are only for three days.

He takes a bite of his pancakes before asking, "What about Blake?"

"What about him?"

"You seem to enjoy each other's company." After a beat, he adds, "He seems like a really nice guy."

For a fraud. But I don't say that. Full of humility, I tell him, "He likes me as a friend." Truthfully, he probably doesn't even like me for that. He just needed someone to glom onto so that it wasn't obvious he was here to deceive.

"I think he likes you for more than that," Kyle says.

Now's my big chance to out Blake for the liar that he is, but for some reason I can't bring myself to do that.

Not yet, anyway.

CHAPTER TWENTY-EIGHT

BLAKE

"I'm sorry, say that again," I tell Gillian. *Is her heart made of pure stone? Has the woman no inner kindness at all?*

"I said that I'd be happy to get you courtside tickets to a Bulls game, but you need to pony up something on your end."

"The boy has *cancer*, Gillian. He's *dying*." How can she not see that it's her duty as a fellow human to do whatever she can to make his last days good ones?

"Is that somehow my fault, Blake?" *Ice. Queen.*

"No," I tell her. "But a normal response to this kind of request would be to bend over backwards and be helpful."

"I'm offering to be helpful," she says. "I just want something in return."

"Fine." Gillian is nothing more than a cold-blooded reptile. "What do you want in return?"

"I want you to write about a woman at the event that you personally find interesting."

She can't possibly mean that. "Come again?"

"I want you to write a first-person account of someone you've met that you would be interested in dating."

"That isn't possible," I tell her.

"Why is that, Blake?" Again, with her "teacher reprimanding a bad kid" tone.

"Because I'm not interested in dating anyone here." *Lies.*

"It's a good thing you're there for another ten days then, isn't it? You still have plenty of time to find someone."

I stand up from the chair I've been sitting on and start pacing around the room. "What is wrong with you, Gillian?"

"Excuse me?" She sounds shocked that I'm standing up to her.

"Why can't you just be a nice person and help a dying kid fulfill a last request? Why do you need to get something out of it?" At this point, I don't care if she fires me.

"What's wrong with being a nice person *and* getting something out of it?" she wants to know.

"A nice person would be willing to do something for a terminally ill kid without having an ulterior motive," I tell her.

"I'm the boss, Blake," she says in that no-nonsense tone of hers that makes me see red. "Therefore, if I see a way to encourage my reporters to give me better stories, it's my job to do so."

A Hail Mary pass would be easier than bargaining with this woman. "What about journalistic integrity? What about reporting a story so that all sides are portrayed by a third party?"

"You're writing a fluff piece for our weekly circular, Blake. You're not doing any hard-hitting reporting here."

Ouch. I know I'm not covering the Middle East peace talks but even so, there should be ground rules. "So, you're looking for tabloid journalism?" Take that, Gillian.

"Call it whatever you want, Blake. But if our readers are not entertained by what we give them, they won't continue to read our publication."

"People read the news for news," I remind her.

"People read the supplemental magazine for entertainment," she responds. "So, if you want those tickets, you'll supply me with one article that is fully about your personal experience at the singles' event and give our readers a firsthand account of what it's really like."

"What if I don't meet anyone that I'm interested in?" I almost whine, trying desperately not to sound as pathetic as I feel.

"Then make her up," Gillian says. "I'll need your answer right now because it's going to take some time to finesse those tickets."

I am so steaming mad that I want to tell her what she can do with her job. In fact, I'm so disillusioned I would happily move back to LA and beg for my position back there. I haven't even unpacked my boxes yet, so it wouldn't be any harder than calling a mover.

But if I did that, I know I would never be able to get Ben those tickets.

"I'll write the article," I tell her. "But I want five tickets."

"Why five? You said you just needed them for the kid and his parents."

"I want five because I'm going to go to the game too and I might bring someone else."

She laughs. "Ah, the woman you're not interested in?"

"I was thinking about asking my dad," I tell her. There's no way Molly is ever going to want to see me again after I write an article about us in the paper. And while I could fabricate someone else, I know the story will only be as good as the heart and soul put into it. For that, I'm going to need to base it on reality. For that, I'm going to need Molly.

"I'll do what I can, Blake," Gillian says, "But your article better knock my socks off."

"Don't worry about me," I tell her. "I know what you want, and I'll deliver. But you'd better do the same. I want those tickets before you run my piece."

"I'll hand them to you personally, as soon as you turn your article in."

I don't have what it takes to be civil for another second, so I disconnect the call without even saying goodbye. How did I not see Gillian for the shrewd manipulator that she is?

But then again, I was so excited about getting my dream job that I wasn't really looking for warning signs. Now here I am, about to get everything I've ever wanted and all I need to do is air my dirty laundry for all of Chicago. Not only that, but I need to air Molly's as well …

Opening my laptop, I start writing.

Here's the thing about being single that no one wants to talk about: you can't still be alone without having made a lot of mistakes. To be single means that you have rejected others, you've been rejected in return, and you've allowed hopes and dreams to build that ultimately hit a wall.

In order to not stay single, you have to open yourself up to risk and be willing to go through all of that again. And that is not easy.

I've had two long term relationships in my thirty-two years. With both, I thought I'd won the jackpot. Both ended in ways I did not see coming.

My first adult relationship was when I was twenty-three years old. Finley and I worked in the same coffee shop. She was an aspiring actress looking for her big break and I was an ambitious sports journalist with no idea how to break into the business.

Finley and I worked together for a month before I asked her out. Our relationship was built on shared aspirations. We fed each other's enthusiasm and consoled each other in times when our greatest desires seemed too far away to reach.

We lived together for two years. I sporadically wrote for various sports websites, and she was cast in the occasional commercial. In my mind, we were in the same place in our careers.

I envisioned mutual success, eventual marriage and children, and a life full of everything we ever wanted. We were going to be a dream couple living our best lives.
Then Finley got her big break, when she was cast in a recurring role on a nighttime crime drama.

I couldn't have been happier for her. For us, really, because I knew her accomplishment meant that I was also on the precipice of triumph. Finley did not see it the same way.

In her eyes, she was a star, and I was a dead weight holding her back from reaching greater heights. And for whatever reason, she didn't feel it necessary to tell me we were through before she'd already replaced me.

I found out what my new status was when Finley's show was nominated for an Emmy award. She told me that they only gave her one ticket so I couldn't go with her. I believed her until her show won. She walked up on stage with the cast to accept their award, then she turned to one of her co-stars and nearly sucked the lips off his face.
I was hurt and humbled in equal measure. I was also gone when she came home that night.

My second relationship ended more amicably, but it was still a shock to my system. You don't invest time and energy and expect things to just fizzle.

Now, I'm here at a singles' convention in Wisconsin wondering how this has become my life. I was angry when I got this assignment because covering events like this is not why I got into journalism. I was even madder when my editor told me she wanted me to write about my personal experience.

Early on, I met a woman that I liked very much but I made the call not to pursue her. Why? Because I was ordered not to tell any of the other participants what I'm really doing here, and I did not want to start something with her based on a lie.

While I want to keep telling the truth and outing Gillian for the manipulating she-devil that she is, I know my boss would have that part edited out. So, I continue writing:

This woman caught me totally and completely off guard. She's more than just outwardly beautiful, too. She's perpetually clumsy, she overshares, and she can be as bristly as a startled porcupine. While some people may find those things faults, I find them endearingly attractive.

For years, I have kept the women I've dated at arm's length. Past heartache can do that to you. But when the right person shows up in your life, it's easy to forget history and jump into possibilities for the future.

I hope I have a future with this lovely lady. Her name is Polly ...

CHAPTER TWENTY-NINE

MOLLY

After breakfast with Kyle, I head toward the great room to chat up some of the lodge's guests. The first people I approach are a mom and dad with their young son. The boy is bald, so I assume they're one of the families Heath Fox and Trina are hosting.

"Hi there," I say. "I don't want to interrupt, but I was wondering if you might answer a question for me." I hurry to add, "My name is Molly, and I work for the lodge."

The father looks up and visibly forces a smile. "I'm Ward." He gestures toward his wife. "This is Francie and our son, Ben."

I point to a chair next to them. "Do you mind if I join you?" I sit down before they can tell me no. "We're working on adding things to the gift shop that guests might like, and I wonder if you have any suggestions."

Francie looks totally hassled by my presence, so I am determined to leave quickly. "I haven't been into the gift shop yet," she says.

Ward explains, "We've been pretty busy since we got here."

Ben, who looks like he'd like nothing more than to take a nap, briefly perks up and asks, "Do they have any stuffed animals?"

"I don't think so," I tell him. "Is that something you'd like them to carry?"

"I left my stuffed beaver at home," he says sadly. "I don't sleep good without him."

I immediately write down his request before asking, "What else do you like about home that you wish they had here?"

"Earbuds," he says before explaining, "I fall asleep with music but my parents like quiet."

I write down earbuds before asking Ward and Francie, "Would you mind if I borrowed Ben for a few minutes?" I point across the hall. "I'd love to take him into the gift shop and see if he has any more ideas."

Ben's parents look at each other in surprise. "I work here," I remind them. "I'm not a creeper."

Francie laughs. "You don't look like one." Then she asks Ben, "Would you like to go to the gift shop with Molly?"

His interest is immediate. "Yes!"

"We'll be here when you're done," Ward tells him.

I reach my hand out to Ben, and he takes it easily. As we walk away, I ask him, "How old are you, Ben?"

"Almost seven," he says.

"That's a big number," I tell him. "Have you started losing any teeth?"

He shakes his head. "But I have a loose one."

"That'll be exciting when the tooth fairy comes," I tell him. "My tooth fairy used to give me a whole dollar when I lost a tooth." Ben starts to giggle, so I ask, "Why is that funny?"

Between snickers, he tells me, "You must be from the olden days like my parents. The tooth fairy gives my friends five dollars."

"Five dollars?" I feign shock like this is an ungodly amount. "What in the world would you do with that kind of money?"

Ben grows serious before saying, "I'm saving to buy my parents a present."

Squeezing his hand, I tell him, "You're a sweet kid, Ben. What do you want to buy for them?"

"I want to hire someone to take a great family picture of us. I want to put it in a nice frame."

"I bet you'll be able to do just that after you lose a bunch of teeth."

His eyes fill with unshed tears. "I don't have time to lose a bunch of teeth."

I feel a sharp pain in my heart when I realize what he's saying. "How about if I take some pictures of you and your parents and then I can order a frame for you to put one in?"

He looks up, surprised. "You'd do that for me?"

"I sure would," I tell him. That's when it occurs to me that picture frames might be a nice touch in the gift shop. I make a mental note to add that to my list.

As soon as we walk into the shop, Ben starts to look around. After a few minutes, he says, "My parents like to do puzzles at night. Maybe you could sell some of those." That's actually a brilliant idea.

"Anything else?" I ask him.

"How about some bear tattoos?"

"Bear tattoos?" I have a hard time suppressing my laughter.

"Yeah! I went to my friend Tommy Wilkes' birthday party, and he had all kinds of cool animal tattoos that his mom helped us put on. The bear was super scary!" I write down fake tattoos on my list.

Ben turns around and inspects the candy shelf. "You need gummy worms. Not gummy bears, worms."

"What's the difference?" I ask him.

"Worms are longer and grosser than bears. Also, you get more candy with a worm than with a bear. That matters," he assures me.

This kid is a veritable gold mine and I briefly consider cutting him in on the profits. "What else?" I ask.

"How 'bout those hand warmer thingies?"

"Gloves?" I ask.

He shakes his head. "No, the thingies my dad has for camping. They're little packs that you sort of smoosh around. They get real hot. I would have liked to have had those when we went snow-mobiling."

I write down hand warmers before asking Ben, "Have you gone zip-lining yet?"

He shakes his head. "I'm kind of scared."

"I was, too," I tell him. "But my friend went at the same time with me, and it made me feel safe."

He looks up thoughtfully. "You mean my dad could go with me?"

"Absolutely," I tell him.

Ben asks, "Can we go back now?"

"You bet. You've given me a lot of great ideas, Ben. Thank you."

When we get back to his parents, my new little friend announces, "I want to go zip-lining with you, Dad. Molly says we can ride together."

Ward looks surprised. "I didn't know if they allowed that here and I haven't had a chance to ask." He adds, "Ben is afraid of heights though."

"I don't love them either," I tell him. "But you really aren't that far off the ground. I'm sure if you didn't like it after one run, you could stop."

"Can we go, Dad?" Ben asks excitedly. "Please?"

Francie interjects, "What about me? Can I come too?"

"Yes, yes, yes!!!" Ben exclaims excitedly. "You can come, too, Molly!"

I hadn't planned to go zip-lining again, but I suddenly have another idea. "How about if I come and take pictures of you all while you're doing it?"

Ben's face brightens like a light bulb has been turned on under his skin. "Yes!" he shouts.

"We don't want to take you away from your job," Ward says.

"It's my job to make sure guests have everything they need," I tell him. That's when it occurs to me that Trina and Heath could hire a photographer to take pictures of the families who come here. My mom always complained that she was never in the photos because she was the one taking them. And in the case of Ben and his family, I'm guessing the memories these pictures will invoke will be cherished forever.

Francie pushes her chair back and says, "Can you give us twenty minutes to go upstairs and get into warm clothes?"

"Absolutely," I tell her. "In the meantime, I'll make sure you're added to the schedule." I hope they can get them in on such short notice, but I'm willing to bet the lodge will do everything they can once I tell them about Ben.

Before they leave, I suggest, "Why don't I get a picture of you all in front of the fireplace?"

Ben claps his hands excitedly. "Can we get one with the singing animals, too?" Ah, the chipmunks.

"We can take pictures wherever you want to," I tell him.

I wind up spending the entire afternoon with Ben and his family. After we went zip-lining—where I also took a bunch of videos—I snapped pictures of them building a snowman, having a snowball fight, and making snow angels. When we finally went back inside, we ordered hot chocolate and warmed up by the fire.

Not only did I have a wonderful day, but I was grateful to get out of my head for a while. After two cups of hot chocolate with whipped cream, I air drop the pictures of the day to Ward and Francie's phones.

Ben walks over to me and whispers, "What about the picture frame?"

"How long will you be here?" I ask him.

He turns to his parents. "How many more days are we going to be here?"

Ward holds up three fingers. Leaning down so that my mouth is right by Ben's ear, I tell him, "I'll have it for you in two days."

His smile is electric. Opening his arms, he leans in and gives me a hug. "Thanks, Molly. You're the best!"

After saying goodbye to Ben and his parents, I go back up to my room to get ready for tonight's mixer. I wasn't excited about it this morning, but I feel like my day has been spent getting perspective on what's important in life. And more than anything, I'd love to be part of a happy family someday.

The only way to accomplish that is to meet somebody to share that family with.

CHAPTER THIRTY

BLAKE

For tonight's get-together, we're meeting in the ballroom for square dancing. I've loved country music since the square-dancing segment we had in middle school gym class. It was hands-down my favorite.

After putting on a pair of jeans and pairing it with a flannel shirt, I look in the mirror and realize that all that's missing is a cowboy hat and boots. Other than that, I could pass for that country singer Cody Johnson.

I decide that tonight I'm going to go down to the mixer ahead of the crowd. I want to make sure that I'm there before Molly shows up. I don't know how I'm going to get her to talk to me, but I have a couple of ideas.

On my way to the elevator, I see Ben's family again. I'm no longer surprised by how often we run into each other. "Ben!" I greet him. "You look like you've had a busy day." This is the first time I'm seeing him without a hat on and sure enough, he's bald.

"I went zip-lining!" he tells me excitedly.

"That's a lot of fun, isn't it?" I reach a hand toward Ben's dad and introduce myself. "I'm Blake."

He smiles knowingly. "Francie told me. It's really nice what you're trying to do for us."

"What's he doing?" Ben wants to know.

"It's a surprise," Francie says. Then she tells her husband, "Why don't you take Ben to our room. I'll be there in just a minute."

After they leave, Francie tells me, "I just want you to know that I'm not holding you to the whole Bulls tickets thing."

"I talked to my boss," I tell her. "And things look promising. I just need your phone number so I can let you know what date your tickets are for, and we can set up how I'm going to get them to you."

Francie looks like she's about to cry. "I don't know what we've done to deserve people doing such nice things for us, but I'm very grateful."

"I'm not doing much," I tell her, "but I have an inkling of what your family is going through." Before emotion clogs my throat, I tell her, "My little brother died when he was only three."

Francie takes my hand in hers and gives it a squeeze. Several moments pass before she lets it go. "Thank you, Blake." That's all she says before she walks off to join her husband and son.

Life is so fragile; you never know how much time you have. As such, it seems horribly frivolous to waste even a moment. Suddenly, Molly is all I can think about, and I can't wait to go downstairs to see her.

When I get to the ballroom, I discover they've done their best to make it feel less elegant and more rustic. There are bales of hay stacked around the room, and the tables are covered in red-checked gingham cloths. They even have a table full of cowboy hats for us to use. I pick up a black Stetson, and it fits perfectly.

Molly walks into the room looking like she didn't get the country western memo. She's wearing another cocktail dress. This one is a black sleeveless number. I'm glad to see that her back is covered because I did not like the stares she was getting when she wore that sexy blue number.

I approach her from behind so she can't run from me. When I reach her side, I gently touch her shoulder to get her attention. As soon as we make eye contact, I can't tell if she's happy to see me or in a panic to get away.

"I'm sorry about this morning," I tell her. "I know I said I was here for work, but it's occurred to me there's no reason I can't be here for pleasure as well."

"What are you saying?" she asks incredulously. "You want me to help you find a girlfriend?"

Shaking my head, I tell her, "I'd like you to dance with me."

"Why?"

"Because I like you and I want to dance with you," I tell her.

"Because you're afraid I'm going to tell people why you're really here and you want to keep watch on me?" Man, is she suspicious.

"Molly," I tell her. "I like you and I want to dance with you. Why can't that be enough?"

She looks down at her dress and says, "I'm not wearing the right thing."

"You look beautiful," I tell her sincerely. Then I take her hand and lead her out onto the dance floor. The band is playing an old Garth Brooks song that I've always loved. I open my arms to Molly and invite her in.

Once we're moving to the music, I lean down and tell her, "You are stunning tonight." She grumbles something about empty compliments, so I double down. "You are easily the most gorgeous woman in the room."

"Quit trying to charm me, Blake. I'm not buying it."

I surprise her by saying, "I don't care if you tell people why I'm here."

She pulls back so she can look me in the eye. "This morning you practically begged me not to."

"That was before I realized I can do my job *and* have fun."

"Are you sure your girlfriend won't mind?"

"Molly," I pull her closer, "Gillian is not my girlfriend. I don't have a girlfriend."

"And you're not looking for one either," she drawls disdainfully.

"I might be." I let that statement dangle in the air for a moment before adding, "If I meet someone I like."

I feel her body tense in my arms before she says, "You like me."

"Very much."

We dance for the rest of the song without saying another word and yet, I feel like we've communicated nonstop. Before another song starts, Trina steps up to the microphone and announces, "Are you all ready to learn some basic square-dancing moves?"

I'm surprised when the crowd lets out a loud cheer. I guess everyone likes to do-si-do. Before handing off the microphone to the band leader, Trina says, "All I know about square-dancing is that it's time to grab your partner!"

We spend the next several minutes watching a couple up front show us the moves. We allemande left, right and left grand, and promenade. Then we learn how to sashay, pass through, and box the gnat. There's thirty minutes of this before we're deemed ready to roll.

Leaning down to Molly's ear, I ask her, "Are you ready?"

"Oh, I'm ready," she tells me.

The band starts to play an old-time classic called "Birdie in the Cage." They start out slowly at first to give everyone a chance to warm up. Then they play the same number again at the regular pace. We laugh as we spin and twirl and practice all the steps we just learned. I can't remember the last time I had so much fun.

By the time the song is over, the whole room is panting from exertion and laughter. I take Molly's hand and lead her off the dance floor. When we're safely out of the traffic flow, I tell her, "I'm really glad you're here."

"Why?"

"Because I'm having the time of my life and I'm having it with you. Molly," I start to say before pausing for a moment. "Things aren't always what they seem, but that doesn't mean they aren't real."

She looks at me with confusion. "I have no idea what you're saying."

"I'm saying that just because you think I'm here for one reason, doesn't mean I'm not here for another reason, too."

She shakes her head. "You are confusing me."

"You think that I'm here to get tips for a coffee shop …"

She interrupts, "Because that's what you told me."

"Right." I still can't tell her why I'm really here and it's driving me crazy. But I swear that once those Bulls tickets are in my hand, I'm going to tell Molly the whole truth. Looking deeply into her eyes, I say, "Please listen to me very carefully because what I'm about to say is one hundred percent the truth."

She doesn't so much as blink, so I continue. "I like you, Molly, and that's for real. I love spending time with you. I think you're funny and gorgeous and quirky …"

"And?" she breathlessly prompts me.

The air positively crackles with energy as I lean closer to her. "And I wonder if you would mind if I kissed you."

I can feel the tingles as they rise on her arms. "You want to kiss me?"

"I really do," I tell her.

"Right here in front of everyone?"

Without breaking eye contact, I nod my head. "If you don't mind."

She leans in toward me and reaches up on her tip toes before answering, "I don't mind at all."

And then, just like that, our lips meet, and I realize that maybe there was a divine plan for my coming to this event. Maybe I was meant to be here for a bigger reason because at this moment, I one hundred percent feel like Molly just might be my person.

CHAPTER THIRTY-ONE

MOLLY

First kisses are notoriously unpredictable. Some are so shockingly bad you know you're never going to kiss that person again; some are nice; and then there are the ones that fill you with every toe-curling emotion under the sun. Kissing Blake falls into the last category.

I've been attracted to him since I first laid eyes on him. And while I'm sure it would have been great had we kissed right there at the train station, the days of getting to know each other have really sweetened the experience.

The hard thing has been that even when I thought Blake wasn't interested in me, I loved spending time with him. So much so that I might have tried to stay friends with him just so I didn't miss out on his occasional presence in my life. Although, I'm pretty sure the friendship angle wouldn't have lasted. I couldn't have watched him date other women.

Having said that, somehow things changed tonight. I don't know what happened that made Blake realize he could work and have a social life, but whatever it was, I'm grateful for it.

I know something shifted in me after spending the day with

Ben's family. Life can be a sweet journey, and it can be a harrowing one. Today reminded me that when it's sweet, you have to live in the moment and enjoy it to the best of your ability.

All these crazy thoughts are running through my head while Blake is kissing me. His lips are so soft and demanding that I don't ever want this contact to end. I'm about to let myself completely drift away into fantasy land when Blake tentatively lifts his head far enough to break contact. I immediately groan at the absence of him.

"Wow," he says.

"Wow, what?" I want to hear him say the words.

"Just wow," he repeats.

"You never know how first kisses are going to be, do you?"

He shakes his head. "I didn't have any doubt that if you ever let me kiss you it would be one of the best of my life."

Awareness floods every corner of my body. The air between us suddenly feels alive, like it's part of a forcefield holding us together. "You've thought of kissing me ..." I want to hear more about this.

"I've thought of little else since the night we met."

"I don't believe you." I remind him, "You were very dismissive of me that night."

His arms are still around me, and the heat of him is nearly my undoing. "I saved you from falling on your face."

"That's true," I tell him, "but once we got into the car to come to the lodge, you barely looked at me."

"I was in work mode." He lowers his eyes to meet mine, and I'm immediately drawn into their green depths. "You know what they say, don't you?"

"All work and no play makes Blake a dull boy?" I guess.

"I was thinking more along the lines of not playing around where you work, but I like yours better." He runs his hands down my arms before gently caressing his fingertips across mine. "Would you like to take a walk with me?"

I would walk to Australia with this man. I'd walk to the moon with him. But I can't seem to open my mouth and tell him that, so I merely nod my head.

As we move toward the door, Trina stops us. "I saw that," she announces.

My face heats up in what must be the mother of all blushes. "It seems that Blake might like me as more than a friend, after all," I tell her.

Blake declares, "Faulty starter, my foot."

Smiling, Trina tells him, "Remember, the thing with faulty starters is they can be fixed. Looks like you took yours to the shop."

Car metaphors really aren't my thing, but I think Trina nailed this one. I don't know why Blake didn't think he could date while getting tips for his coffee shop, but I'm glad he figured it out.

"I appreciate you asking me to join your event," I tell Trina. "I have some ideas for you about the shop as well as some other things."

"Let's talk about that tomorrow," she says. "For now, go and enjoy your night."

Blake and I walk out of the ballroom hand in hand. He leads me toward the great room where there are two vacant chairs next to the fire. Once we're situated, he says, "This is the most romantic environment I can imagine."

I look around at the giant Christmas tree and the wreath hanging over the fireplace. There are six stockings suspended from the massive wooden hearth. "My sister teased me about coming here and meeting a lumberjack."

"So that's where the whole lumberjack thing came from. I must confess, I'm a little relieved that's not your type."

"Who says that's not my type?" I bat my eyes flirtatiously at him.

"It had better not be." He sounds jealous, and I love it.

"What do you think my type should be?"

He closes his eyes like he's deep in thought before opening

them again. "I was thinking you need a guy who knows how to make a great cup of coffee."

"Maybe one who writes dystopian love stories on the side."

He looks briefly confused before saying, "I don't think it matters what he does for a living so long as he's sitting right here with you."

Reaching out, I take Blake's hand in mine. "Good thing the guy I'm sitting with does both."

He hesitantly asks, "What if I'm not really writing a novel?"

"Why would you have said you were if you weren't?"

"I told you before that my goal was to be here incognito."

"By lying to people?"

"I like to think of it as more of an embellishment," he says. "The truth is that I like to write but I haven't done it a lot lately."

"If you like to write, then you should write," I tell him. "I've recently realized that life is too short not to follow your heart in all things."

Blake laces his fingers through mine. "I've come to the same conclusion." After a beat, he adds, "My mom likes to remind me there aren't endless chances to meet your person."

"I think she's right," I tell him. "But at the same time, you can't force yourself to make it work with someone you know isn't right."

"Like Kyle for you," he says.

"Like Kyle," I agree.

The fire makes a loud popping sound that momentarily breaks into the bubble of our conversation. Blake points to a loveseat that a couple just vacated. "Why don't we go sit over there?"

Standing up, he leads me over to our new perch. As soon as we sit down, he puts his arm around my shoulder which makes me feel like the luckiest girl in the whole world.

Sounding nervous, Blake says, "I think Kyle is planning on making another play for you."

"He already did."

Leaning to the side so that he breaks contact between our

bodies, he implores, "Why would you do that? You know you deserve better." Before I can put his mind at ease that I'm not at all interested, he continues, "Once a cheater always a cheater."

"Relax, Blake." Then I come clean. "I let Kyle think there might be a chance because I was trying to make someone else jealous."

His eyes widen as realization hits. "You were trying to make *me* jealous?"

"I was," I confess. "But I was starting to think it wasn't working."

"I didn't want to lie to you, Molly," Blake says. "I didn't want to start anything based on a lie."

"It's a good thing you told me the truth then, isn't it?" Blake's shoulders remain tense like there's something else he hasn't told me. "You *have* told me the truth, haven't you?"

"I've told you what I can," he says cryptically.

"Blake, you're making me anxious. Are you in the witness relocation plan or something?" I joke. At least I hope it's a joke.

Changing the subject, he says, "I'm more in the Los Angeles recovery plan."

Not wanting to ruin the magic of the night by asking more about what he's not telling me, I ask, "How long did you live there again?"

"Ten years."

"I go out there once or twice a year to work for hotel chains opening a new branch. It always seems nice, if not a little unrealistic. You know what I mean?"

"Oh, I know. LA is the land of illusion. Everyone tries to sell you on an image, and reality rarely comes into play."

"I prefer the Midwest where you know what you're getting," I tell him.

He clears his throat nervously. "I wonder what my life would have been like had I never moved out there."

"That's funny," I tell him. "I've always wondered what my life would have been like had I left Chicago after college and gone somewhere else."

"Do you think we would have ever crossed paths had either of us done those things?" he asks.

"I think it depends."

"On what?"

Turning so that I'm fully facing him, I answer, "On whether or not we're each other's person."

The look Blake gives me ricochets through my body like I've taken a direct hit from a lightning bolt. The hairs on my arms stand at attention and prickles of electricity stab at my skin. "The only thing that truly matters," he says, "is what's right here in front of us."

Lowering his head to mine, he once again captures my mouth in the sweetest kiss imaginable. I force myself to not worry that there's something he's not telling me. In fact, I want time to stop right now so that I can ride the wave of possibility and see if it doesn't lead exactly to where I hope it will.

CHAPTER THIRTY-TWO

BLAKE

Kissing Molly is my new favorite hobby. Forget hobby, I want it to be my new profession. I'm pretty sure we could take the gold if the Olympics ever added kissing to their roster. I'm confident that we'd be so great, if we could convince Nike to sponsor us, they'd be forced to change the company swoosh logo to a pair of lips.

Molly and I never do go back into the ballroom. Instead, we sit in front of the fire for another two hours. I learn a wide variety of things about her, such as, she orders her pizza with extra onions and garlic; she broke her leg skiing when she was twelve; and she's watched every episode of *I Love Lucy* at least five times, but closer to twelve for her favorites.

I share that I hate corn—which is almost sacrilegious when you live in the Midwest; that I am allergic to mussels; and that I dream of spending a month in Singapore where I would zipline every day at a place in Sentosa. I have yet to experience a sixty-mile-an-hour descent but I'm ready.

"I'd need a diaper if I did that," Molly jokes.

I laughingly agree. "I'm pretty sure I would, too. But it would be worth it to fly at that speed."

"Have you ever jumped out of an airplane?" Molly asks. "You seem like the type."

"While I appreciate your belief that I could do such a thing, the answer is no," I tell her. "I went up with some buddies once, but I was the only one who didn't leave the plane."

"You mean the pilot jumped, too?" I love Molly's sense of humor.

"Luckily, no, but even if he had, I think I would have taken my chances trying to land the plane before throwing myself out an open door at fourteen thousand feet."

Molly changes the subject. "Where did you live when you were in LA?"

"Brentwood."

"How did you afford *that* on a barista's pay?" She sounds surprised, which she should because Brentwood is not cheap. Even when you're renting a condo like I did.

Avoiding the truth *again*, I tell her, "Every town has a ghetto."

Luckily, she doesn't push for more information. Instead, she asks, "Where do you live in Chicago?"

"Wrigleyville."

Squinting her eyes, she shakes her head and declares, "You must make one heck of a cup of coffee."

Hurrying to take the focus off me, I ask her, "Where do you live?"

"Gold Coast. I'm on Oak Street."

"That's a nice neighborhood, too."

"I grew up in Evanston," she says. "I stayed there for college at Northwestern before moving into the city."

"I went to Loyola," I tell her.

We spend nearly another hour sharing details of our lives. By the time eleven o'clock rolls around, I feel like I've known Molly forever. When she yawns for the third time, I tell her, "I think it's past your bedtime."

Nodding wearily, she says, "I don't want to leave, but you're right. I'm never up later than ten."

"Even when you're on a date?" I ask.

She snorts. "I haven't been on a date since Kyle and I broke up."

"Are you serious?" I can't imagine that Molly isn't asked out daily.

"Even though I know Kyle and I would have never made it in the long run," she explains, "it was pretty soul crushing to be cheated on. I guess I've just felt too vulnerable to risk something like that happening again."

I want to punch Kyle right in the face for hurting Molly so badly. Yet, I don't mind that she's not been spending her time with other men. "What's weird," I tell her, "is that I don't think Kyle's a bad guy at heart. I just think he made some poor choices."

She surprises me by agreeing. "I don't think he's a bad guy, either. I know he regrets what he did to me, but I'm still a fan of how karma has returned the favor."

"Justice has a way of rearing its head, doesn't it?" And suddenly I worry about my own karma for lying to Molly about why I'm here. I hope there are some loopholes that cover my current situation.

"Have *you* ever been dumped so spectacularly?" Molly wants to know.

I tell her about Finley and how I found out about her affair along with the rest of the country during the Emmy Awards.

"Finley Adams?" she asks, seemingly amazed that I had once been part of such a duo.

"Yup."

She surprises me by saying, "I don't mean to be a hater, but I never saw her appeal. She always seems like she's overacting."

Leaning in, I give Molly a quick kiss. "Thank you for not thinking she's amazing. I've been over her for years, but it seems I'm always hearing people singing her praises and it starts to grate on me." Molly yawns again, so I tell her, "Let's go."

As we walk toward the elevator, she asks, "So, what do we do now?"

"I think we're going up to bed." She looks startled, so I clarify, "Each of us in our own rooms."

Smiling sheepishly, she says, "I meant, what do we do about the singles' event?"

Ah, I see. She wants to know if we're declaring ourselves a couple and bowing out from meeting other people. While I have no interest in other women, I still have to be there. "I'm still working, so I need to check out the action. I was hoping you might join me."

"I'd like that."

"But you should know that I'm not looking for myself anymore."

"Oh?"

"No, ma'am," I assure her. "I've met the person I want to get to know better."

Molly leans into my side. "Me, too." Then she says, "My sister is not going to believe this."

"Will she be disappointed I'm not a lumberjack?"

Molly laughs. "Probably, but she'll get over it once she meets you." She hurriedly adds, "Not that you need to meet her."

Putting her mind at rest, I say, "I would love to meet your sister, whenever you'd like to introduce me to her."

We take the elevator up to the second floor without talking. It's remarkably pleasant and not all that common to enjoy someone's company without the need for conversation. When we get to Molly's room, I give her a small peck before asking, "Do you want to have breakfast with me in the morning?"

"I would love that," she says. "And Blake …" I wait expectantly to hear what she says next. "Thank you for not lying to me anymore. I can't ever be in another relationship with someone who doesn't tell the truth."

Well, crap. Stumbling over my words, I tell her, "I never want to lie to you, Molly."

"Good, because that's one thing I will not put up with." She kisses me quickly on the cheek before opening her door. "I'll see you in the morning."

"Good night," I tell her. I'm still standing there long after she's gone. How in the world have I gotten myself into this situation? Even if it means risking my job, I want to be honest and tell Molly everything, but if I do that, I won't be able to help Ben. And that little boy reminds me of my family's most challenging ordeal. As such, I'm going to have to continue to keep the truth hidden. I hate the deception, but I don't really see a way out of it right now.

I inhale deeply before releasing a ragged breath. I say a silent prayer that Molly will understand why I did what I did and that she will forgive my transgressions. Even though it's happened remarkably fast, I know without a doubt that I want to pursue a future with her.

CHAPTER THIRTY-THREE

MOLLY

As soon as I get into my room, I close the door and pick up my phone. Ellen answers after only one ring. "Molls, are you okay? Why are you calling so late?"

I'm practically giddy as I tell her, "I think I just met my lumberjack."

"Wait, what? Are you serious? You met an honest-to-God lumberjack up there?"

I unzip my dress and step out of it while telling her, "He's not really a lumberjack, he's a barista."

"He makes coffee for a living?" She does not sound impressed.

"He's from Chicago," I tell her. "But he's lived in LA for the last ten years."

"Is he a starving actor or something?"

"No. He's a barista."

"Molly," Ellen sounds disappointed, "you can do better than that."

"I really like him, Ellie. He's kind and sweet, and oh, boy is he easy on the eyes."

"How old is he?" she demands abruptly.

I try to remember if he told me how old he was when he moved to LA, but assuming it was right after college, I tell her, "Thirty-two, I think."

"And he makes coffee for a living."

"Who cares what he does, Ellen? He's lovely."

"Does he live in Elk Lake? Because if so, you'll rarely get to see him. Maybe you should distance yourself now before you get in too deep."

I don't know why, but I thought my sister would be more open-minded than this. Although, as I recall, the thing she liked most about Kyle was that he was a lawyer. I remind her, "Kyle made a ton of money, and you know what happened there."

"Yes, but …" She seems to be at a loss for words, which is not like Ellen at all.

"Please be happy for me, Ellie. Trust that I can pick my own guy and just let it go."

"But you've just met him. How can you know he's *your* guy?"

Crawling into bed, I tell her, "I met him the night I got here. He's staying at the lodge for a work thing."

"What kind of work thing requires a coffee maker to stay at such a nice place?" Wow, Ellen really is a snob.

"I don't know the particulars," I lie. "This might be nothing more than a flirtation, but I'm having fun, so that's a good thing, right?"

"I guess …" Yeah, she's not convinced.

"How are you doing?" I hurry to ask. "Are you at Mom and Dad's?"

"I'm here."

"What about Henry? Have you heard from him?"

"Not a word."

She sounds surprised, so I tell her, "He's probably in shock."

"I don't know why. He's the one who broke up with me."

Nestling under the covers, I remind her, "Yeah, but he thought you were going to get engaged. I'm sure your lack of excitement threw him off."

"You're saying this is my fault?" Ellen accuses. It's clear her dander is up.

I don't want to hurt her feelings, and I will always be there for my sister, but facts are facts. "Isn't it?"

"I thought you always had my back. I didn't expect this from you."

"Didn't expect what, Ellen?"

"Betrayal."

Oh brother, I thought I was calling my sister to have a good talk, but that's not how things are going. "Ellen," I say. "You knew Henry had children when you met him. Not only do you know his kids, but you love them. How in the world is it his fault that you decided you don't want to be with him because he's a great father?"

"I said I'd marry him," she practically spits.

"No one wants to feel like the person they love is ambivalent toward them. And I'm pretty sure that's exactly how you sounded when you half-heartedly agreed to marry Henry."

"You weren't there. You don't know how I sounded."

"But I know you, Ellie," I tell her firmly. "And from what you told me, Henry must be hurt beyond belief. If you want him back in your life, then it's on you to make that happen."

She huffs loudly in my ear before saying, "Oh, go make a cup of coffee." She hangs up without saying goodbye.

Even though I feel horrible for my sister, I have to laugh at such a ridiculous comeback. She must know this is her fault. That doesn't mean I don't love her and support her choices, but I think she's making a major mistake here.

I plug my phone into the charger before reaching over and turning off the light. Then I pull the covers up and force my sister's plight out of my mind. Ellen will decide whatever she decides, but right now I want to relive every moment of my night.

Closing my eyes, I drift off to sleep faster than I have in ages. I dream that I'm a princess locked in a tower watching as my handsome prince, Blake, rides across the countryside to save me.

He rides, and rides, and rides for what seems to be hours, but he never gets any closer. I call out to him, "Prince Blake, what's keeping you?"

I don't hear his answer because a storm moves in. It starts to thunder and rain. Blake keeps riding but the distance between us starts to increase. How is that even possible? Turning around, I run across the room and sit down at an ornate vanity. In true absurd dream form, I stare into the mirror and talk to it. "Mirror, mirror, on the wall, who is the happiest couple of all?"

I expect it to tell me that it's me and Blake, but instead, it says, "Ronald and Olivia are the happy pair. It is a fairytale ending they will share."

Ronald and Olivia? What are they doing hijacking my dream? "You're wrong, mirror!" I pick up a hairbrush and throw it into the glass and watch as it shatters.

Undeterred, the mirror says, "Glass is easy to break, but the repair is impossible to make."

I shout, "What does that even mean, you stupid mirror?"

The voice in my reflection changes into my sister's. "Lies are lies that cannot mend. Truth untold will be the end."

It's been two years since Kyle left me, so I'm clearly not one to jump into a relationship. In all that time, I haven't so much as flirted with another man. But kissing Blake feels like coming home to a place I never dreamed possible.

Rolling over in bed, I think about how Blake lived in Brentwood, and is now in Wrigleyville. Neither of these locations suggest he's struggling for money. Then I recall how he confessed that he's not writing a book. There must be something he's keeping from me because both of his recent addresses suggest he's making more money than someone who pours coffee for a living.

The rest of the night is spent in one fever dream after another. In one of them, Blake is a frog who, no matter how many times I kiss him, refuses to turn into a prince. In another, he's Lord Farquaad from Shrek, and while I'm not a sizest, the fact that he's nearly two feet shorter than me leaves a negative impact.

Even in my sleep I can't help but wonder why I'm not having fabulous dreams of our future. And while there's a definite fairy-tale aspect to my visions, they're all dark and foreboding.

Is it possible that Blake isn't the man I think he is? Is he still lying to me about something?

CHAPTER THIRTY-FOUR

BLAKE

I dream of Molly all night. I see us exploring Chicago together, traveling the world, and even getting married someday. I wake up feeling like a million bucks. At least until I remember that she doesn't know what I'm really doing here.

Grabbing my laptop from the nightstand, I open it and start to write.

Starting to date someone new is full of risk, but it can also be full of excitement. A new love interest is invigorating. It's the unknown becoming known, like slowly unwrapping a Christmas present. Once the paper is off, you're left wondering if the box will hold a dozen of the best vintage baseball cards of all time, or if you'll find yet another home-made sweater full of holes that your grandmother didn't sew together?

Last night, Polly and I shared our first kiss. It was wonderful and amazing. It felt like the beginning of something special. Which, if I'm being honest, scares me. I did not come to this

event believing that it was anything more than a sham—a way
for Trina Rockwell to keep meddling in the lives of single
people and making money while she was at it.

But now that I've met someone I really like and want to get to
know better, I'm forced to consider that maybe Trina knows
what she's doing. She definitely comes up with fresh, out-of-
the-box activities—like last night's group square dancing
lesson ...

In a rare moment of charitable thinking, I'm about to give mad
props to Trina, but there's a knock on my door. On my way to
answer it, I stop in front of the mirror to tame the bedhead I have
every morning.

After making sure I'm somewhat presentable, I open the door.
It's early, so I'm surprised to see Molly standing there. She looks
gorgeous in her fuzzy red turtleneck sweater and skinny jeans,
and it's all I can do not to pull her into my arms. "Molly." I step
back to let her come in, but she doesn't move. Instead, she just
stands there with her mouth hanging wide open. "Are you okay?"
I ask.

"I ... um ... I'm ... well ..."

"Having a stroke?" I tease.

She points toward my bare chest and manages to utter, "You're
naked."

Looking down at my plaid flannel pajama pants, I assure her,
"Not naked. I just don't have a shirt on."

"Wh ... Why? I mean, why? Why don't you have a shirt on?" I
wonder if she's this flustered with everyone or I just make her
nervous. I hope it's the latter because that would mean she has
feelings for me too.

Her expression is so odd, you'd think she'd never seen a man's
bare chest before. "I just woke up. I haven't even gotten out of bed
yet."

She surprises me by saying, "But it's ten thirty."

"Are you serious? I never sleep this late." I step back into the room. "Do you want to come in? I'll throw on some clothes so we get down to the dining room in time for breakfast."

"I ... um ... no. I'll just stay here."

"Suit yourself," I tell her before blowing her a kiss and shutting the door. Molly is adorable when she blushes, which is something she's been doing nonstop since I opened the door.

Hurrying to my closet, I grab a fresh pair of jeans and a grey cashmere sweater. I barely got the chance to wear warm sweaters in LA, so I'm loving the heck out of doing so now that I'm back in the Midwest. Once I'm dressed, I run into the bathroom and brush my teeth. Then I add a splash of my signature aftershave.

When I step out into the hallway, Molly is leaning against the wall like she's using it as a support to keep her from falling to the floor. "You ready?" I ask.

"Uh ... um ..." She leans in toward me and practically inhales my neck. "Y ... you smell great!"

I bend down and sniff her back, letting the tip of my nose touch the delicate skin at the base of her neck. Then I lift my head so that my mouth is resting next to her ear. "You smell pretty incredible yourself."

She visibly shivers. I love having such an obvious effect on her. "Th ... thank you."

"You mean thump queue?" I tease, remembering our first encounter on the train.

Her blush is delightful, but she doesn't comment.

"Before we go down to the dining room, Molly, I wanted to make sure you understood what's going on here."

A look of panic crosses her face. "What's that?"

"I want you to understand how much I like you," I tell her with a slow grin.

"Oh."

"And I wonder if I might give you a small, good morning kiss to remind you." I assure her, "I just brushed my teeth."

"I ... um ..."

Her chin bobs up and down slightly, which I take to mean that she's okay with it. Lowering my mouth to hers, I let my lips briefly touch hers before starting to pull back. But she doesn't let me break contact. She moves with me until our bodies are pressed against each other.

"You still like me this morning, huh?" she asks breathlessly.

"Very much," I assure her. "Do you still like me?"

"Mmmm."

Taking her hand, I say, "We have to get our order in by eleven or we'll have to eat lunch." Then I pull her in the direction of the elevator.

Once we're inside, she declares, "I'm getting the chocolate chip pancakes. How about you?"

"That sounds good," I tell her. "Why don't I get the Swedish pancakes, and we can share?"

She nods her head. "Perfect."

We're at our table and seated with only five minutes to spare, so we order right away. I ask for a cup of coffee and Molly gets a hot chocolate. She divulges, "I've had at least two hot chocolates every day since I've been here."

"Sounds like you know a good thing when you find it," I tell her. *Not unlike me finding her.*

She giggles. "I was planning on being really good and not having a lot of sweets, but I went off the rails and now I don't even know where the rails are."

"The holidays are the time for decadence," I assure her.

"So," Molly says, "you're going back into the trenches today."

I feel a guilty heat under my collar while answering, "I want to find out what else Trina has up her sleeve that we might be able to incorporate at the coffee shop."

Molly looks over my shoulder. "Isn't that Thor sitting over there? And Krista, too?" I turn around and sure enough, Krista and Thor are sitting near us at separate tables.

"I wonder why they're not sitting together," I say.

Molly exhales loudly before announcing, "That's probably our fault. Or rather *your* fault."

"My fault? How do you figure?"

She glares at me meaningfully. "You're the one who broke up their first date when you started acting like you were interested in Krista."

"Ah, yes. But I was really interested in you."

"You had a funny way of showing it," she murmurs sardonically.

"That's because I'd decided not to pursue anyone while I was here. As such, I was trying to give you and Thor some time to connect."

"So, you were never interested in Krista romantically?"

"I was not," I assure her. "But I have an idea, if you're game."

"What's that?"

Standing up, I tell her, "I think I should go ask Thor to join us and you should ask Krista and once we're all at the same table, we can update them on our new status. That way, they might decide to reconnect."

"Our new status?" she asks flirtatiously. "What might our new status be?"

I give my shoulders a brief shrug before telling her, "I was thinking we should tell them that we've paired off and that neither of us is available."

Her smile is positively blinding. "Let's do it!" She practically sprints toward Krista before I've even taken a single step.

Once Molly reaches her destination, I head to Thor's table. "Hey, man," I say. "How about joining me for breakfast?"

I don't think he saw me coming because he startles when he hears my voice. "Hey, Blake. How are you?"

"Really good," I tell him. "Would you like to join me?"

Pushing away from his table, he stands up and grabs his plate. "I'd love to."

I lead the way to Molly's and my table, with Molly and Krista only seconds behind us. When Krista sees me, she stops dead in her tracks. "You …" she accuses like I just ran her dog over with my car.

"Krista!" I say, hoping to sound friendly, but not too friendly.

Addressing Molly, she says, "I'm not sure this is such a good idea."

Molly takes her arm and pulls her toward the table. "I think it is. There's something that Blake and I want to tell you both."

Krista sits down, but not before scooting her chair as far from mine as she can. Thor sits down normally.

I open my mouth to tell them what's going on, but Molly beats me to the punch. She says, "Blake and I have decided that we're going to take ourselves out of the dating pool."

"What, why?" Krista asks. Then she points between us and guesses, "Are you two dating?"

"I knew it!" Thor claps his hands together loudly. "I knew you were into Molly!"

"I was," I tell him. "I didn't want to come on too strong right out of the gate."

"So, you asked me to go hot tubbing with you instead. How flattering." Krista doesn't sound the least bit complimented.

"I wanted to make sure I talked to a few women before settling down with Molly here." I say this like I was choosing a kitten at the animal shelter and not a love interest.

Molly seems to take it that way, too because she kicks me sharply under the table, causing me to cry out in pain. She says, "Blake and I should have never joined you two for breakfast. You seemed like you were having such a nice time …" She lets her insinuation hang in the air—that they should reconnect.

Thor clears his throat somewhat uncomfortably before telling Krista, "I really did enjoy spending time with you."

"I enjoyed spending time with you, as well." After a beat, she adds, "I've seen you talking to some other women. Have you met anyone special?"

Thor winks at her. "I thought I did but then Blake stole her away from me."

Raising my hands out in front of me like this is a stick-up, I apologize. "I'm sorry if I messed anything up between the two of you."

Thor is quick to ask Krista, "What do you say we take off and spend the day together? Maybe go for a hike?"

"That's sounds very nice, Thor." Krista pushes her chair back before addressing Molly. "Thank you for inviting me to join you." Then she turns and stares daggers at me. "Blake." That's all.

Once Thor and Krista leave, I tell Molly, "That was fun. Who do you want to set up next?"

She looks around the room like we're really going to do this, but then she responds, "I haven't talked to that many people. You're the one who's been making the rounds. I think you're going to have to take the lead."

The waiter stops by and drops off our food which prompts me to say, "I'll think about it, but for now I want to enjoy my date with you. How does that sound?"

"So good," she practically purrs.

Meeting Molly is the last thing I expected when I came here, but I'm not complaining. Playing stupid, I ask her, "Are you talking about me or the pancakes?"

Molly cuts into her pancakes and takes a bite. She releases a groan of appreciation before answering, "Clearly, I'm talking about the pancakes."

Molly Anders is well on the way to capturing my heart, and I can only hope she feels the same way about me. If this were a fairytale, we'd be nearing the "And they all lived happily-ever-after" portion of the story.

Unfortunately, this isn't a children's book and there's still a big secret between us that needs to be told.

CHAPTER THIRTY-FIVE

MOLLY

After Blake and I eat a scrumptious breakfast accompanied with copious flirting, he asks, "How about if we go snowmobiling today?"

"I need to do a little work," I tell him. "Would you mind if we caught up a bit later?"

"It's almost noon now," he says, "so why don't we just meet at tonight's dinner at five. Does that give you enough time?"

"That's perfect." I tentatively lean over and give him a kiss. The thing with kissing someone you've only just started seeing is that you don't want to be pegged as the needy one by always being the first to instigate physical contact. Having said that, I can't seem to keep my lips off Blake. Thankfully, he doesn't seem to mind.

Once I'm back in my room, I check the internet to see if the picture frame I ordered yesterday has arrived. According to the site, it's already been delivered to the front desk. I have no idea how it got here so quickly, I'm just glad it has.

I hurry downstairs to pick up my package. Trina is talking to one of the desk clerks. I approach her and say, "Good morning! Do you have a minute to chat?"

She nods her head. "I sure do."

"Let me just grab something and I'll be right with you." I tell another man behind the desk what I'm there for and he immediately hands the package over.

Then I turn to Trina. "Where should we go?"

"Let's sit in the great room," she says. "I can't get enough of that Christmas tree."

"It's really spectacular," I tell her. "I haven't put mine up at home yet so I've been enjoying yours a lot."

Once we're sitting at a small table in the corner, I open the envelope I'm holding and put the contents on the table in front of us.

She looks down at it. "You bought a digital picture frame?"

"I did." Her brow furrows in confusion so I tell her, "I think you should carry these in the gift shop." Then I elaborate, "Thanks to your and Heath's generosity, a lot of the families that come here have children who are having a hard time. And a vacation like this is the kind of thing they would really appreciate remembering."

"What a fabulous idea!" she says.

"I spent the day with a family yesterday who have a young son that I think might be terminally ill."

She nods her head. "I'm afraid that could be any number of people."

Opening the box, I pull out the picture frame, then I take my phone out of my purse. I plug the USB connector from the box to my phone and I transfer the files of the pictures and video that I took of Ben's family yesterday. Once I'm done, I hand the frame to Trina.

Her expressions softens as she watches the still images of such a happy little family move into footage of them zip lining, then playing in the snow. "This is remarkable, Molly. Seriously."

"I always have the best intentions of transferring my pictures to the digital frame that I bought." I add, "The one that's still in the box it shipped in three years ago."

She laughs. "Life has a way of getting in the way, doesn't it?"

"Yes, and I'm single with no kids. Imagine how hard it is for these families to get something like this done."

"It sounds like you're suggesting more than selling picture frames."

Nodding my head, I tell her, "I am. I think you should consider hiring a photographer to spend a couple hours with each family and then make them a frame of their own."

"Oh, Molly, I love that idea!"

"And the families could always add more pictures as they go."

Trina looks like she's about to cry. "This is exactly why you're so good at your job," she says. "You've looked beyond the surface and found something that will make people's time here a lifelong memory. We could still carry the frames in the gift shop for regular guests, but I really love your idea of helping the people whose trips we sponsor."

"This kid broke my heart," I tell her. "He's been saving his money so he could buy a frame for his parents."

"His name is Ben, right?" Trina asks.

I nod my head. "His parents are Ward and Francie."

Her expression turns serious. "Ben has leukemia. Heath heard about their family from his brother."

"Is it really hopeless?" I ask, both wanting to know the answer, and not. I can't stand the thought that such a child is living on borrowed time.

Trina shrugs. "I'm not sure. I know that Heath has asked a friend at Sloan Kettering to look at Ben's files. There's a chance there's a clinical trial he might be right for."

A chill shoots through my body that starts at the top of my head and zings down my arms. "I'm sure anything that gives his parents hope would be amazing."

"It's hard though, right? I mean, you don't want people to lose hope, but they still have to prepare for the worst."

"When do you think Ward and Francie will find out if Ben qualifies?"

"They're supposed to hear before Christmas," she says. "Heath has offered to sponsor them in New York if they get in."

"You two are really amazing, do you know that?" I ask her. "So many people don't even know how to begin to help others and you guys are doing it on a huge scale."

"We're lucky that we can," she says.

"Yes, but a lot of people who can, don't. You two should give a seminar and teach them how it's done."

Trina smiles modestly. "If you have any more ideas like this, please let me know. In the meantime, you and Blake, huh?"

"I can't even believe it," I tell her. "I thought he'd friend-zoned me the second we met."

Crossing one long leg over another, Trina leans back in her chair. "He isn't the kind of guy I expected to sign up for one of my events."

"What does that mean?" Does she suspect he's here to steal her ideas? Does she know something about him that I don't?

"He hasn't spent his time with just women. He's been talking to everyone like he's interviewing them or something."

If she only knew that's exactly what he was doing, but I'm not going to tell her. I don't think Blake's getting ideas will take anything away from Trina's business, but she might still feel like he's ripping her off.

Veering the topic away from why Blake's here, I tell her, "I think he and I might have helped to get Thor and Krista back on track today."

"Nice." Then she says, "I hope the two of you will keep coming to our get-togethers. If for no other reason than to show the others what's possible."

"Oh, we're coming," I tell her. Turning my head, I see that Ben and his family have walked into the room. "I'm going to give Ben his frame."

Trina holds up one finger before standing up and walking

toward the Christmas tree. She removes one of the bags under-neath and hurries back to me. "We put a bunch of staged presents under the tree. Why don't you put the frame in here?"

"Thank you," I tell her as I slip the frame back into its box and then insert it into the bag. "Do you want to come with me?"

She shakes her head. "No, this is your gift to them. I'm going to go to my office and get to work on trying to hire a photographer. If I'm lucky I might be able to find one to start right away."

"That's fast!"

"This is the perfect time of year to capture some beautiful memories," she says. And then she's off.

I'm amazed there are people like Trina and her fiancé, and I decide in this moment to do more for charity than I have. If everyone did something small, the whole world would be the better for it.

Approaching Ben's family, I smile and wave. Poor Ben looks rough this morning, but as soon as he sees me, he smiles brightly. "Molly!"

"Hey, buddy." I wink at him and lift the bag. "Your gift for your parents arrived this morning."

He takes it enthusiastically before turning to his mom and dad. He tells them, "Molly helped me get your Christmas gift."

"It was all Ben's idea," I tell them. Francie and Ward both look like they're about to cry. Then I lean down and whisper in Ben's ear, "It's a digital frame. I already put in the pictures we took yesterday."

His eyes open wide with excitement. "Seriously? Can you show us?"

I lead the way to a small seating area near the fireplace. Once we're all seated, I tell Ben, "Let your parents open the bag and then I'll show you."

Francie's hands start to tremble as she unties the bow on the bag. Then she pulls out the box with the frame. "Oh!" she exclaims. "What a wonderful gift!"

"Open it up!" Ben encourages her.

Francie opens the box before sliding the frame out. "Just hit the power button on the side of the frame," I tell her.

As soon as she does, pictures of yesterday start popping up. Tears immediately stream down her face. This is my cue to leave, so I quietly stand up and walk away, giving this little family some privacy.

As I walk across the room toward the lobby, I can't help but feel grateful and humbled by how beautiful life is. No family deserves the kind of heartache that Ben's family is experiencing, and yet they're doing their best to really live in the moment and make the most of each other. I wish people would do that before there was a crisis.

Then, as though some kind of horrible magic has occurred, I look up and watch as my sister Ellen walks through the front doors. What in the world is she doing here?

CHAPTER THIRTY-SIX

MOLLY

I cannot believe my eyes. Running across the lobby, I call out, "Ellen?"

She looks up and spots me. "Molly," she says sternly like she's mad at me.

"What are you doing here?" I demand.

"I'm here to get my money back," she replies heatedly.

I feel like I've landed back in the middle of one of my crazy dreams from last night. "What money? What are you talking about?"

"I'm talking about my Christmas gift to you. It turns out it's a dud."

"What Christmas gift?" I'm so confused right now.

"I bought you a spot at Trina's singles' event."

My head starts to spin. "No, they had a cancellation, and I was asked to fill in as a replacement."

"That's the excuse Trina and I concocted because I knew you'd never come here otherwise," Ellen announces.

"But I've been hired to do a job here."

"The job is for real," she says. "Trina just scheduled you for it at the same time as her singles' event to get you here."

"So, what?" I ask skeptically. "This was some kind of pity present or something?" I don't know whether to be mad or happy. I mean, things have turned out spectacularly well for me, so I should be feeling a world of gratitude. But at the same time, I really hate that my sister has been feeling sorry for me. Or worse yet, convinced that I could never find someone on my own and rooked someone else into her matchmaking shenanigans.

"I wouldn't call it a pity present," Ellen says. "It's more like some outside help to get you back into the land of the living. Unfortunately, it didn't work."

"But it did," I tell her. "As much as I can't believe you did this, I met a really nice man."

"A barista …" she hisses like he's a freeloader or a bum.

"Oh, my god, Ellen. You are such a snob."

"I just want to make sure that whoever you wind up with is your equal," she says. "Now, are you going to show me to our room or are we going to stand here all day?"

"You're staying *with* me?"

"You told me I could." She reminds me, "On the day you left, you invited me to join you."

"Yeah, but you were going to be with Henry …" *Shoot, I temporarily forgot about Henry.*

I take her suitcase from her and start to roll it in the direction of the elevator. We walk side by side in a cloud of frustration and anger. I'm frustrated with Ellen and she's so angry at me.

Once we get to the second floor, I lead the way to my room. Opening the door, I walk in and declare, "We'll have to call down and see if they can send up a cot."

"If you want to sleep on a cot, then call them," she says challengingly. "But I'm sleeping in the bed."

I watch as my sister moves her suitcase next to mine before kicking off her shoes and climbing onto my bed. "I'll share with you if you want," she hesitantly offers before patting the mattress next to herself.

I join her and surprise myself by saying, "Thank you."

"For what?" she goads.

"For your gift," I tell her. "Don't get me wrong, I'm offended to the core by it, but I'm grateful. If I wasn't here, I would have never met Blake."

"Which is why I want my money back!" Ick. Actual spittle hits my cheek when she yells this.

Shaking my head, I ask, "Are you really this prejudiced against hard working people?"

"I'm not at all prejudiced," she says. "I don't care what people do as long as they're gainfully employed and not making moves on my sister."

"So, my happiness doesn't enter into this at all?" I ask.

"Of course it does, but being that I'm the one paying, my happiness matters too."

"Then go back home and tell Henry you love him. Take care of your own stupid life and stop meddling in mine." I have never talked to my sister like this before and I'm feeling mighty powerful right now.

"My stupid life?"

"Yes, Ellen. You have your own life to mess up; quit interfering in mine."

"Well!" she huffs. "How's that for gratitude?"

I take one of the pillows off the bed and throw it across the room like I'm having a tantrum. "I'd be grateful if you'd leave well enough alone and let me enjoy my gift."

"I want to meet this *coffee* man," Ellen declares. She says the word coffee like it's a slang term for heroin.

"No."

"What do you mean, no? You can't tell me no. I'll meet him if I want to."

I know she can make that happen. Especially if she confronts

Trina to get a refund. I suddenly have an idea. "I'll introduce you to Blake, but first you have to do something for me."

"What?"

"You have to come into town with me. There's someone I want you to meet."

"Are you high?"

"Don't be insulting, Ellen," I tell her. "Come into town with me, and when we get back, I'll introduce you to Blake."

My sister exhales like she's trying to hurl a wad of gum across the room. Then she gets up from the bed and grabs her shoes. "Fine, let's go."

I slide into my loafers and take my coat off the hanger. On the way downstairs, I tell Ellen, "Elk Lake is adorable. You'll love it." She simply grumbles and huffs alongside me.

When we get to the lobby, I discover that the shuttle is waiting out front. We get in and it's Paul from my first couple of rides. "Hey, Paul," I tell him. "My sister and I are going to Bride's Paradise on Main Street."

He smiles kindly. "Sounds good. Will you need more than an hour?"

"Probably not," I tell him. "But I'll call the lodge if we do."

Ellen doesn't say a word to me as we drive into town, so I jabber on like I'm her personal tour guide. "Elk Lake decorates like it's the North Pole. They seriously outdo themselves. Dad would love it!"

Ellen doesn't deign to speak until Paul pulls over in front of the store. "So, you've decided to marry this coffee maker?"

"What? No!" She is truly acting ridiculous.

As we walk into the shop, Melissa calls out, "Molly! I'm glad you came in!"

"Thank you," I tell her before asking, "Is Sammy here today?"

"She is. Would you like me to get her?"

I nod my head so Melissa waddles across the room. Moments later, she comes back out with her stepdaughter in tow.

Sammy's smile is radiant. "Molly! How's it going up at the lodge?"

"I met a very nice man," I tell her.

"I knew you would."

Sammy looks toward my sister, so I say, "Melissa, Sammy, this is my sister, Ellen. She's just come up from Chicago."

Melissa stretches out her hand first. "I'm happy to meet you, Ellen."

"Why?" my sister asks grumpily before saying, "I mean, hi. I guess I'm happy to meet you too."

I roll my eyes, so Melissa knows that I'm aware my sister is being horribly rude. Then I tell Ellen, "Melissa is Sammy's step-mother. Melissa is married to Sammy's dad."

"So?" Ellen growls. "Why should I care?" If Emily Post were still alive, she'd hit my sister over the head with her etiquette book.

Ignoring her question, I ask Sammy, "Would you please tell my sister what you told me about Melissa the other day?"

The red-headed teenager looks confused before asking, "You mean about my loving Melissa as much as my birth mom?"

"Yes, that." Then I turn to Ellen. "Did you hear that, Ellen? Sammy, who is Melissa's *stepdaughter*, loves Melissa as much as her real mom." Ellen remains quiet, so I tell Melissa and Sammy, "Ellen's boyfriend just proposed to her, and she said no because she doesn't want to be second to his kids."

Ellen hisses, "I didn't say no."

But at the same time, Sammy asks, "Didn't you know he had kids?"

Ellen is clearly not pleased that I outed her, so I answer for her. "Oh, she knew. But my sister is so self-centered that she thinks she should always come first."

Melissa interjects, "I don't think it's about coming first or second. It's more about becoming a family and making your *family* the priority."

I fling my hand out toward Ellen with such vigor I nearly hit her. "See? This is how it's done. You're so wrapped up in yourself that you've completely missed it."

"I have not," Ellen declares with a fraction of her previous heat. "I love Henry's kids."

"Then why are you competing with them?" I want to know.

"I'm not competing ..." But then reality hits her like a blow to the side of the head. "I don't *want* to compete with them."

"Then don't," I tell her. "Marry their dad and become part of their family. Then you'll *both* put family first.

I can't quite decipher what Ellen is feeling, but she no longer seems to be angry with me. Instead, she asks Melissa, "How long have you been married?"

"Just over a year," she answers. "I met Sammy and her dad when they moved up here two years ago."

Sammy moves closer to Melissa before touching her step-mom's stomach. "And now I get to be a big sister. How cool is that?"

Ellen's head moves up and down almost imperceptibly. "That is cool."

Turning to my sister, I tell her, "You and Henry and his kids can be a happy family, too. And if you decide to have children of your own, then you can be a *big*, happy family."

Her nostrils flare like they do when she's trying to suppress an emotion. "Are you done?" she asks me.

"That depends entirely on whether or not you've taken my point," I tell her.

"I have."

"Then I assume you'll want to leave right away so you can go make things right with Henry. Maybe accept his proposal with a little more grace?"

My sister side-eyes me like she's considering it, but then she says, "I'll go home when I'm good and ready."

Ellen has always been stubborn, but this is taking things too far. "Why wouldn't you go now and put Henry out of his misery? I'm sure he's dying to make up with you."

"Because I have something to do here first," she says.

"You mean, interfere in my life."

Ellen turns to me with a look of great concern. "You're my sister, Molly. I care what happens to you. It's my job to look out after you."

"No, it's not," I tell her. "And it's time you transfer some of this motherly concern onto real children. Henry's children."

"Maybe," she says. "But first I'm going to meet this coffee boy."

Hurray.

CHAPTER THIRTY-SEVEN

BLAKE

Being that Molly had to work, I decide to attend today's group activity by myself. It turns out it's a charades tournament. And while I like watching charades—because come on, it's hysterical—I hate playing.

Hoping to stay out of the action, I find a corner of the ballroom to sit in. Maybe if I keep my head down, no one will notice me.

Trina moves toward the fifteen people who have shown up and announces, "We need to break into four groups. The winner of the best two out of three will play the winner of the other group. The losers will play as well so we can determine all four places."

A woman I haven't talked to yet raises her hand. "What's the prize for first place?"

Trina tells her, "You get to eat dinner with our first bonafide couple of the event!" The group doesn't seem overly enamored with the idea, so Trina continues, "You can ask them all kinds of questions about how they knew they found the person they wanted to exclusively get to know better."

All I can think is, who in the world wants to eat with Olivia and Ronald? I mean, I'd seriously throw the game just to get out of that. Trina starts to create four teams but then realizes she's one person short. Instead of filling in herself, she looks around the room and points at me. "Blake, you're on team three!"

Scooting my chair closer to the wall, I tell her, "I'm not playing. I'm just watching."

Her eyes narrow menacingly before she orders, "No, you're playing. You're here in the room which means you're participating in today's activity."

I suddenly wonder if people wind up dating each other out of sheer fear of what Trina will do to them if they don't. Standing up, I slowly walk toward the group the matchmaker has declared mine.

When I get there, I introduce myself. "I'm Blake," I tell them.

The woman who wants to eat dinner with Olivia and Ronald as much as I do says, "I'm Maya." She points to the other pair. "Charlie and Sheryl." Without bothering to lower her voice, she adds, "I think they might be on the way to being the next couple of the event." Little does she know that Molly and I have already claimed that slot.

I nod my head toward Charlie, a ginger with a gigantic forehead, and then to Sheryl, who is a tiny mouse of a woman. She can't even be close to being five feet tall. "Hey," I tell them before confessing, "I'm really bad at this game."

Charlie waggles his enormous head back and forth cockily, while saying, "Don't worry, I *own* charades."

"Maybe you can play on your own then," I joke.

He doesn't think I'm funny and he tells me as much. "Ha, ha. I can't guess at my own performances."

I really should have not come to this today. But then, remembering why I'm here, I decide to make the most of it. "What do you do for a living, Charlie?"

"I'm a contortionist."

"Really?" A contortionist? I knew such people existed, but I've never met one before. "What do you do with that?"

He proudly tells me, "I work with a troupe. We hire ourselves out and perform at various functions."

I can't imagine what those would be, so I ask him, "Like the circus?"

"We've worked at the circus. We also do parties and conventions. Pretty much any place a singer would perform."

An image of Charlie opening for Hozier pops into my head, and I release a loud bark of laughter. I immediately feel bad and try to pawn it off as enthusiasm. "That's really cool, man!"

He doesn't seem convinced, but luckily the other team we're playing comes over. I know a couple of them from previous discussions. Emberly, a tall Black woman who looks like that 1980s super model Iman, announces, "Let's get going, I have a massage in two hours."

Please, God, do not let this last two full hours. I won't make it.

Charlie walks over to the table holding our box of clues and immediately takes one. The other team takes offense, and Emberly, their apparent leader, announces, "You don't just get to go first. We need to toss a coin or something."

Charlie puts the clue back before reaching into his pocket and pulling out a quarter. "Do you want to toss or call?" he asks her.

"You toss, I'll call," she says. When the coin is in the air, Emberly calls out, "Heads!" then switches that to, "I mean tails!"

When the coin lands, Charlie flips it over and gives the other team a death glare before saying, "It's heads. We go first." Then he walks over to the box and takes a clue. No one in our group contests the fact that Charlie will act first.

It turns out Maya is a vigorous charades player whose plan for success is to yell out as many guesses as she can before Charlie even starts. "*Saved by the Bell*! Elton John! The Taj Mahal!"

I lean over and tell her, "Charlie is showing us that it's a book."

"*The Brothers Karamazov*! *The Shining*! Icebreakers!" Oh. My. God. The good news is there's no way I'm going to have to suffer through a meal with Ronald and Olivia because there's no way we're going to win.

True to my prediction, nearly *three* hours later, we are declared the fourth-place team and I'm finally put out of my misery. I leave the ballroom sure that I will never play this game again. Ever. Even if someone offered me a million dollars to do so.

By the time I get back to my room, I only have a few minutes to get ready for tonight's dinner and have to hurry with my shower. I change into a pair of black dress slacks that I pair with a light-weight turquoise cashmere sweater. Then I walk out the door.

I know I was supposed to meet Molly downstairs, but if she's in her room, there's no reason we shouldn't walk down together. After all, we're going to be the official second couple of the event and couples show up together.

I knock on her door and wait for a solid two minutes before knocking again. "Molly," I finally call out. Nothing. She must have already gone down, so I head toward the elevator on my own.

I feel happier than I've felt in a very long time—even though I've spent my afternoon playing a game that now rivals water-boarding in its level of appeal to me. By the time I walk back into the ballroom, I'm practically giddy with excitement. I've missed Molly more than I thought possible.

Before I can find her though, Trina approaches me. "Did you have fun this afternoon?"

"Not in the slightest," I tell her somewhat testily.

"Well, Molly wasn't there …"

"No, she wasn't."

"And you must have missed her enormously, especially since you two are the first couple of the event."

"We're the *first* couple? What about Ronald and Olivia?" I start to panic that my reward for making it through this afternoon alive is spending more time with these people. And even though that's why I'm here, I'd planned on taking the evening off to enjoy some time with Molly.

Trina tells me, "I haven't seen Ronald or Olivia in a couple of days. I'm starting to wonder if they've left the lodge."

My whole body cringes as I ask, "So, it's me and Molly?"

Slapping me on the back, she says, "You got it!"

"Do we have to sit at a special table, or can I sit anywhere?"

She points. "Front table by the microphone."

The paper had better give me a bonus for going through this hell. But then it occurs to me that Molly is my bonus. I had no intention of meeting anyone that I wanted to date, but she stumbled and tripped her way into my life, and I'm absolutely smitten.

As soon as I sit down, I see Molly walk into the room. She looks radiant in yet another black cocktail dress. She's busy chatting with a shorter woman and they don't stop talking until they reach me. Molly looks nervous and I immediately wonder what's up.

I lean in to kiss her, but she pushes me away, saying, "B … Blake, hey. Hi."

Uh oh, is she having second thoughts about us? I move away from her and say, "Hi. Who's your friend?"

Molly looks like she's on the border of a panic attack when she says, "This isn't my friend, this is my sister, Ellen."

"Ellen!" I greet with perhaps a bit too much enthusiasm. "How nice to see you."

"Why?" she demands with her fists resting on her ample hips. Her stature reminds me of a correctional facility officer in a bad B movie.

"Because you're Molly's sister?" This comes out more a question than a statement.

"I'm not that happy to meet you, Blake," she tells me.

Molly hisses under her breath, "Give him a chance, Ellen."

I pull a chair back for Molly to sit down while Ellen takes care of herself. I have no idea what's going on here, but I sense this is not going to be an easy meal. Once we're seated, the winning charade team starts to show up.

Emberly stands by an empty chair and stares at me. "You're part of the first couple of the event?" She sounds totally disbelieving.

I stand up and pull her chair out for her while saying, "Emberly, I'd like you to meet Molly." Then I tell Molly, "Emberly and I played charades this afternoon." With a pointed look, I add, "Trina promised everyone that the winning team could eat with us and ask us questions about being the first official couple here."

Molly looks like she just swallowed her tongue. "Oh." After I sit down, she leans into me and says, "This is horrible timing."

I'm not sure why she's upset, but I can only guess she likes making a spectacle of herself about as much as I do. Which is not at all.

One other person from the winning team shows up. He introduces himself. "Hey, I'm Aspen. I'm a ski instructor in the winter and a barista in the off-season."

Molly's sister announces, "Two of you at the same table? Doesn't anyone make their own coffee anymore?"

It's obvious that Ellen has decided not to like me, and now I have my first inkling why that is. She doesn't like my career choice. Little does she know that I make an awful cup of coffee.

Hoping to engage her on a topic that she finds interesting, I ask, "What do you do, Ellen?"

"I write for *Chicago Wind* magazine," she says proudly. "I wrote a piece on the Elk Lake Lodge when they first opened."

Beads of nervous sweat immediately pop up on my forehead. I'm here on assignment working for the same freaking paper. The only reason Ellen doesn't know me on sight is because I've only been in the office a couple of times. Holy heck. I have the worst luck.

I somehow manage to choke out, "That sounds very interesting."

Molly interjects, "Blake enjoys writing, as well." It's clear she's hoping to help us find some common interest. Which, now that I know where her sister works, is the last thing I want to happen.

"What do you write?" Ellen asks, like she's pretty sure I find signing my own name a challenge.

"I ... um ... well ..." I'm starting to sound like Molly. "I'm thinking about maybe writing a dystopian love story."

"You can't be serious." Yeah, she's not impressed.

"With a sports angle," I tell her. "I love sports."

Ellen's eyes narrow to slits as she asks, "There's something about you that's familiar."

"You might have been into the coffee shop where he works," Molly tells her. "Perky Cups?"

"Perky Cups? That's not the name of a coffee shop in Chicago."

"How do you know that, Ellen?" Molly grumbles. "Have you had coffee at every place in the Loop?"

She scoffs. "No, but I do get my bras at a place called Perky Cups in Wrigleyville."

Holy crap. That must be why the name popped into my head. I must have walked by it or something.

Molly turns to me. "You live in Wrigleyville."

Before I can think of how to dig my way out of this hole, Ellen announces, "You really do look familiar to me, Blake. What's your last name?"

I blurt out, "Walker," at the same time Molly says, "Walsh."

Ellen pushes her chair back and stands up like she's going to attack me. "Blake Walsh?" she barks. "I know who you are and you're no barista!"

Molly looks at me with pleading eyes, like she can't believe I lied to her. "I can explain," I tell her.

But before I can do so, Ellen shouts loud enough for everyone in the room to hear, "He's a reporter! We work at the same newspaper!"

CHAPTER THIRTY-EIGHT

MOLLY

I stare at Blake as confused as if I were trying to solve a calculus problem. Which would be a real stretch for me, as the farthest I got in math was trigonometry. "You're a reporter?" I lash out.

Before he can answer, another woman at our table stands up and accuses, "You're not looking for a relationship! You're here to spy on us so you can tell everyone how pathetic we are!"

I've been so caught up in the fact that Blake lied to me, it didn't even occur to me that he's here in an official capacity. "Do you even work at a coffee house?" I ask.

Shaking his head, he says, "No, I don't."

"So, you're not here to find out how to help single people meet one another?" He shakes his head again. "You're writing a story about Trina's event?" I can't wrap my head around that.

"That's why I'm here," he says. Then he looks at Ellen and adds, "I was instructed to remain incognito and not tell anyone who I was."

Ellen visibly blanches but she remains silent.

"I told you that I would never date another liar," I yell. "And you assured me you weren't one."

Blake's face pales. "I never *wanted* to lie to you."

"If you don't want to lie to someone, Blake, then you don't lie. That's all there is to it."

"I couldn't tell you the truth …" He doesn't seem to know what to say after that, so he simply looks at me with a pitifully pained expression on his face.

Ellen decides this is the perfect time for her to rejoin the conversation. "Sportswriters make decent money."

I turn my head in her direction so quickly I nearly get whiplash. "Are you for real?" I shriek.

Ellen shrugs. "At least he's not a barista."

The other barista at the table, Aspen, wants to know, "Dude, what's wrong with being a barista?"

My sister responds, "Nothing if you're twenty and you're hard at work getting your engineering degree." Not knowing when to leave well enough alone, she asks him, "Are you twenty, Aspen?"

"I'm thirty-four and I think you're a real witch," he tells her. Honestly, he's not wrong. That's exactly how she's acting.

It's my turn to go after Ellen. "Are you saying that you think it's okay for me to date Blake now?"

"Yeah, why not?"

"Because he lied to me, Ellen."

Tipping her head from side to side, she decides, "I can see how it might look that way, but he was really just working undercover."

"I told him I would never date a liar, Ellen. And I can't believe you would want me to after what Kyle did to me."

"Kyle cheated on you," she says like I don't already know this.

"Kyle *lied* to me," I insist. "He told me that he loved me and that he couldn't wait to have a future with me, and all the while he was seeing Amelia."

Blake interjects, "I never wanted to lie to you. In fact, I was going to tell you the truth but then my boss said she wanted me to write about a personal experience I was having …"

I don't let him finish his sentence. "You asked me out to be fodder for a story?"

"No, no, no," he says quickly. "I liked you before she asked me to do that."

"Did you ask me out before she told you to write about a personal experience?" A slow head shake this time. "So, you've agreed to write about us? When did you plan to get around to telling me that?"

He shamefacedly answers, "As soon as I turned in the article. But there's more to it than that, Molly."

"I don't care, Blake." I stand up so quickly I don't realize I'm clutching the tablecloth.

When I lift my fist in rage, I pull the entire thing upward and upset several full glasses of water and wine spills everywhere. I'm unbothered by the mess. I just continue my rant. "If I forgave you, I would essentially be telling you it's okay to lie to me. And it is NOT."

The whole ballroom is now staring at us, including Kyle, who somehow feels the need to join in the fray. He strides across the room and stands right in front of me. "I know I made a mistake, Molly. And I know I told you I wasn't ready to date again. But I *am* ready! And you're the woman for me!"

I cannot believe this is happening right now. The man I was so excited about is nothing but a lowdown sorry excuse for a human. And to make matters worse, my cheating pig of an ex is trying to win me back.

"Go straight to hell, Kyle," I tell him as I gesture wildly with the clutched tablecloth.

"But I thought we were friends now." He sounds horribly confused as he adds, "I thought you'd forgiven me."

"I don't forgive you, Kyle. You and Blake are two sorry peas in a pod, and I don't care what happens to either of you!" Then with all the dignity I can muster—which honestly isn't much considering I'm covered in red wine and have just made the biggest scene of my life—my support tablecloth and I stride out of the ballroom with my head held high.

As soon as I reach the door, I realize I have something else to say. As luck would have it, all eyes are still on me. Spinning around to face the room, I announce, "It takes real courage to do what you're all doing. It takes faith in love to put yourselves out there like this. I have a lot of admiration for all of you, and if you don't want to be made a laughingstock, I think you should stay as far away from Blake Walsh as you can!"

A roar of cheers fills the airs, which further ignites my sense of injustice. I point at Kyle and add, "Kyle Rogers cheated on me after dating me for an entire year. If you have the sense that God gave a slug, you'll stay away from him, too!"

And with that, I storm out of the ballroom. My whole body is shaking so badly, I'm not sure how I don't fall right over the table-cloth. But for the first time since arriving in Wisconsin, I don't even stumble. I just glide.

I don't get far before Trina catches me. "Molly." She sounds so concerned that I almost burst into tears. "Are you okay?"

"Not even a little bit," I tell her. "In fact, I know you hired me for two weeks, but I can't stay here for another minute if Blake is going to be here."

I expect her to tell me that she's kicking his sorry butt out of her event, but instead, she reaches for my checked hero cape and replies, "I totally understand. I don't see why you can't finish your proposal from home."

"You're letting him stay?" I bluster.

"I don't care that he's a reporter. After all, any press is good press. This is a great way to bring attention to what I'm doing here."

"You should be livid! He lied to you, too."

"Molly," again with the concerned and caring tone, "I knew from the start there was something off about Blake."

"How?"

"I don't know," she says, "I guess because he was working the room like he was hosting a party. He talked to everyone, not just the women."

"And you're not mad? How can you not be mad?"

She answers, "This is my first singles' event at the lodge, and I already have a reporter from a big news outlet here. In my book, that's a win."

"I can't forgive him," I tell her. "I won't."

"I don't blame you. You've been hurt before and that doesn't help. Having said that, are you sure this isn't something you can't overlook?"

"You're a matchmaker, Trina," I tell her. "Do you often suggest that people date liars?"

"I think this situation is a little bit different, Molly. Just try to keep your mind open."

I shake my head forcefully. "No. There are some things you don't compromise on, and this is one of them." I stick my hand out to shake hers before saying, "I appreciate the job. I'll send you a final list of ideas by the end of the week."

I'm about to turn and walk away, but then I remember something. "My sister's here. She wants her money back for my spot in this farce."

But before Trina can respond, Ellen walks up to us. "Great event, Trina," she tells our host. "Seriously, if I were in the market for a man, I might give something like this a try for myself."

"Are you actually insane?" Yeah, I'm back to shouting. "You told me today you wanted your money back."

Ellen sheepishly confesses, "I didn't actually pay anything. Trina volunteered to host you when I was up here writing an article about the lodge."

I'm surrounded by liars. "If you didn't pay, then what are you doing up here, Ellen? You said you came to get your money back."

"I wanted to meet Blake. I couldn't believe that of all the men you were meeting, you were going to settle for a guy who made coffee for a living."

"Well, I'm not settling for him, or anyone. In fact, at this moment, I'm pretty sure I'm never going to date again."

Ellen and Trina both look at me like I'm the most tragic person in the world, and it's seriously ticking me off. Women are supposed to have each other's backs. We're supposed to stand up for each other and fight for each other, not tell each other it's okay for a man to lie to us.

And if nothing else, Blake is a liar and a fraud and that is not going to work for me.

CHAPTER THIRTY-NINE

BLAKE

Tonight was a total flop. An absolute disaster. A complete catastrophe. I could go on, but I'm depressed enough as it is. I only stay in the ballroom for a few minutes after Molly leaves. I want to give her enough time to make a clean getaway. Yet staying here any longer makes me susceptible to the wrath of the crowd, and the villagers are starting to circle.

As I'm getting ready to go, Emberly approaches me. "I used to be a model. I'd love to cover fashion shows for the newspaper you work at."

"Emberly," I take a deep breath before continuing, "I have absolutely zero pull at *Chicago Wind*. In fact, I'm fairly certain when my boss hears about tonight, I won't even have a job."

She reaches in her purse and pulls out a business card. Handing it to me, she asks, "Can you at least give this to your editor?"

People are so mercenary when it comes to pushing their own agendas. Yet, I suppose I sort of admire that. If you don't look out for number one, who's going to do it for you? Taking the card, I tell her, "I'll do that." Then I practically spring for the exit.

Once I'm in my room, I text Gillian.

ME

Have you secured the tickets yet?

She responds fifteen minutes later.

VAMPIRA

I have them. And you can have them when you hand over your articles.

ME

I'll be back in town tomorrow. I'll give them to you then.

VAMPIRA

The event doesn't end for several more days.

ME

I've had enough.

VAMPIRA

I'll be the one to decide that, Blake. If I'm not pleased, you're going back.

I hate when people feel like they need to have the last word, so I leave her message on unread. Passive aggressive? Most definitely. But I'm not going to give Gillian the satisfaction of knowing that she won.

I don't want to run into Molly until she's calmed down, which is why I'm pacing in my room like a caged animal. As such, the knock on my door takes me by surprise. The only person it could be is Molly, and knowing the mood I left her in, if I open it, I might be on the receiving end of a hot pot of coffee.

I let her knock again before I hear a voice that isn't hers. "Open the door!" It's Ellen.

Opening the door, I snap, "What now? Are you going to set my room on fire?"

She pushes me into my room before following. "Don't be a drama queen, Blake."

"A drama queen?" Stabbing a pointer finger in her direction, I practically yell, "You don't even know me, lady."

She rolls her eyes. "Settle down. I'm on your side."

"If tonight was you being on my side, remind me to never make an enemy of you."

She strides across the carpet and sits down at the table. "I've got no beef with you, Blake. In fact, Gillian thinks you're great. She says you're the perfect addition to the paper."

"Gillian thinks I'm a gigantic pain in the butt," I tell her.

"I'm sure you are. But that doesn't mean you're not also good at your job."

"Why are you here?"

"I'm here to help. I think you and my sister might just be a good match."

Sitting on the chair across from hers, I tell her, "I don't think your helping is a good idea."

"Why? I know everything about Molly. If anyone can get past her defenses, it's me."

"She's never going to forgive me for lying to her," I say. "And honestly, I don't blame her. I have not been on the up and up, and that was the main reason I'd decided I wasn't going to flirt with anyone here."

"Yet, you clearly broke that rule," she needlessly tells me.

"Your sister is hard to ignore."

"My sister," she replies, "is a catch. But she's also been hurt badly, and she doesn't know how to come back from that."

"And I made that even harder for her. Which is not what I wanted to do."

Ellen waves off my comment. "Molly is just gun shy. She should have gotten right back on the horse after that idiot Kyle, but she second-guessed herself and then she lost herself. All she needs is some time to realize that you were just doing your job. I'll work on her."

"I'm leaving tomorrow," I tell her. "I can't stay here knowing how much I've hurt her."

"She'll be happy to hear that. She wanted to leave, but this way we can stay and have some sister time."

I was kind of hoping Ellen would tell me to stay and she'd help me work things out now, but she knows her sister better than I do. If Molly needs space, I'll give it to her. "I'll check out at ten, if you want to make sure she doesn't see me."

Ellen stands up. "Good. Now hand me your phone."

I hand it over and watch as she types her phone number in. Then she calls herself. "Now you have my number. We'll stay in touch."

Ellen walks out of the room without a backward glance. While she and Molly have completely different personalities, it's clear that neither of them are pushovers. I can only imagine what their parents are like.

After Ellen is gone, I brush my teeth and get into my pajama pants before sitting on the bed and opening my laptop.

The road to happily-ever-after is often fraught with disaster. Take tonight. I got caught in a lie, and Polly found out. As a result, she rightfully ended things with me.

I came to Trina Rockwell's event at the Elk Lake Lodge certain it was a waste of everyone's time. And while things didn't work out for me, several couples seem to be well on their way to a happy ending.

Take Arnold and Olive. He works for the government, and she has a thriving career caring for animals. They are two unassuming people who, on the surface, don't seem like they'd be a match. I'm not sure where they would ever cross paths in the real world, but here, they have managed to find enough common ground to become a couple.

I also met a circus performer who has matched with a dental hygienist. Then there's the television show producer and the schoolteacher. Unless these people hang out in the same coffee shops, or have mutual friends, chances are they would have never met.

Not only does the Elk Lake Lodge offer them a beautiful, rural retreat, far away from the hustle and bustle of their daily lives, but they are also able to meet other singles outside their normal daily scope.

Trina Rockwell creates structure for people to get to know each other, and then she gives them enough space to pair off to share personal time. I did not want this assignment when it was given to me. I'd made my decision about what it would be like before having any evidence to back up my opinion.

I'm happy to discover that I was wrong. And while this event did not work for me personally, my lack of success is on my shoulders alone. Polly may not have been interested in me had I been honest with her from the start, but at least our budding friendship would not have been based on a lie.

I suppose if I had any advice to give, it's this: If you book a spot at one of Trina's retreats, make sure you're genuine in your desire to be there. Present yourself honestly and without artifice. Keep an open mind and an open heart. And most importantly, treat everyone with the respect they deserve.

Closing my laptop, I feel a heaviness of heart that I haven't felt in ages. In the last few years, I've dated my fair share of women. Some nicer than others. But none of them have inspired the desire in me to settle down again. None of them, except Molly. And I fear that I've irreparably damaged any chance for us to share a happy ending.

CHAPTER FORTY

MOLLY

I don't know where Ellen took off to, but she's not gone for long. When she comes back to our room, she announces, "I ran into Blake. He's leaving tomorrow."

I stop packing mid-sweater. "*He's* leaving?"

She nods her head once. "He said to tell you how sorry he is."

"Where did you run into him?" I all but jump down her throat.

"In the hall. He was on his way to his room." She hurries to add, "He feels really bad."

"He should."

"Molly," my sister says as she crosses the room and hops up on the bed. "Journalists often need to practice anonymity. It's the only way for them to get the real story."

"He's writing about *us*, Ellen. Don't you think I should have known that was going to happen?"

She shrugs. "Not necessarily."

"You don't think it's my business to know my personal life is being used to entertain the public?"

She blows her nose before saying, "We have to run everything through legal. Nothing he was going to write would have broken any laws."

"Are legalities the only litmus test you use for deducing a good relationship? If so, it's no wonder Henry broke up with you."

Her face contorts into a look of pure shock. "That was mean."

"But not against the law." I throw her words right back at her.

"You know, I was glad that Blake is leaving because I thought it would give the two of us some nice time away together. But if this is how you're going to act, then I'm going back to Chicago, too."

"Good," I hiss at her. "Go."

In response, she calls downstairs and asks for a room for the night. When she hangs up the phone, she says, "The lodge is fully booked so I'm going to have to stay here. But don't worry, I'll be gone in the morning."

Ignoring her, I turn around and walk into the bathroom. As I start the shower water running, I realize this isn't Ellen's fault. Well, it is in the sense that I'm here at this time because she finagled me a spot at the singles' event. But it's not her fault that Blake lied to me.

Getting into the shower, I let the hot water rain down on me. My skin is so sensitive it feels like hot pin pricks stabbing at me. I let the water envelope me until my skin starts to prune. Then I get out and towel off.

After slipping into my nightgown, I walk back in the room. Ellen is on her phone doing her best to ignore me.

"I'm sorry," I tell her. "I know it's not your fault how things worked out. I just don't like your standing up for Blake."

"I'm a journalist, Molly. I do what Blake did all the time." She asks, "Remember Davis Fulton?" At my blank expression, she reminds me, "The musician who was accused of sexual harassment by his assistant?"

"Oh, yeah, him." It's no wonder I forgot with how inappropriate the music and film industries are. It's like you haven't arrived until you've been accused of aggravated assault.

"I pretended to be his new assistant to get the scoop on the guy. He didn't find out who I really was until I quit and my article ran."

"And that wasn't illegal?" I want to know.

"It would have been had I signed the confidentiality agreement he gave to me. But I put off doing that. It's not my problem he trusted me when I told him I gave it to his agent."

"But you were searching for the truth to help people." I hate that I'm starting to see her point. "You know, so that no one else fell victim to the guy. How is what Blake is doing helping people?"

"He's finding out if this is a decent event for single people to invest their money in. How is that *not* helpful?"

I let that sink in for a minute before deciding. "Fine, he's helping people. But he should have never started something with me based on false pretenses."

"He knows that," Ellen says. "But you were simply too irresistible to stay away from."

Climbing onto the bed next to her, I crawl under the covers. "Don't try to flatter me. It won't work."

"I'm not trying to flatter you. I'm simply suggesting there might have been some mitigating circumstances, that's all."

Changing the subject, I ask her, "What are you going to do about Henry?"

She sighs loudly. "I don't know."

"But what about Melissa and Sammy? Don't you think they made it look like this whole stepfamily thing can be good?"

"You know they do, which is why you introduced me to them. But Henry has three kids. Three little kids who haven't even gone through puberty yet. That's going to be rough no matter how you look at it."

Snuggling deeper into my nest, I tell her, "It'll be a lot easier with you joining the family now. They already know you and love you, Ellen. That's not going to change if you marry their dad."

"Maybe." She doesn't sound convinced. "I was hoping that you and I could stay here for a few days together. What do you think?"

"That sounds nice," I tell her. "So long as you don't talk about Blake."

"Fine, but I have a condition of my own." As if I can't see this coming from a mile away. "No talking about Henry, either."

"Fine," I tell her snippily.

Ellen gets under the covers next to me. "Remember when you were really little, and you would wake me up in the middle of the night to get you ice cream?"

"Remember how you always did it?" I laugh. "That was really cool of you, Ellie."

She scoffs. "I only did it so you would go back to sleep." She cuddles in next to me. "It's funny how life turns out, isn't it?"

"You mean how the men in our lives have been so disappointing?"

"Only a couple of them," she says, which makes me think she might be realizing that she doesn't want to lose Henry. She adds, "I was thinking more of how special it is that I got a younger sister. I'd just about given up hope of having a sibling and then boom, in comes this dark-haired little cherub to love."

"You're a great big sister, Ellen. I'm lucky to have had you." That's the truth. Ellen doted on me and bent over backwards to do fun things with me. When she went away to college, she let me come and stay weekends with her. When she graduated from college and got her own apartment, I would go and stay for a week at a time during my summer break.

I've complained a lot about how controlling Ellen is, but as I look back, I realize she was just trying to protect me. She was trying to make my world safe. And I love her for that. I just wish that now that I'm grown, I could do the same for her.

I suddenly have an idea. Getting out of bed, I grab my phone and go back into the bathroom. If this works, then maybe, just maybe, I can repay some of the debt I owe to my sister.

CHAPTER FORTY-ONE

BLAKE

Gillian stares at her computer screen intently before saying, "Not bad."

Not bad, my foot. I just turned in three articles that rock socks like a fox on a box eating lox. I may owe my love of the written word to Dr. Seuss.

Sticking my hand out toward her, I demand, "I'll take those tickets now."

Instead of handing them to me, she says, "Your last article isn't complete. The one about you and Polly." She pauses long enough to ask, "Is that her real name?"

"I'm not going to give you her real name." Then I ask, "How is the article incomplete? I told you about our first kiss, I told you about how she broke things off with me. What more do you expect?"

"I want the finale! I want the making up and getting back together."

"Under no circumstances will I write anything more about me and M ... Polly. I gave you what you wanted, which was a review of the Elk Lake Lodge's dating event. I did my part." Sticking out my hand, I tell her, "Now do yours."

Gillian reaches into her desk and pulls out a small white envelope. "You know, if you told her the only reason you wrote about her was to help a sick boy, I'm willing to bet she'd forgive you."

"I thought that was all top secret."

"You can't write about it," she confirms. "But you could tell Polly."

Making a grab for the tickets, I tell her, "She's not happy that I was writing about us, but her main complaint is that I didn't tell her why I was at the event. I made up some lie about being there undercover for the coffee shop I worked at."

Gillian scoffs. "What coffee shop would pay for you to participate in a two-week-long singles' getaway?"

"It doesn't matter," I tell her. "I came up with a good story and Molly believed me."

"Ah, so her name is Molly! What's her last name?"

"Her last name is none of your business, Gillian." Taking the tickets from her, I ask, "Do I still have a job?"

"Of course you still have a job. Why wouldn't you?"

"Do I still have a job writing about *sports*?" I clarify. I will not do another one of these filler pieces even if it means saving my career.

"You do. In fact, you should plan on starting the first of the year. Charlie has decided his last game will be on New Years' Eve."

I release the breath I'd been holding. "Finally. Thank you."

"But I still want you to tweak the last article and give me the happily-ever-after our readers will be counting on."

I concede, "If there's a happily-ever-after, I'll write about it. But that's a big if, considering Molly isn't talking to me."

"Christmas is a time for miracles, Blake. Don't give up."

I think about that as I walk out of Gillian's office. I'm not a fan of those cheesy movies where people's eyes meet across the room and they just know they're looking at their soul mate. I particularly detest the ones where two unsuspecting people meet and fall in love while picking out a Christmas tree. How unrealistic is that?

But if Christmas could bring a miracle that would let Molly forgive me, I'd stand in a block-long line and sit on Santa's lap myself to thank him. Taking the tickets out of the envelope, I slowly count them. There are five, like I requested.

Walking over to a loveseat in the lobby, I sit down and text Ellen.

ME

I have an extra courtside ticket to the Bulls game on Christmas Eve. What are the chances that you could convince Molly to go to the game?

ELLEN

Slim. Molly hates basketball.

ME

Seriously?

ELLEN

Maybe hate is too strong of a word. Why? What do you have planned?

I don't have anything planned yet, but I have the beginning of an idea.

ME

I have five tickets. Three of them are for a family I met at the lodge who have a sick kid.

ELLEN

You don't mean Ben's family?

ME

How do you know about them?

ELLEN

Molly introduced them to me this morning at breakfast. Is that who you got the tickets for?

ME

Yeah. Ben is pretty sick with leukemia.

I can't help but wonder how Molly knows Ben's family.

ELLEN

What if we get Francie and Ward to ask Molly to go with them without using your name?

ME

That would be brilliant! Do you think they'd do it?

ELLEN

You got them courtside tickets to the Bulls, Blake. I'm sure they'd love to help.

ME

Do you want me to text them, or will you ask?

ELLEN

I'll ask. That way I can fill them in on the whole story.

ME

Thank you, Ellen. That would be amazing.

ELLEN

Don't thank me yet. I'll try to find them and talk to them today.

ME

Tell them I'll leave their tickets at Will Call. I'll leave Molly's too if they can convince her to go.

I was not Ellen's biggest fan last night in the ballroom. But then she came by my room and offered to help me patch things up with her sister. Now, she's going above and beyond to get Molly to the Bulls game. I pick up my phone and go to a search engine to find out who's who in the Bulls organization. I find their publicist's name and write her an email.

Dear Sharon,
My name is Blake Walsh and I'm the new sports reporter for *Chicago Wind*. I have a big favor to ask …

CHAPTER FORTY-TWO

MOLLY

Ellen left me two hours ago to get a diet soda from the vending machine down the hall and she hasn't returned yet. I finally decide to go search for her, but she's not on our floor. I find her sitting in the great room, talking to Ben and his parents.

Walking over to them, I look at her and say, "I thought you were coming right back."

"Molly, hey! I was, but then I ran into Francie, Ward, and Ben." She smiles at them all.

Francie says, "Sit down, we have something we want to ask you."

I sit in the rocking chair next to my sister. "What's up?"

Ward says, "We'd like to thank you for taking those beautiful pictures of us and putting them in a frame."

"We'll cherish it always," Francie says, her voice choked with emotion.

"You're most welcome," I tell them. "And honestly it wasn't that much."

"We got some good news this morning," Francie says. "Ben

has been accepted into a clinical trial in New York. We're going to leave right after Christmas."

That must be the trial Trina told me about. "That's wonderful news!" I tell them. Then I look at Ben and say, "You'll love New York. Try to go ice skating in Central Park if you're up to it."

Ben looks tired but he still manages a small smile. "That sounds really cool. I've never been to New York before. I think they have a big apple there. I'd like to go see that."

Ward playfully pats Ben's arm. "New York is called the Big Apple. There's no real apple that I know of." Then Ben turns to me and says, "We just scored some courtside tickets to the Bulls game on Christmas Eve. We were wondering if you'd like to join us."

Basketball really isn't my thing, but I really like these people, especially Ben. "I'd be honored to join you, but wouldn't you rather take a friend of Ben's?"

Ben says, "You're my friend, Molly. So, I *would* be taking a friend."

That has to be the sweetest thing I've ever heard. "In that case," I tell him, "I'd love to come."

"We're leaving earlier than we'd planned so we can get home and pack for New York," Francie says. She hands me a piece of paper with her phone number on it. "Text me your number so we can arrange all the details." Then she stands up and signals for Ward and Ben to do the same. "Come on, gang, we need to make tracks."

Ben runs over to me and throws his arms around me. "Bye, Molly! Thanks for everything! I'll see you at the game." Then he hurries off with his parents.

"What a nice family," Ellen says. "They told me what you did for them. You're a good egg, Molly."

"I do my best," I tell her. "Do you think Mom and Dad will be mad that I won't be home for Christmas Eve?"

"Not at all. Especially when they find out why you won't be there."

"What about you?" I ask. "Where are you spending Christmas Eve?"

"With Mom and Dad, of course."

"Ellen," my tone carries a warning, "what about Henry and the kids?"

"What happened to not talking about Henry and the kids? Besides, I'm still thinking about that," she says. "I liked Melissa and Sammy, and you're right—they make step-parenting look like a dream—but Henry has three kids and an ex-wife who hates him. That's a whole different story."

"You're a piece of work, Ellen," I tell her.

"I'm the one who has to live my life, Molly. So, please let me make my own decisions."

"Fine," I tell her. "I need to go talk to Trina about a few things. Why don't I meet you upstairs in a couple of hours?"

Ellen stands up and surprises me by reaching out to give me a hug. "I don't mean to be grumpy; I just want to make sure I make the best decision for me."

I watch my sister walk away. She *should* make the decision that's right for her. The problem is that I don't think she will. At least not without a little persuasion. Walking toward the far side of the great room, I sit down next to the singing chipmunks and pull out my phone.

I couldn't get a hold of Henry last night, so I hit the icon with his face on it.

"Molly? What's up? Is Ellen okay?"

"She's fine, Henry. How are you?"

"Did she tell you what happened?" he asks carefully.

"She said that you proposed and she accepted in the most unenthusiastic way possible."

He snorts. "That's about it. I mean, who says, 'Why not?' when the person they love proposes to them?"

"Ellen," I tell him laughingly.

"I thought she'd be so happy. I mean, we've talked about having more kids together and time isn't exactly on our side."

"She's scared," I tell him. "Don really did a number on her."

"If I ever run into that guy, I hope I'm in my car so I can do the most damage."

I totally understand Henry's anger. He's such a sweet man, but Don's actions have a way of bringing out the Incredible Hulk side in all of us. "I have an idea, Henry."

"What's that?"

I grab a throw on the back of the chair I'm sitting on and lay it across my legs. "What do you say you and the kids go to my parents' house for Christmas Eve dinner and surprise Ellen?"

"I don't know about that. I mean, Ellen might not be receptive. We didn't leave things on a good note."

"I'm with her now," I tell him. "We're at a lodge in Wisconsin."

"She's not in Chicago?" He sounds surprised and a little hurt. "She never leaves town without telling me."

"How about if you come up here?" I ask him. "The two of you can talk about everything away from your home base. Sometimes that's all we need for clarity."

"I'm pretty sure wherever you're staying is booked up this time of year." He sounds nervous but hopeful.

"It's completely full," I tell him. "But I'll leave the day you arrive, so you can stay with Ellen in my room."

"I don't want to kick you out," Henry says haltingly.

"I need to go home anyway," I tell him. "Things didn't go well for me here and I have a lot to think about."

Luckily, Henry doesn't ask me what happened. Instead, he says, "Thank you, Molly. I appreciate everything you're doing."

"I want you for a brother-in-law," I tell Henry. "You and Ellen are perfect for each other and I think you just need a few days away from everything to realize that."

"Text me the info. I can be there tomorrow."

I say goodbye to Henry and then text him the deets on the Elk Lake Lodge. My next stop is Trina's office. I'm nervous to see her because, between me and Blake, she wanted him to stay, and he's the one who left. Now, I'm about to tell her that I'm leaving too. Knocking lightly on the door, I say, "Trina, it's me, Molly."

"Come in," I hear her call out.

I open the door to find her sitting at her desk surrounded by studio lights. I turn to the side and see a guy about my age standing behind a camera. He's taking pictures of Trina.

"I can come back," I tell her.

She stands up and gestures me toward her. "Don't be silly. This is Noah. He lives in Elk Lake, and I just hired him to take pictures for us at the lodge."

Noah smiles shyly and waves. "Hey."

"That was fast work," I tell her.

"There's no sense putting off the execution of a good idea." She turns to Noah. "Can you give us a few minutes?"

Noah puts his camera down on her desk. "No problem. I'll just be outside when you're ready."

After he leaves, Trina says, "He's taking some headshots of me for our brochure. He'll take some of Heath when he gets back from the city." I was wondering why I hadn't met Trina's fiancé, and now I know why.

"I'm planning to go back to Chicago today," I tell Trina.

Sitting down again, she says, "But you don't have to go now. I understand that Blake left."

"I'm certainly not going to stay and keep going to your event," I tell her. "And I finished the report for your gift shop. I emailed it to you this morning."

"I saw it and it looks great," she says. "But why don't you and Ellen stay on and have some fun?"

"Because," I start to say before taking the chair across from hers, "Ellen's boyfriend is going to come up and take my place." I explain, "They broke up when he proposed last week. Ellen loves him, but she's scared."

"Oh, I see." Trina turns to her computer and starts to type. "What's his name?"

"Henry," I tell her.

"And what are Ellen's and Henry's favorite foods, do you know?"

I list several of Ellen's favorite things before asking, "Why?"

Trina smiles mischievously. "I'm going to do everything that I can to make sure they have the stay of their lifetime."

"Trina, you're too good." Then I tell her, "I want to pay for their room."

"Nonsense," she says. "We expected you to be here for at least four more days, so there's no new guest expected for that room."

"Yes, but you shouldn't have to pay for Ellen and Henry."

"It's Christmastime, Molly," she says. "Christmas is the perfect time for happy endings."

My heart sinks into my chest. She's right. Christmas is a time for all good things to come to fruition. Too bad that's not how it's working out for me.

CHAPTER FORTY-THREE

MOLLY

I don't stay in Elk Lake long enough to see Henry. In fact, I don't even tell Ellen that I'm leaving. I just pack up and roll out of the room while she's in the shower. I do, however, leave her a note, so she won't think I disappeared into thin air.

The train ride back into the city is nothing short of depressing. Happy, festive people are everywhere. They're smiling and wearing Santa hats and animatedly discussing holiday plans. Couples are walking hand in hand and carrying shopping bags that are surely full of presents for loved ones. Meanwhile, I'm going home to my boringly sterile beige apartment that hasn't even been decorated.

When the train pulls into Union Station, I'm overwhelmed by a horrible sadness. I have no idea why I'm so bent out of shape over Blake. Yes, I had high hopes of a possible future together, but we didn't know each other well, and certainly not for long. There's no reason I should let his treachery affect me like it has.

Blake is handsome, lovely, funny, and nice, but I probably just saw those characteristics amplified. Maybe I did that because I was finally ready to get back into the dating scene, and not because he was as perfect as I thought he was.

Taking a cab to my apartment, I stare out the window and try to force myself to enjoy all the decorations. It's my favorite time of year in Chicago. I need to stop letting thoughts of Blake take center stage in my brain and ruin that for me.

When the cab pulls up to my building, I get out and briefly drop my suitcase off with the doorman. Then I head to the market on the corner where I buy a fresh wreath for my door, along with a poinsettia plant and some staples for my refrigerator. I'm going to go home and force myself into the Christmas spirit, even if it kills me.

When I get back to my building, Martin, the doorman, tells me, "I'll bring your suitcase up for you in a few minutes. You have a delivery at the desk you might want to pick up."

I stop at the desk and find that I've been sent a giant vase of red roses. There must be fifty of them. I open the envelope with my name on it, but the card isn't signed. There's just a simple message.

Christmas is a time for miracles.

Tears spring up in my eyes. That's the same thing Ellen told me right before I left for Elk Lake. I line my grocery bags up my arms so that my hands are free to carry the flowers.

I love my sister's optimism, but there are no Christmas miracles for me this year. Maybe next year, if I'm really good. Once I get to my apartment, I open the door and discover a Christmas tree has been set up in my living room by the window. Flipping on the light switch causes hundreds of tiny colored lights to flicker on and illuminate the glass ornaments that adorn it.

I pull my phone out of my purse and call Ellen. "What have you done?" I ask her.

"What have *I* done?" she flings. "What have *you* done? Why is Henry here?"

"He's there so that the two of you can work things out before too much distance makes everything weird." Then I tell her, "I love my tree and flowers."

"I'm glad you love the tree," she says, "but I didn't send flowers."

"Are you sure?" I ask her.

"Of course I'm sure." I hear her giggle before she says, "Henry says thank you."

"Are you going to thank me, too?" I ask her.

"Maybe," she says. Her voice lowers. "I'm just really scared, Molly. I mean, what if things go spectacularly wrong?"

"Like they did with Don?" I know that's what she's really worried about.

"Yes, like that."

"You can learn from the past, Ellen, but you can't stop taking chances. You can't stop believing that good things can happen to you."

"You did," she accuses none too kindly.

"I may have stopped believing in a fairytale ending for myself, but I've decided that it's time to give love a chance again."

"With Blake?" she asks excitedly.

"No, not with him."

"Not with Kyle?" She sounds horrified.

"Not him, either," I tell her. "I've decided that next year is going to be my year to make some big changes." I list the few that I've come up with. "I'm going to start dating again. I'm going to travel less and accept more jobs closer to home. And I'm going to go see every romcom that comes out. Because honestly, if things can work out for a hooker and a billionaire, then surely, they can work out for me, too."

"Ah, *Pretty Woman*," she says dreamily before telling me, "You can't call them hookers anymore. They're sex workers now."

"How is that any classier?" I want to know.

"I don't think it's a matter of class. More an accurate description of the job they perform."

"Fine. If things can work out between a *sex worker* and a billionaire, then there must be hope for me."

"You might not even have to wait until the New Year," Ellen says mysteriously.

Kicking off my loafers, I curl up on my couch in front of my beautiful Christmas tree. "I'm not going to go on a date before then," I tell her. "Plus, New Years is less than two weeks away."

"Just keep an open mind, Molls," my sister says. "Remember what I told you before I left."

"Christmas is a time for miracles," I repeat. "Which was the message on the roses that I received."

"Truly?" She sounds surprised, so maybe they weren't from her.

"Truly," I tell her. "And you know what, maybe it is. Maybe there's a miracle with my name on it. I'm just not quite ready to get my hopes up. This has been a tough week."

"The good thing about fish," Ellen says, "is the sea is full of them. Maybe Blake isn't your guy, but there's definitely someone out there who is."

I hope she's right. "I think Henry's *your* guy, Ellen. He loves you, his kids love you; you need to trust that love."

She's quiet for several moments before saying, "Maybe. I guess that's what we're going to spend the next few days figuring out."

After hanging up with Ellen, I go into the kitchen and put away the groceries I just bought. Then I pop open the bottle of champagne I picked up on a whim and carry it back to the couch.

Sitting down, I raise my glass toward the tree and toast, "To Christmas miracles!" Not that I think I'll get one this year, but I think it's a solid possibility for next year.

Kyle may have taught me not to trust easily, but I've also learned that I can't let him ruin future encounters for me. If Ellen can come back from her tough road—which was honestly much worse than mine—then surely, I can put on my big girl panties and get on with things.

I continue to toast in front of my Christmas tree all the sentiments I hope will come true in the coming year. I toast, "To Ben! May his clinical trial kick cancer's butt so he can live a long and happy life!" I toast to Ellen and Henry. Then I add my parents and various friends to the list. I finish off with one that I almost can't say out loud.

In the barest of whispers, I say, "To Blake. Thank you for helping me to figure out it was time to move on."

CHAPTER FORTY-FOUR

BLAKE

I have always loved Christmas Eve. In my family, it's a bigger deal than Christmas day, which means my parents are not thrilled that my first one home won't be spent with them.

My phone rings while I'm sitting at my dining room table wrapping Christmas gifts. I look at the screen and see it's my mom. She's probably calling to yell at me, which is why I decide not to answer it. But once it goes to voicemail, she calls again. I'm pretty sure this could go on all day, so I finally pick up. "Mom, hi!" I try to sound happy to hear from her.

"I can't believe you're missing Christmas Eve dinner to go to a basketball game."

"That's my job, Mom. I didn't schedule the game." I may have misled my parents into thinking I was working tonight, which is the only excuse they would have accepted.

"I know, I know. But I'm still not pleased."

"Are you guys planning on watching the game?" I ask.

"If your sister and dad want to. You know basketball isn't my thing." My mom's *thing*, as she calls it, is baseball, and she would miss anything, including Christmas Eve, if the Cubs played this time of year.

"I'll be over bright and early tomorrow morning," I promise.

"I thought you were coming tonight after the game." She sounds disappointed.

And while I could probably make it over there tonight, I hope things go so well with Molly that we'll be busy making memories of our own. I made us a reservation at a fancy steak house not far from the United Center where the Bulls play. The foods editor at work needed to cancel her reservation and I was lucky enough to be standing nearby to overhear this. I begged her to let me take it over. I may have also promised to return the favor with tickets to a future sporting event of her choice.

I only have a couple of hours to get everything in line for tonight, and I'm more nervous than I've ever been regarding a woman. The only time I was close was senior year of high school when I asked Shilo Hunter to prom. I really hope tonight goes better, because Shilo said no.

I hurry to shower before putting on a pair of jeans and a Bulls sweatshirt. Then I put the five Santa Claus hats I bought into a shopping bag, along with some other things I put together for Ben. I have things to work out at the stadium, so my Uber picks me up almost an hour before I'd normally leave.

I managed to pull a few more strings when Sharon, the press agent from the Bulls, called me back. She was able to talk to the team, and they agreed to bring Ben onto the court after the game. That's an honor that gives me chills just thinking about it.

When I arrive at the stadium, I text Sharon to let her know that I'm there. She meets me within minutes at Will Call. Sharon is middle-aged and very no-nonsense looking. She's wearing a red blazer with matching frames for her glasses. Her gray hair is pulled back into a sharp ponytail. Walking right up to me, she says, "Blake Walsh?"

"That's me." I stick my hand out to shake hers. "I really appreciate everything that you're doing to help me."

Ignoring my hand, she says, "The only reason I'm doing it is because of Ben. The other thing is a bunch of romantic drivel as far as I'm concerned." Before I can respond, she adds, "But it's Christmas Eve and it will make for good television, and that's my job."

Oooookay. Note to self: Sharon isn't the warm, fuzzy type. "I still appreciate it," I tell her.

"Yeah, fine. Follow me." She leads the way into the stadium and then walks across the court to show me where we'll be sitting. Pointing upwards, she says, "The Jumbotron is there. We'll make sure we get great video of Ben and his family, and I'll email you the edited footage after Christmas."

"That's really going above and beyond, Sharon. Thank you."

"Yup." Then she walks me through how the team is going to approach Ben and tells me, "His parents can go onto the court with him, but tell them not to ask too many questions. This isn't something we normally allow, and I want to make sure there aren't any snags."

"What about the other thing?" I ask. For clarification, I add, "You know, the romantic drivel."

She rolls her eyes. "That will be at halftime. Make sure you're both here and no one is in the bathroom."

"I'll do my best," I tell her. Which is clearly not what she wants to hear.

"No, Blake. You will not do your best. You will both be here and ready. Comprende?"

I understand that Sharon could be a general in the army if she chose to. In fact, I wouldn't be surprised if military training was part of her past. "Gotcha," I tell her.

"You will have complimentary waiter service if you want to eat or drink anything. I'll comp your bill, so you don't have to pay."

"Wow, that's seriously very generous of you," I tell her. Especially because a hot dog at a basketball game will cost you fifteen bucks.

"Don't worry, you'll be able to return the favor sometime in the future."

"Oh?" *What have I gotten myself into.*

Sharon assures me, "There will be times when I need some good press for my guys. I'll be coming to you then, so don't be surprised."

"Okay." I know these things are standard in my business, but Sharon says this in such a way that she sounds like the godfather in the mob, and she's just made me an offer I can't refuse. And believe me, I don't.

Screwing up my courage, I tell her, "I have another huge favor to ask."

"No more favors."

"Oh, okay."

"I'll leave you to it," Sharon says, before adding, "Don't screw anything up."

This woman is seriously terrifying. I can only hope Molly doesn't trip and fall into the game or spill a beer on the court or something equally clumsy. Worst case scenario, she might still make a scene when she sees me. She doesn't know I'm the one who set up this night.

I figure the best way to handle everything is to not be sitting at my seat when Ben's family and Molly arrive. That way, I can stroll in right before the game starts and not give Molly the chance to storm out.

Walking off the court, I go stand near where the team will enter. I've covered hundreds of games, but I'd be lying if I didn't admit to feeling thrilled to be back in Chicago at a Bulls game. I remember when I was twelve, my dad brought me to one, and Jay Williams high-fived me on his way onto the court. I didn't wash my hand for a week.

I take a deep breath to steady my nerves. Tonight is my do or die night as far as Molly goes. As a warmup, I've been sending her flowers every day for the past week, but I haven't signed any of the notes. As for the messages, for some reason I've relied on platitudes that seem fitting in our situation: you can't judge a book by its cover, time heals all wounds, love conquers all. And probably the most inspired: it's always darkest before the dawn.

I wonder if Molly's enjoyed the flowers or if she's been worried she has a stalker. In retrospect, maybe I should have signed the notes. But had I done that, I'm pretty sure she would have thrown them all away. This way, she might have actually gotten some enjoyment out of them.

The stadium is filling fast, and the excitement of the coming game is permeating the air around me. I'm still standing in the same spot when I see Ben's family walk in with Molly. She's so beautiful she takes my breath away.

"Hey, man," I hear to my left. I keep my eyes on Molly and step aside.

This time I hear, "Yo, Blake."

I look up and see Christian Woods from the Lakers standing over me. "Christian!" I greet enthusiastically. "What's up?"

"Basketball?" he laughs. Then he says, "I hear you left us to come home."

"Once a Chicago boy, always a Chicago boy," I tell him.

Offering a fist bump, he says, "It's good to see you, man."

And that's when I have another idea …

CHAPTER FORTY-FIVE

MOLLY

I'm standing at Will Call at the United Center when I see Ben running toward me. I bend down and open my arms to him. When we connect, I pick him up and spin him around. "Hey, big guy, how are you?"

"I'm so excited," he tells me. "I think this is going to be the best day of my whole life." My heart clenches when he says that. I hope Ben lives to see days much more exciting than this one. Like his wedding, the day his children are born. The day we colonize the moon …

"I'm pretty excited, too," I tell him before handing him the giant foam finger I bought for him. He looks at the Bulls logo on the palm, and exclaims, "Cool!" Then he puts it on and turns to show his parents.

I give Francie and Ward both a hug before asking, "How are you guys doing?"

Francie says, "We're all packed for New York. Heath Fox is letting us stay in his penthouse, if you can believe it." I can believe it. Heath and Trina are two people who really walk the walk in life.

"When do you leave?" I ask.

"Tomorrow," Ward says. "Ben's first appointment is the day after Christmas."

I think about one of the flower bouquets I got this week and announce, "It's always darkest before the dawn." I can only hope that's the case for Ben.

As for the flowers, I loved getting them at first, but then they started to feel kind of weird. I'm pretty sure Kyle is the one sending them, and there's no way I'm going to buckle and date him again.

He's been texting too, which makes me want to change my number. In fact, I finally told him that's what I was going to do if he didn't stop. He did, but the flowers kept coming. I'm not sure what it's going to take for him to leave me alone, but I've decided that if he doesn't cut it out soon, I'm going to text him pictures of the arrangements in the garbage. I wish he'd been this determined to have me in his life when we were together.

As we cross the court to get to our seats, a wave of excitement hits me. Our seats are nothing more special than folding chairs, but they're right on the court, and even I know those are almost impossible to come by.

Ben sits between his parents, and I sit at the end. Once we're seated, a waiter comes by and offers to bring us food. In true Chicago fashion, we all get the deep-dish pizza. The adults order beer and Ben gets a root beer. Ben shouts over the noise of the stadium. "We don't even have to stand in line for food!" I find that pretty exciting as well.

The stadium fills quickly, and the players are all warming up when someone sits down next to me. I turn to look who it is and almost swallow my tongue. "Blake?" I croak. "What are you doing here?"

"I'm the one who got Ben's family the tickets," I tell her.

Ben jumps up from his seat and runs over to hug Blake. He says, "You're the best, Blake. Thank you!"

Blake hands him a large bag and says, "This is for you. I thought you might want to open it before the game starts."

Ben hurriedly rips into the bag and pulls out a Bulls sweatshirt that he immediately puts on. Then he takes out five Santa Hats with the Bulls logo on them. Handing them to each of us, he gushes, "This is the best Christmas ever!"

When Ben goes back to his seat, I lean over and hiss in Blake's ear, "I didn't realize that you knew Ben's family well."

I can't quite define the look on his face. It's sad, with a touch of longing and perhaps a good amount of hope. I try not to let it get to me. Blake tells me, "I kept running into them at the lodge. Francie told me what's going on with Ben and I wanted to do something to help."

While I think that's nice, I'm still annoyed. "How did you get such great tickets?" I ask like he had to have stolen them or something.

"My boss got them," he says. "But they came with a price."

As much as I don't want to talk to him, I want to know what that price was. "Did you have to sell your spleen?"

He grimaces while answering, "I had to write an article based on my personal experience at Trina's singles' event."

Holy heck. He wrote about us to help Ben? "That's why you wrote about us?" And while I suppose that's honorable, didn't I have some say in it?

He nods his head slowly. "I couldn't tell you because I couldn't risk you getting mad at me and outing me before I got the tickets."

"So, you lied to me to help Ben?"

"No," he says. "I lied to you before then. But I made it worse trying to help Ben."

My brain is spinning a million miles an hour and I don't know how to process everything. Instead of trying, I turn my attention to the game and do my best to ignore Blake. But that's harder than you might think. I feel the heat of him next to me like I'm sitting by a space heater set on turbo.

The start of the game is a total blur, and I can't focus on it. Instead, I eat my pizza and drink my beer. I occasionally look over at Ben, who is having the time of his life. As halftime approaches, I realize I'd better get up and go to the bathroom before the line is a mile long.

Leaning over to Francie, I tell her, "I'm going to hit the ladies'."

But before I can walk away, Blake's hand shoots out and grabs my arm. "Where are you going?"

Pulling my arm back, I snap, "To the bathroom. Not that it's any of your business."

"You can't go now," he says, sounding panicky.

"I can go the bathroom whenever I want to, Blake, and you can't stop me." I move to pull out of his grasp, but he holds on for all he's worth.

"Please don't go now or you'll miss it."

"Miss what?" I bluster.

"I have a surprise planned."

"For Ben?"

"Yeah ... um ... I have a surprise planned for Ben."

Sitting down, I tell him, "It had better be quick because I don't want to wait in a huge line."

"You won't have to," he says. Pointing across the court, he adds, "There's a private club for people with seats like ours. The lines shouldn't be that long."

Of course there's a private club. I can't imagine how much people pay to sit courtside. If I wasn't here with Ben, the cost of my ticket would have been a waste. When the buzzer blasts to signal halftime, we watch as the Bulls dancers take the court. The music starts to play as the scantily clad women shake their booties and assume poses I'm pretty sure I'm not bendy enough to ever achieve.

When they're done, I try to stand up again, but Blake takes my hand and yanks me down. Then I hear the crowd start to chant my name. Looking up, I see my name pulsing across the

Jumbotron. Then the camera pans to my face. What's going on here? I turn to look at Blake and growl, "Is this your doing?"

Before he can respond, a member of the Lakers walks across the court and stands right in front of me. He's holding a huge bouquet of red roses that are like the ones that were sent to my apartment the day I got home from Wisconsin. *My secret admirer is a professional basketball player?*

The giant of a man turns to the crowd to try to quiet them down, but it doesn't work. If I had to guess, they might think he's about to propose to me or something. *Please don't ask me to marry you, whoever you are.*

Luckily, he doesn't. Instead, he practically shouts, "Miracles happen at Christmastime!"

What in the world is going on? I don't have long to wait because someone comes up and hands Blake a microphone. For the love of God, what now?

Blake taps the microphone to make sure it's on before he starts to talk. In my wildest dreams, I never could have come up with something like this.

CHAPTER FORTY-SIX

BLAKE

I am so nervous right now my armpits feel like uncapped fire hydrants. I have no idea what Molly is going to say, but if her reaction to seeing me tonight is anything to go on, I could be in real trouble here. But no matter. I've put this thing into motion and I'm going to see it through.

Taking the microphone, I tap on it lightly. When I hear the amplified noise, I know it's go time. Standing next to Christian, I lean in and say, "I'm good, man. I've got it from here."

But instead of walking away, the giant basketball player signals across the court and the entire Lakers team comes over. Christian tells me, "No way, man. We're not leaving a friend in his moment of need."

I'm oddly touched by their show of support. I know most of the players from my years interviewing them, but still, this goes above and beyond. However, if Molly's expression is anything to go on, it's also extremely intimidating and perhaps not entirely welcome. But there's nothing I can do about that now.

Turning to Molly, I speak loudly and clearly. I tell the crowd, "My name is Blake Walsh and I'm the new sportswriter at *Chicago*

Wind." There's a tentative amount of applause which makes it clear people have no idea what's going on. And really, why would they? This is an unprecedented spectacle, even for a Bulls game.

Speaking into the microphone again, I say, "My mom always told me that Christmas is a time for miracles. And folks, that's what I need tonight."

Molly's eyes shift from the left to the right like she's searching for an escape route. I hurry to say, "I recently met a wonderful woman that I'd like to get to know a lot better. The problem is that I lied to her and now she wants nothing to do with me."

The crowd boos me in unison, as only a Chicago mob can do. Molly seems to enjoy this part because she stands up and lifts her arms up and down to encourage their hate. Then she takes the microphone from me. "I met Blake at a singles' retreat. He pretended he was interested in me, but it turns out that's only because his boss told him he had to write about a woman there." Their boos turn to hisses.

Taking the microphone from Molly, I tell them, "I liked Molly from the start, but because I knew I needed to keep the reason I was there a secret, I decided not to ask her out."

Molly leans into the microphone and shouts, "He friend-zoned me and then told me about all the other women he was interested in!" I'm going to need a police escort to get out of here in one piece.

Stepping away from Molly, I defend myself. "I did not tell her about other women. I tried to set her up with another guy."

People are starting to get to their feet and darn if I'm not hit by a flying hot dog. Christian takes the microphone from me and shouts, "None of that! This man is my friend! As much as he's making a mess of things, he's trying to tell this lady something. Now everyone settle down and let the man talk."

Nothing about tonight is going how I thought it would. Nothing. But at least the crowd sits back down. Taking the microphone back, I tell Molly, "I am very sorry for not telling you why I was at the lodge. If I could go back in time, I'd simply quit my job and ask you out. But I can't go back. All we can do is go forward."

The crowd finally likes something I have to say because they start to cheer. Please let it be for me.

"I think you're wonderful, Molly. I love your smile, your sense of humor, all the crazy things you say. I even love how you're constantly tripping over things. I sent you flowers every day this week to let you know how much I like and admire you."

She steps toward me and says, "You didn't sign the cards. How was I supposed to know they were from you?"

Shaking my head, I tell her, "I knew how mad you were at me, and I wanted you to enjoy the flowers before you tossed them."

She crosses her arms and nods her head. There's a lot of murmuring, but the crowd doesn't seem to know which one of us to support. Before they can turn on me again, I say, "I made a big mistake, and I promise that if you give me a second chance, I will never lie to you again."

Her toe is tapping like she's keeping rhythm to a drumbeat. She looks around and the crowd starts to chant again, "Do it! Do it! DO IT!!!"

But it isn't until Ben walks over to Molly and takes her hand that I have any hope. Molly leans down and lifts him up. The microphone picks up his sage advice. "You gotta do it, Molly. Ben is a nice guy. Sure, he messed up, but we all do sometimes." He adds, "I never pick my shoes up when I take them off after school and my mom and dad get frustrated with me, but they still love me."

The Bulls aren't supposed to do anything with Ben until after the game, but I spot Ben's favorite player, Colby White, walking in our direction. He stops in front of Molly and reaches his hands out to take Ben from her. Then he leans into the microphone and says, "You gotta listen to the little dude, Molly. He knows what he's talking about."

The crowd starts to cheer like the Bulls just won the game with a three-pointer at the buzzer. Colby lifts Ben up above his head and declares, "We're winning this game for Ben!" And the crowd goes even wilder.

Not to be outdone, Christian takes the microphone from Molly and says, "I'm afraid the Lakers are taking this one, White." He hands me the mic then reaches out and takes Ben from Colby's hands. "Ben is our good luck charm, so *we're* gonna win for him!"

I don't even think Christian knows who Ben is, but that doesn't stop him. He's not going to let the Bulls think they've got this one in the bag. But honestly, at this point it doesn't matter who wins because Ben feels like king of the world right now with two famous basketball teams fighting over who's going to win the game for him.

When everyone quiets down a little, Colby points between me and Molly before asking Molly, "So what's the verdict. You gonna give Blake another chance or what?"

Ben gives her the thumbs up which spurs on Colby and Christian to do the same. Molly finally says, "I'm scared."

Ben tells her, "Me, too, Molly. Me, too. But we both have to do what we have to do."

Molly's eyes fill with tears before she looks at me. "Would you really quit your job if you could go back in time?"

"I'll quit it now if you want me to," I tell her.

After several long moments, she finally nods her heads and says, "Okay. I'll give us a chance, but so help me, Blake, if you ever lie to me again, I'm going to have Colby here slam dunk you right through that hoop over there."

Colby is clearly on board with this idea because he comes over and picks me up like he's going to follow through with Molly's orders. Then he laughingly ruffles the hair on my head before practically dropping me on the ground. He must have been watching the clock because the buzzer sounds to signal the end of halftime.

I don't even watch the second half of the game. I spend the whole time holding Molly's hand and telling her how sorry I am. I tell her that I think she's wonderful, and I thank her repeatedly for giving me another chance.

She says, "I liked you from the moment you saved me from falling on my face."

"Which time?" I tease.

"Every time," she tells me. "But that's why this whole thing is so scary."

"I promise on everything that's important to me that I'll never lie to you again, Molly."

She nods her head slowly before leaning closer to me. Then she takes me by surprise and kisses me right there at the Bulls game. The kiss is sweet and special. It's full of hope and possibility. I'm about to pull her closer when we hear the crowd start to chant our names. Breaking apart, we look up at the Jumbotron to see that we're front and center on the Kiss Cam, which signals us to give them the kiss they're demanding. And by golly, we give an all-star performance.

Tonight I learned that Christmas really does bring miracles. It brought Molly back to me, and this time, I'm not going to screw things up.

CHAPTER FORTY-SEVEN

MOLLY/ONE YEAR LATER

"Pass the french toast!" Ellen shouts down the length of the dining room table.

Blake picks up the tray and sends it in the direction of my sister, who is eight months pregnant and eating like she's gestating quadruplets. Luckily, she's only got twins in there.

Blake blows me a kiss before mouthing the words, "Merry Christmas."

I cannot believe how many wonderful things this last year has brought. Blake and I have been nearly inseparable since the Bulls game last year. True to his word, he hasn't lied to me once. Although, I wish he would have when I asked him if my new pants made my butt look big. At least after saying yes, he reminded me that nobody likes a bone but a dog. That's when I decided he meant it as a compliment.

Henry stands up and raises his orange juice glass into the air. "I would like to toast to my lovely wife Ellen, who has blessed me not only by marrying me, but by giving me twin boys."

My dad calls out, "Here, here!"

My mom adds, "Next Christmas is going to be wild!"

Henry's kids are here with us, and they're as excited as their dad about the additions to their family.

After we finish breakfast, we head off into the living room to open presents. Blake already gave me mine last night, and I love it. It's a gold necklace with two hearts entwined together like they're one.

After all the gifts are opened, I stand up and announce, "We need to get over to Blake's parents' house and then we're taking off to the lodge." We've decided to visit the Elk Lake Lodge every year at Christmas to remember where our love affair started.

My mom jumps to her feet. "Let me wrap up a fruit cake for you to take."

My dad announces, "I bought them a bottle of scotch. It's on the counter."

We hurry to say goodbye to everyone and wish them a very Merry Christmas before heading out the door. As soon as we get into the car the phone rings. I look at the screen and announce, "It's Ben."

"Hey, Bennie," I answer. "How are you doing?"

"Great!" he says "I got new ice skates, and a new basketball, and a fish tank!"

"You must have been a very good boy this year," I tell him. And I know he was. He's not had an easy time with his treatment, but the artemisinin regimen he was put on seems to really be helping.

"You know I was!" Ben says. "I just called to tell you guys that I love your present and I can't wait to see you on New Year's Day." Blake and I bought Ben and his parents Bulls tickets to the rest of this season's games. Their seats are right next to ours.

Ben says, "Mom wants to talk to you, so I'll see you in a week!"

Francies takes the phone and says, "Merry Christmas, you two!"

"Merry Christmas to you guys," we say in unison.

"We got some news yesterday that I wanted to share with

you." Blake and I sit quietly waiting to hear what she has to say. "We got a call from Sloan Kettering regarding Ben's latest test results."

I sit so still my heart feels like it's stopped. Reaching over, Blake takes my hand and squeezes it while we wait. Francie says, "They had to run the tests twice because they weren't sure the results were correct. It seems that they are."

I can't wait another second, and I practically yell, "Tell us already!"

Francie inhales deeply before saying, "Ben is in full remission. There's no cancer left in his body."

Emotion explodes out of me like the business end of a cannon. "Yes!!!"

"That's the best news ever, Francie. The best." Blake's voice is full of emotion.

After we hang up, we sit in the car, unmoving for several minutes. Blake finally says, "I'll never doubt it again."

"What won't you doubt?" I ask him.

"That miracles really do happen at Christmas." Then he leans over and gives me the sweetest kiss imaginable.

I've learned so many things this year. I've learned to trust again. I've learned to have faith that good will win out. And I've learned to treat every day like it's a gift. I know that our futures are entwined and I'm excited to see it all play out. Every day since Blake and I have gotten together has felt like its own special miracle, and I will never take him or us for granted.

COMING SOON: PITY PLAY

Pity Play is coming in February, 2025!

Pre-order your digital copy here.

ABOUT THE AUTHOR

USA Today Bestseller Whitney Dineen is a rock star in her own head. While delusional about her singing abilities, there's been a plethora of validation that she's a fairly decent author (AMAZING!!!).

After winning many writing awards and selling nearly a kabillion books (math may not be her forte, either), she's decided to let the voices in her head say whatever they want (sorry, Mom). She also won a fourth-place ribbon in a fifth-grade swim meet in backstroke. So, there's that.

Whitney loves to play with her kids (a.k.a. dazzle them with her amazing flossing abilities), bake stuff, eat stuff, and write books for people who "get" her. She thinks french fries are the perfect food and Mrs. Roper is her spirit animal.

Join her newsletter for news of her latest releases, sales, and recommendations. If you consider yourself a superfan, join her private reader group, where you will be offered the chance to read her books before they're released.